"Are you out of your ever-loving mind?" Edward shouted.

He saw Laurel's lower lip tremble and tried not to feel sympathy. After all, within minutes of walking off the street and into his office, this pretty, penniless, wide-eyed waitress had actually proposed marriage to him—as if that would guarantee his legal services and solve all her problems.

Him! Solid, stolid attorney Edward White!

Who did Laurel think he was, the White Knight?

Even if he had been, Edward wasn't at all certain he'd attempt to rescue this particular damsel in distress. She was obviously a tad eccentric.

So why on earth was Attorney Edward White's firm, no-nonsense, professional mouth watering at the thought of championing Laurel Heffington Miller's utterly improbable cause?

Dear Reader,

Fall is to be savored for all its breathtaking glory—and a spectacular October lineup awaits at Special Edition!

For years, readers have treasured Tracy Sinclair's captivating romances...and October commemorates her fiftieth Silhouette book! To help celebrate this wonderful author's crowning achievement, be sure to check out *The Princess Gets Engaged*—an enthralling romance that finds American tourist Megan Delaney in a royal mess when she masquerades as a princess and falls hopelessly in love with the charming Prince Nicholas.

This month's THAT'S MY BABY! title is by Lois Faye Dyer. *He's Got His Daddy's Eyes* is a poignant reunion story about hope, the enduring power of love and how one little boy works wonders on two broken hearts.

Nonstop romance continues as three veteran authors deliver enchanting stories. Check out award-winning author Marie Ferrarella's adorable tale about mismatched lovers when a blue-blooded heroine hastily marries a blue-collar carpenter in *Wanted: Husband, Will Train*. And what's an amnesiac triplet to do when she washes up on shore and right into the arms of a brooding billionaire? Find out in *The Mysterious Stranger,* when Susan Mallery's engaging TRIPLE TROUBLE series splashes to a finish! Reader favorite Arlene James serves up a tender story about unexpected love in *The Knight, The Waitress and the Toddler*—book four in our FROM BUD TO BLOSSOM promo series.

Finally, October's WOMAN TO WATCH is debut author Lisette Belisle, who unfolds an endearing romance between an innocent country girl and a gruff drifter in *Just Jessie*.

I hope you enjoy these books, and all of the stories to come!

Sincerely,

Tara Gavin, Senior Editor

Please address questions and book requests to:
Silhouette Reader Service
U.S.: 3010 Walden Ave., P.O. Box 1325, Buffalo, NY 14269
Canadian: P.O. Box 609, Fort Erie, Ont. L2A 5X3

ARLENE JAMES

THE KNIGHT, THE WAITRESS AND THE TODDLER

Silhouette®

SPECIAL EDITION®

Published by Silhouette Books
America's Publisher of Contemporary Romance

SILHOUETTE BOOKS

ISBN 0-373-24131-3

THE KNIGHT, THE WAITRESS AND THE TODDLER

Copyright © 1997 by Deborah A. Rather

Printed in U.S.A.

Books by Arlene James

ARLENE JAMES

grew up in Oklahoma and has lived all over the South. In 1976 she married "the most romantic man in the world." The author enjoys traveling with her husband, but writing has always been her chief pastime.

Dear Reader,

They say that love is blind, but over the years I've come to doubt the veracity of that statement. It seems to me that, rather than failing to see what is obvious, real love often sees *more* than the human eye reveals. Love sees all the possibilities and brings with it the power to transform even the plainest Jane—or, in this case, the dullest Edward—into all that engages and excites the human heart. Love gets beneath the skin to the beauty of the soul and bares that beauty for all to see. It's precisely that transforming power of love that drives us to open our hearts, sometimes even before we can open our minds, and makes us more than we knew we could be. So it is with Edward and Laurel.

Laurel is a woman in need of a champion, and in dull, responsible, predictable Edward she sees him. With the eyes of love, Laurel sees not so much a big teddy bear in need of a make-over, but the large stalwart heart of a hero. The power of love frees that heart and in doing so transforms its possessor into a thrilling, passionate, even stylish, modern-day knight with a law book under one arm and an adorable redheaded little imp under the other. Say that love is blind, if you will. I say that love not only has X-ray vision but the power to bring out the nobility and beauty that reside in the heart of every lover. May it always be so.

God bless.

Arlene James

Chapter One

Laurel shifted nervously in her chair, crossing her slender legs and tugging demurely at the hem of her short, straight skirt. Her worried eyes skimmed the polished interior of the waiting room, taking in the gleaming wood paneling with its picture-frame molding, the lush plants in brass and ceramic planters, the discreet indirect lighting, the comfortable wing chairs upholstered with butter-soft, navy blue leather, and heavy, pristine glass-and-brass tables. The carpet underfoot was made of thick, hunter green wool. The elaborately framed prints on the wall were genuine works of art, the window treatments a stylish blend of burgundy, blue and green, draped and looped and pleated with thick gold tassels and fringe. The waiting room of the office of attorney Edward White was lavishly and expensively, if unimaginatively, decorated, as befitted its stately Turtle Creek address. No business location in the entire Dallas area evoked such images of status, prestige and old money.

Was it a mistake to come here? she wondered for the umpteenth time. Would the family name carry enough weight to convince him to help her? Unanswerable questions. Only one thing did she

know for sure: no one outside of the select, necessary few could know about Barry. She shuddered to think what her ex-husband would do if he knew about the boy. Bryce would undoubtedly take him away from her and use him to ensure that she did not fight for what was rightfully hers, and she would, indeed, give up everything for Barry. Yet, how could she protect that sweet, bright child without money? Her thoughts drifted to Danny Hardacre and his obscene proposal again. Involuntarily she shuddered. Suddenly she realized that the gentleman sitting opposite her was watching openly over the top of his newspaper.

Glancing at her wristwatch, she forced a sigh and again shifted in her chair, rocking to one side and uncrossing her legs. In an effort to avoid his curious gaze while buoying her own spirits, she looked down at her shoes. She liked her shoes. They were the perfect shoes for this outfit. She smoothed the white-and-gold braid decorating the stand-up collar of her military-style coat dress and smiled down at her olive green patent leather shoes with their big white buttons barred with gold. How many olive green patent leather ladies' high heel shoes were there in the world? Why, she might have the only pair in Dallas.

She heard a warm chuckle and lifted her head to look at the room's only other occupant. He was a tall, slender man with dark, wavy hair, handsome, sharpish features and a decided sparkle in his eyes. Snappily dressed in a cream silk sport jacket, tan slacks and a matching T-shirt, he wore costly Italian leather loafers without socks. His grin was quick and knowing.

"I don't believe I've ever seen a pair of shoes just that color," he said, nodding at her feet.

Laurel smiled, taking his statement as a definite compliment. "Thank you. I got them from a friend, a designer, during the spring market show at the apparel market. I had just finished this dress, and the shoes were a perfect match for it—utterly perfect." She shrugged happily, momentarily distracted from her larger worries.

The gentleman closed the investment magazine that he had been perusing and twinkled a smile at her. "So you're a fashion designer?"

Laurel's spirits instantly plummeted. She looked down at her

toes in an effort to hide her disappointment. "Oh, no," she said as casually as possible. "I mean, I have the training, but I've never actually *worked* at it."

"Ah, then you design just for yourself."

It was more statement than question, and Laurel couldn't hide her surprise at the astuteness of it. "How did you know?"

He chuckled again. "A guess, really. I once dated a designer. I've never known anyone else so pleased at finding just the right accessories for an outfit."

Laurel struck a disgusted pose. "Was it that obvious?"

His grin told her that it was.

She sighed. "It's silly, I know, and frivolous, but I can't help myself. I just feel better when I'm well dressed, and—"

"I didn't say that," he interrupted. "I'm something of a clotheshorse myself. The right clothing won't make a bad situation better, but it won't hurt, either. It's just..."

"What?"

"It isn't going to impress him."

Him? She lifted both delicately penciled brows in confusion. "Who?"

"Ed."

"Ed?"

"White. You know, Edward White, the attorney in whose office you're waiting."

"Oh!" She smiled, then the message penetrated, canceling the flash of relief that had accompanied understanding. "Oh." Was it hopeless then? Had Hardacre been right after all? She pictured her divorce lawyer: fiftyish with a desperate air about him, receding hairline, pockmarked skin, a short, stocky build and those awful polyester pants and baggy sport coats. If he'd owned a tie that was not stained, she hadn't seen it.

She tried not to think of Daniel Hardacre, not even as her last resort, but he had warned her that no one else would take on her case for the simple reason that she could not guarantee payment for services rendered. He had then offered to represent her in her pursuit of justice, but only if she would marry him. She'd had enough experience in divorce court to know that any spouse of hers would be entitled to half of all the moneys acquired during

the course of the marriage. Daniel could have collected half of her inheritance for his trouble and had her at his mercy in the bargain. She had told herself very reasonably that half was better than none, but she couldn't do it. She couldn't marry Daniel Hardacre, not even for Barry.... Not yet. Perhaps if he promised to forego even the smallest intimacies of marriage she could manage it, but then she'd somehow have to hide Barry. She could never trust Hardacre to keep quiet about him. Yet, only money and a good deal of it would make it possible to adequately hide the boy from a husband, and Danny did not have even a few hundred to advance her. She might be able to keep him quiet by bartering her body, but the very idea made her skin crawl. No, she would not think of Danny Hardacre, not even as a last resort—not yet.

Determinedly, she swallowed down such thoughts and tried to focus on something positive. An outstretched hand entered her field of vision. She jerked her gaze up to find her companion smiling apologetically at her.

"My name's Parker Sugarman," he said gently, letting her know that he'd noticed her distress.

She made herself smile and slipped her hand into his. "Laurel Heffington Miller."

He lifted a brow at her maiden name. "Mrs. Miller, is it?"

"Not anymore," she stated with pronounced satisfaction.

He laughed and pumped her arm up and down. "Nice to meet you, Laurel Heffington Miller."

A giggle bubbled up. "Same to you, Parker Sugarman."

He sat back and folded his arms, considering her. "You're a very interesting young woman," he announced finally. "I like that."

She dropped her gaze, warmed by that unexpected statement of praise. "Thank you."

A long silence followed, during which it occurred to Laurel that here sat a golden opportunity. She licked her lips and eased her gaze up. "You seem to, ah, know Mr. White."

Parker Sugarman nodded. "I've known him for years."

Laurel leaned forward slightly. "Is he a good attorney, do you think?"

"The best, and an even better friend."

She bit her lip, afraid to be encouraged. "Would you say that he's, um, generous?"

Parker Sugarman's gaze suddenly became speculative. He nodded carefully. "In his own way, yes."

Laurel took a deep breath. "Would he want to help someone in trouble, do you think?"

He tilted his head, and the tone of his voice dropped a notch. "Are you in trouble, Ms. Miller?"

She grimaced. "I probably didn't phrase it properly. My problem is...of a financial nature."

"Ah." He seemed to relax and waved a hand negligently. "Well, if this financial problem has legal complications—"

"It does."

"Then you couldn't do better than Edward to advise and represent you."

She nodded, trying desperately to take hope from that, but her list of disappointments was long. Six other attorneys had turned down her case so far. Why should Edward White be any different? What she needed was a courageous advocate, one obsessed with righting wrongs and seeing justice dispensed, one who wasn't cowed by the specter of opposing attorney Abelard Kennison. What she needed was a white knight in lawyer's clothing. At least Edward White had the right surname, but would he help her just because it was the right thing to do? If her present surroundings were any indication, he could certainly afford to do so, but she could have said the same about several of those who had already turned her down.

Absently, she ran both hands through her short, pale blond hair, disarranging the precise middle part and the twin curves of the longish bangs that framed her forehead and eyes and, unbeknownst to her, making a spiky lock at the crown stick straight up. Parker Sugarman cleared his throat and, when she looked at him, pointed to the crown of his own head. Laurel rolled her eyes upward, suddenly realized to what he was alluding, and quickly smoothed down the errant lock.

"I shudder to think how many times a day I do that," she confessed, blushing.

Parker shrugged. "I wouldn't worry about it. You're pretty enough to get away with it."

Laurel's already large, bright green eyes, widened at the smooth compliment.

Parker Sugarman burst out laughing. "I'm sorry. You're just so expressive. I have a little girl, Darla, and she's like that. Her eyes don't just widen, they nearly pop out of her head. I find it very appealing. She's so...unaffected, honest. It's...refreshing."

"Thank you. I think."

He laughed again. "You're welcome."

Laurel smiled, at ease once more, comfortable enough, in fact, to change the subject. "About Mr. White..." she said hopefully.

Parker folded his hands in his lap in a show of good-natured resignation. "What would you like to know?"

"Anything. Everything."

He slid his gaze sideways, pretending to search his memory. "Well, let's see. He's thirty-six, single, an only child. His parents live in Boca Raton, both retired attorneys. Did I mention that he's single?"

"Yes, as a matter of fact, you did."

Parker Sugarman examined his nails. "What I should have said is that he's never been married."

"Oh?" Was it her imagination, or was he putting special emphasis on Edward White's marital status?

"Mmm. He was engaged once." Parker's tone was entirely too nonchalant.

"Was he?"

"To a lovely woman," he went on.

Where the devil was this going? she wondered. She waited a long moment and then, knowing that she was supposed to, asked, "What happened?"

Both his tone and his smile were unrepentantly smug. "I married her instead."

Laurel's chin nearly hit her lap. "Good heavens!"

He shrugged, grinning. "They had already broken up. Besides, it was for the best. They weren't suited."

"No?"

"No." He leaned forward and dropped his voice to a conspir-

atorial whisper. "Between you and me," he told her, "Ed's a trifle—how do I put this?—um, stuffy...if you catch my meaning."

Laurel frowned, not catching his meaning at all. "I thought you were his friend."

"I am! His very best friend. It's just that Ed is dependable to the point of boredom."

Laurel bristled in defense of a quality whose lack she knew all too well. "How can you call being dependable *boring?* It's the hardest thing in the world to be!"

"Maybe the word I should have used is *responsible.*"

"Same thing!" Laurel insisted. "Heavens, if I'd been as dependable and responsible as my grandmother wanted, I wouldn't be here now!"

"Oh, really?" He seemed inordinately pleased by that.

Laurel's frown deepened. "I think you're being unfair to your friend."

He shook his head. "Look, all I'm saying is that too much work and no play makes Edward a dull boy."

"My father used to say that about himself," she revealed sternly, "and he died trying to climb a stupid mountain because it was there. He took my mother with him, too."

"Yes, I think I heard about that. I'm sorry."

She shrugged, refusing to be mollified. He had offended her sensibilities. How dare he call dull and boring the very qualities she had struggled all her life to cultivate! Unsuccessfully. She bit her lip, her eyes misting with tears. Maybe she didn't deserve her inheritance. Maybe Danny Hardacre was the best she could expect both as an attorney and a husband. Now that was a truly depressing thought.

Parker Sugarman reclaimed her attention, sliding to the forward edge of his seat and bending toward her. "I didn't mean to upset you, and I wasn't implying that Edward is of less than sterling character. The fact is, I'm concerned about him. He works too hard. Do you know what my friend Edward needs?" he asked eagerly.

She shook her head, frowning still.

"Something to shake him out of his rut, or maybe some*one*, a

woman perhaps, preferably a *wife*." He smiled unrepentantly. "Just not mine."

Laurel's jaw sagged while her brain tried to formulate a reply. Before she could marshal her thoughts, however, the heavy, leaded glass door that led into the reception area opened. A large, rumpled man stepped into the room. He was a big, powerful man with shaggy caramel brown hair that fell haphazardly over a high, broad forehead and a thick drooping mustache that hid his upper lip. His eyes, in contrast, were a pale, glowing blue. He put her in mind of a big, huggable, rather bedraggled teddy bear, and yet she sensed that beneath that expensive, conventional, poorly tailored suit was a body of stone. She made a pointless but automatic mental note: He should never wear gray. It detracted from his golden coloring. Hmm, and a double-breasted coat would slenderize his broad body and emphasize the amazing width of those shoulders, lending greater emphasis to the aura of power....

"I beg your pardon." His deep voice cut into her reverie.

Laurel opened her mouth to make some standard reply, found it already ajar and snapped it shut with an audible click of teeth. Color flamed in her cheeks, but she could not avert her gaze. He stared down at her.

"Do we have an appointment? I'm sure my secretary would have announced you."

Laurel's blush intensified. "Oh, well, she was g-gone when I arrived."

He frowned and turned a cloudy gaze on Parker Sugarman. "Parker, this will only take a moment." Abruptly his gaze switched back to Laurel. "What time was your appointment?"

Laurel gulped. This was always the hardest part for her, but she knew only too well that if she had called ahead for an appointment, she would have been instructed to bring a consultation fee with her, a fee she couldn't pay. Without it, she would have been turned away, appointment or no. Slipping in after the secretary had left for lunch was her only hope. She got unsteadily to her feet, intending to equalize their positions somewhat. She could not help noticing that the top of her head came only to the tip of his nose. Without her high heels, she would have reached

no farther than his chin. She gripped her small gold handbag in both hands, knuckles whitening with the effort.

"I, um, only have my lunch hour."

He grimaced. "I see. Well, unfortunately, I already have a lunch date. Perhaps you could call later for an appointment."

"Oh, please, couldn't I have just a few minutes of your time?" she wheedled.

"I'm sorry. Let me see you out." He turned away from her, moving to open the door once again. "Parker, are you coming?"

Laurel shot Parker Sugarman a desperate, pleading look. He smiled, got up and motioned for her to follow. He held the door for her, nodding encouragement as she slipped by into the reception area. Edward White was walking down a short hall toward a door that led out onto the sidewalk, extracting a ring of keys from a pocket.

"Hey, listen," Parker called to him, "I really only have a few minutes anyway."

"No matter," Edward said. "We don't see each other often enough anymore."

Parker shot Laurel an enigmatic look and hurried after Edward. "True, but you know how it is, Kendra has to go in early, and Darla will need me." Edward stopped and turned around. Parker smiled lamely. "Sorry, old buddy, but you kept me waiting a half hour, and the family does comes first."

Edward sighed and shot an irritated glance at Laurel. "Give me a break, will you? I was on the phone."

"And I'm sure it was very important," Parker said, clapping him on the shoulder, "but I still have to go. You'll understand when you have a wife and family of your own."

Edward White snorted. "That'll be the day."

Parker's smile was as broad as his wink when he slid it over one shoulder at Laurel. "Besides, you're needed here."

Glowering, Edward stepped close to Parker and spoke quietly into his ear. Parker chuckled, clapped Edward on the shoulder again and stepped away. Turning, he lifted a hand in farewell to Laurel. "Nice to have met you, Laurel Heffington *No-Longer-Mrs.* Miller."

She returned his wave. "I hope so, Parker, and...thank you."

"My pleasure." He moved jauntily toward the door, grinning, and pushed his way through it.

Edward tossed the unused keys into the air and caught them in the same hand, looking her over from top to toe in the process. "How long have you known him?"

"Parker Sugarman?"

He nodded, just once. She glanced at her wristwatch and shrugged. "About fifteen minutes."

He lifted a brow and seemed to relax a bit. "He's married, you know."

"So he said, repeatedly."

Attorney White nodded, to himself this time, and swept a hand through his hair. "Well, I can give you a few minutes," he said, "but only a few."

She beamed him her brightest smile.

He looked, for a moment, as if she'd poleaxed him, but then he scowled and muttered, "Just keep it brief. I'd like to get some lunch out of my lunch hour."

"Very brief," she assured him, following as he led her past the secretary's desk toward his office. Pausing at the large, cherrywood door, he extracted another, smaller set of keys and let himself in, flipping on overhead lights as he moved out of sight. Laurel timidly entered and swept a gaze around his office.

Unlike the waiting and reception areas, no professional decorator had stepped foot in here. The walls were plastered and painted white where they were not lined with simple, functional bookshelves. A tweed sofa in neutral tones had been shoved up against a vast, bare window in the wall facing the desk. A maple coffee table, its surface marred with a deep gash stood before it. Both table and sofa were stacked with folders, books and papers. The massive cherrywood desk behind which Edward White now stood was likewise covered with piles of documents, as were the tops of the metal file cabinets that stood in the corners of the room, flanking the desk.

Edward nodded at one of a pair of leather-and-chrome chairs. Laurel stepped in front of it and sat down. Only then did he seat himself in the big black leather armchair behind him. It creaked and tilted ominously with his weight.

"Now then, Ms.... What is your name again?"

"Laurel. Laurel Heffington Miller. Call me Laurel, if you please."

If her maiden name meant anything to him, he gave no sign of it, merely nodding in acknowledgment. "All right, Laurel, how can I help you?"

She took a fortifying breath. "You can agree to represent me in a civil suit against my ex-husband, seeking control of my inheritance, which is valued, roughly, at four million dollars."

He lifted a brow at that. "Am I to understand that your ex-husband now has control of an inheritance belonging to you?"

"Yes."

"And you want it back."

She tilted her head uncertainly. "Actually, I never had it—not control of it, anyway."

He rocked forward and templed his fingers, elbows braced against the edge of his desk. "You'll have to explain that. If it's your inheritance, why does he have control of it?"

"Because my late grandmother set it up that way."

"She left your inheritance to him?"

"No, she left him in control of *my* inheritance, and the divorce apparently did not change that."

He picked up an ink pen and made some random marks on a yellow legal pad at hand. "At what point did your grandmother intend for you to take over control of your own inheritance?"

Laurel looked down at her hands. "According to Abelard Kennison, she didn't."

She heard the creak of his chair, followed by a fulminating silence, and then, "Abelard Kennison. Well, well, well."

Laurel pushed her gaze up. "You know of him, then?"

He waved a big hand fitted with a heavy gold class ring containing a large, oval green stone. "Everyone even remotely connected with the practice of law in this city knows of Abelard Kennison."

"And most are frightened of him," she said softly.

"For good reason," he replied. "Kennison is a shark in court and out."

"Are you frightened of him?" Laurel asked.

His smile was tight and small. "Why would I be?"

Laurel gulped. "Would you be frightened of him if you had to go up against him in court?"

He leaned forward, forearms laid across the blotter on his desk. His pale blue eyes were cold as stone. "Let's just say that it takes a shark to know a shark, and let it go at that."

Oh, yes, she could see it now, the shark, safely caged, just waiting for a chance to bite. Laurel let out a breath she hadn't known she was holding. "Then you'll help me?"

"I didn't say that. Why don't you tell me why your grandmother felt you were incapable of handling your own inheritance?"

Laurel wrinkled her nose. "She didn't approve of me."

"Oh? And why is that?"

She lifted a shoulder in a halfhearted shrug. "She said I was just like my father."

"He's the one who died climbing that mountain in Tibet, isn't he?"

So he did know. "He and my mother," she confirmed.

He leaned back in his chair. "Damned stupid thing to do if you ask me."

Laurel's brows shot up in surprise. "Me, too!" she blurted.

"A man with a family ought to be more sensible," he said.

"I agree," she hastened to assure him.

Those blue eyes suddenly impaled her. "Then why did your grandmother think you were like him?"

Laurel sat back in dismay. She hadn't alleviated his doubts at all. He was just trying to catch her off guard. Frowning, she said, "I wasn't happy after my parents died—or before, for that matter. They were always off on some adventure or other, and my grandmother controlled my life. She wasn't an easy person to get along with, my grandmother. Nothing I did seemed to please her, and I guess I got in to some pretty rough stuff trying to get my parents' attention. Then they died, and I knew there was no way I'd ever please grandmother. I guess I rebelled, and frankly, my grandfather encouraged me. But then *he* died, and there was no one left but Grandmother. I honestly tried to build a real relationship with her then, to win her approval. I even married in

order to please her, and what a mistake that was! Then she died, too, and I realized that I was completely at his mercy, my husband's that is—his and Abelard Kennison's. And they planned it that way, Mr. White, as God is my witness, I swear they did!''

''So you divorced Mr. Miller,'' he surmised.

She nodded. ''His name is Bryce. Kennison brought him into our house as a kind of caretaker. Grandmother's health was failing, and she trusted Kennison unreservedly. So did I, for that matter.'' She lifted her hands, beseeching Edward White's understanding. ''He said he wanted to help me. He said he'd help me gain my grandmother's approval. I didn't realize until later that he'd planned for me to marry Bryce all along, that it was part of his plan to get his hands on my inheritance. I even suspect that some of the charities that he convinced Grandmother to leave the majority of her funds to are fronts. I think he got the lion's share with his dummy corporations and bogus charities, so why should he get my share, too?''

Edward White arched one thick, chocolate-colored brow. ''Those are pretty strong charges.''

''I swear it's all true. Please, can't you help me?''

Edward spread his hands. ''This sort of thing is an expensive proposition, Ms., uh, Laurel. I'll need a sizable retainer and—''

Laurel shook her head, eyes closed. ''I can't. That's the problem. You see, I don't have a cent to my name other than a small salary and what tips I get as a waitress.''

He was silent so long that she sneaked a peek at him. He was staring at her—and frowning. Her heart sank. ''Are you telling me that you got *nothing* in the divorce?''

She nodded miserably. ''Nothing. My attorney said it was the only way to get it done without a protracted legal fight. He said we'd deal later with the matters of the inheritance and the house.''

''Your grandmother's house?'' he asked in a tone of disbelief. ''The Heffington house? The mansion in Highland Park?''

Laurel spread her hands in abject affirmation. ''My ex lives in my family home,'' she said, a catch in her throat, ''on *my* money, while I work at a diner and barely make the rent on a studio apartment down off Central Expressway.''

White lurched back in his chair, tilting and wobbling precari-

ously. "And who," he asked in a hard tone, "was the Neanderthal who represented you?"

She looked down at her hands, knowing all too keenly what a fool she'd been and muttered, "Daniel Hardacre."

"Holy—" He bit off the next word, shaking his head. "Lady, you have a talent for getting involved with the very people you ought to avoid. Hardacre is a slime, and very likely on the Kennison payroll, or haven't you figured that out yet?"

Of course. She bit her lip, saying in a small voice, "A friend of my grandmother's recommended him. Bryce probably put her up to it, but I didn't know that then. I didn't even realize until it was too late that he was intentionally mishandling everything, and even then I thought he just wanted to marry me."

"*Marry you?*"

She nodded. "After the divorce, he said he'd help me get my inheritance if I'd marry him, which meant, of course, that he'd get half of everything."

"Well, at least you had sense enough not to go for that!" White said sarcastically. Then he pushed his hands over his face and shook his head. "I can't believe this."

"All right, I'm an idiot!" Laurel snapped. "You think that's anything I hadn't figured out on my own? The question is, will you help me?"

He glared at her over the tips of his fingers for a moment, then dropped his hands and softened his gaze. "I'll look into it," he finally said.

Disappointed, Laurel pressed for deeper commitment. "Does that mean you'll represent me?"

"It means I'll look into it," he said smartly.

Laurel chewed the inside of her cheek, consumed with the fear that he was just trying to let her down gently. Saying he'd look into it was far from agreeing to help, and she knew it only too well. It was the money, of course, or rather, the lack of it. If only she could guarantee him funds.... But then, couldn't she? As long as they won, she could guarantee him any amount he wanted, right up to half of everything. It was certainly worth that much to her. In fact, it was worth more than that. If she could just come out of it with the house and enough to keep it up, she'd be happy.

At least Bryce and Kennison wouldn't get it, and she'd be able to take care of Barry properly. She'd have to continue hiding him, of course, perhaps for many months to come yet, but she'd been doing that all along. On the other hand, Edward White might not even care. He might not even expect her to keep up appearances. Unlike Hardacre, he wasn't in the least attracted to her. He might well be willing, even eager, for her to go her separate way immediately.

For a moment, she couldn't believe what she was considering, but why not? She took a long hard look at him. Yes. Better him than Danny Hardacre. Much better than Danny Hardacre.

"There is a way," she mumbled, spirits lifting.

"I beg your pardon?"

Emboldened by the sheer sense of what she was about to propose, Laurel straightened and engaged him with her clear green gaze. "There is a way to guarantee your fee."

"Well, that couldn't hurt," he began, "but—"

"I'll pay you one million dollars," she interrupted flatly.

He shook his head as if trying to unblock his ears. "But you just said—"

"Two million dollars!" she repeated, sliding to the edge of her chair in her excitement. "Two and a half! Just think of it as a partnership."

"What on earth are you talking about? What partnership?"

"Us! The two of us! We can do it, I know we can."

"Do what?"

"Get my inheritance. We, *you* can get my money and my house. You bring your expertise to the effort and I'll bring my zeal and an iron-clad guarantee of cold hard cash! What do you say?"

"I'm still trying to figure out what *you're* saying!" he exclaimed.

"It's so simple when you think about it," she told him. "And to think that Danny gave me the answer! Only, Danny wasn't the right man for the job. Danny couldn't win against Kennison. You can."

His chair slammed down in exasperation, and he leaned so far forward that his upper body stretched almost all the way across

his desk, bringing their faces into proximity. With mere inches between them, Laurel felt a thrill of recognition unlike any she'd ever felt before. This was right. She knew that this was right. Edward White only knew that she had confused him. Poor Edward. He wasn't letting himself feel it. He hadn't sifted through the logic of it yet, but she would make him see the sense in this, and finally, *finally*, she'd have her life in her own hands. The prospect, the very idea of winning a fight that seemed to have lasted her own life long, left her trembling.

"Will you please explain yourself?" he gritted out, and she smiled, gratitude and serenity filling her.

"It's all so simple," she told him breathlessly. "In fact, it's perfect."

"*What* is perfect?" he demanded tautly.

She took a deep breath, looked him square in the eye and said, "Edward White, will you marry me?"

Chapter Two

For several long seconds, Edward merely stared, his mind shuffling her last words over and over in an automatic attempt to make something of them other than what he'd heard. Something sensible, something sane. Finally he gave up, accepting that he'd heard correctly even if he couldn't accept the idea framed by the sound. Anger roared through him. Who did she think she was? Did she think her looks and her name made her desirable to every man with whom she came in contact? Or did she hold herself so cheaply that she'd play whore—for that's what she was proposing—to any man who promised aid? He knew only one way to find out.

He got up out of his chair and calmly walked around the desk to lean against its edge right next to her chair. He made himself smile down at her. The face turned up to him appeared guileless, even trusting. He folded his arms. "Well, let's see," he said lightly. "Hmm." He bent down, angling his body in order to place his hands on the arms of her chair. "How do I know I'd be happy, married to you?" he asked silkily, and then he grabbed her and hauled her up against him. "Let's find out." Ignoring the

almost comically widened eyes, he set his gaze on her slackened mouth and planted his over it.

She gave a small, seemingly involuntary squeak but offered no real resistance. No doubt she needed a real lesson, this spoiled little rich girl, and he was, inexplicably, of a mind to give it to her. He slid his arms around her, locked them and tilted his head, slanting his mouth across hers. Her gasp gave him just the entry he needed, and he stabbed his tongue inside. Dimly he was aware of her arms lifting and her hands closing in the fabric of his jacket. And then, somehow, he seemed to lose track. At some point, his embrace softened. His hand splayed, one between her shoulder blades, the other in the small of her back. What had started as invasion became, unintentionally, exploration, so that his tongue swept around the silky cavern of her mouth and his lips melded with hers. Her fists released their twin holds on his jacket and relaxed, sliding up to the nape of his neck. Her body melted against his, revealing slender, but surprisingly lush curves.

Desire unlike anything he'd ever felt before lodged in his groin and spread upward, eager and insistent. He slid his hand down to cup her bottom and press her pelvis to his. She caught her breath and a second later sighed into his mouth. It was like putting a lit match to tender. He shuddered and pulled her tighter against him, so tight that her feet left the floor, her legs tangling with his as he leaned back, hovering awkwardly over his desk. Slowly he realized that he was teetering on the very brink of control. A moment more of this and he'd lay her down on the desk, shove up her skirt and—

Abruptly he rocked up onto his feet and pushed her away, holding her upright by his hands clamped around her arms. For a long, shocking moment, her bright green eyes stared up at him unseeingly, her lush, slightly swollen mouth curved into a dreamy smile, and then, gradually, focus returned and with it came, not outrage but dismay.

"Oh-oh," she said, slender fingertips coming up to cover her mouth. "Oh, my God."

She sagged, and he released her. She plopped down into her chair, still staring as if not quite believing what had just passed between them. He knew exactly how she felt, and that more than

anything else irritated him mightily. He spun away and strode around his desk, shouting, "Are you out of your ever-loving mind?"

When he turned to face her, even with the desk between them, she visibly shrank back into her chair. He pushed a hand through his hair, appalled to find that his hand was shaking. This was her fault, her fault entirely, and he attacked as much from habit and training as anything else. "Is that your answer to everything? Just marry the first lawyer you meet?"

"You're not the first," she said timidly.

"No? Just how many others have you proposed to, then? Two? Four? God in heaven!"

She stiffened a trembling lower lip and clamped her jaws shut. He planted his hands flat on the desk blotter and leaned close, almost touching his nose to hers. Lord, she had huge, green eyes, lashes as long as broom bristles and a perfect, pretty little mouth. And that he noticed made him even angrier. He tried to tangle his mind around the issue at hand. The little idiot had actually proposed marriage to him! Worse, he apparently wasn't the first! He could imagine the talk around the bar committee tables if it got out that he was representing a hot little number—a Heffington, no less—who'd proposed marriage to half the attorneys in town! He put on his best shark's face and dropped his voice into the sonic boom range.

"Just how many attorneys have you proposed to, *Mrs. Miller?*"

"N-none...e-except you."

He pressed her; it was instinctive. "What about Daniel Hardacre?"

"He proposed to me," she said quickly. " I didn't propose to him. And I turned him down," she added firmly.

Edward's steel-trap mind told him the significance of that much more quickly than he'd have preferred. She'd turned down Hardacre and proposed to *him*, only to him—and then when he'd kissed her, she'd turned to molten fire. Pushing that thought away, he grimaced and dropped down into his chair again, grumbling, "Rating higher than Dan Hardacre is hardly cause for celebration."

She looked down at her lap, long, mascaraed eyelashes lowering. "You're right, of course." Her voice was thick and watery, as if muted by tears.

He made up his mind that if she so much as sniffed he was throwing her out of his office, but to his surprise when she looked up again, she appeared sad but perfectly composed. For some reason that irritated him, too. "This is insane!"

Her bright green eyes snapped angrily at that, but she put her words together carefully. "I only thought that with the community property laws what they are, you'd be guaranteed at least half my inheritance."

He could only shake his head. "You are insane, aren't you?"

Her hands curled into fists against the chrome arms of the chair. She dropped her gaze, but he had to admire the steel in her voice. "It would guarantee your fee so you could take my case."

It had been a long time since he had encountered such desperation, a long time indeed. His clients were usually too well-heeled to be truly desperate. He slashed his eyes to the stapler on the corner of his desk and said gruffly, "Have you ever heard the term 'contingency case'?"

She sat very still. "Yes. I'm told that it is usually reserved for personal-injury cases."

"Usually but not always. Here's how it works," he said, keeping his eyes on that stapler, "If we should win, I'd get a third."

"But I've already offered you half—"

"A third," he repeated sternly. "That's the law."

"Oh."

Seconds ticked away into silence while he tried to decide where he was going with this. He wasn't really considering taking this mess on, was he? Not after that kiss, surely. And yet, something about her got to him, *beckoned* him. And there was Abelard Kennison. He'd give six years off his life to nail that so-and-so. Then she said, "So you're saying that you'll take my case on contingency?"

The rebuff was reflex. "I'm not saying that at all. I'm just saying that *if* I *should* decide to take the case, I *could* take it on contingency."

"Ah." She picked at an invisible piece of lint on her skirt. "And, um, when will you decide one way or another?"

He shrugged. "Like I told you earlier, I'll look into it. If all is as you say *and* I think I can do anything for you, I may—*may*—sign on."

He heard the deep sigh that she heaved and tried not to feel sympathy. She had proposed marriage to him, for pity's sake! Marriage! Who did she think he was, the White Knight? Even if he had been, he wasn't at all certain that he'd have attempted to rescue this particular maiden. She was obviously a tad eccentric, to put it kindly. Marriage, holy cow! Plus, he had nothing but her word that she'd been robbed—that and the fact that Abelard Kennison was involved.

His professional mouth watered at the thought of taking a bite out of old Abe. Kennison's very existence was an affront to every honest, dedicated attorney in the state, and Edward couldn't deny even to himself that he'd love to be the one to bring Kennison down. Just knowing what Kennison would put Laurel Miller through on the witness stand was enough reason to give Edward pause, especially after the lack of good sense that she'd just displayed. He couldn't in good conscience put either one of them through that unless he knew he had a real chance to win. He made up his mind—sort of. A thorough investigation was in order. Marriage definitely was not.

He became aware, belatedly, that she was talking, and tuned in.

"...how I can thank you," she was saying. "You don't know how many other places I've been."

"Suppose you tell me."

"Six."

"I want names," he said coldly. "Make me a list of every attorney who turned you down and what reason he—or she—gave."

"All right. Shall I do it now?"

"Yes." He tossed her a pad and pencil. She began writing. "Also, I'll need addresses and telephone numbers where I can contact you."

"I don't have a telephone at my apartment, but you can always

get a message to me through the diner," she said distractedly, then poked the tip of her tongue out of the corner of her mouth as she concentrated on writing down the information he had requested. It was a sweet, juicy, tiny bit of rose pink that Edward couldn't help noticing.

Disgustedly, he shook his head, wondering how a Heffington came to be waiting tables in a common diner, but he let the curiosity pass. All in good time. Her grandmother must be spinning in her grave, though. It was common knowledge that the old girl had been extremely high in the instep. Laurel laid the yellow tablet on the desk and placed the pencil carefully on top of it. He gave her a dismissive nod, saying, "I'll be in touch."

Carefully schooling her face against the disappointment that had momentarily marred it, she got up, gathering her little bag into one hand and extending the other. Cautiously he rose to his feet and swallowed her slender, graceful hand with his much larger one, surprised to feel the slight roughness of her palm, proof the lady did indeed work for a living. He liked that for some reason. Irritably he reminded himself what had just transpired. Marriage. Of all the asinine ideas.

Of course, in all fairness, that asinine kiss had been his idea. Also, he admitted reluctantly, he had once proposed just such a marriage of convenience himself. At the time, it had seemed reasonably expeditious, but look how it had turned out! His fiancée—ex-fiancée—was not only married to, but in love with, his best friend! He shook his head, failing to realize how long he'd held Laurel's hand until she gently pulled it free. Hastily he cleared his throat and bent over his desk, busily shuffling papers.

"I'll be in touch," he muttered, and she thanked him again on her way to the door. He gave her a nod, then collapsed into his chair. From behind the open door, she hesitantly said, "Um, y-you never a-answered me."

"Yes, I did," he snapped, repeating angrily, "I'll be in touch." For a long moment, she stared at him around the edge of that door, and then she nodded and slipped away, pulling the door closed quietly behind her. She was long gone before he realized what she'd meant. He hadn't, actually, answered her marriage

proposal, but surely she didn't think... He wouldn't want to place bets on what that woman might think.

He had a flash of those enormous eyes and immediately recoiled from the picture. Either she was the single most desperate individual he'd ever met, or out of her mind, and he didn't care to ponder which. Reaching for the legal pad, he quickly scanned what she'd written. Seeing nothing there to alarm him, he quickly made notes containing the information she'd given him. Reading over it, he numbered the items on the list in order of importance, with her late grandmother's will rating number one. He'd begin there. Satisfied with his organization, he linked his hands behind his head and kicked back, wondering who he ought to call in on this, someone very discreet and very thorough. A name popped into mind and right out again, for that was when he saw her, standing at the bus stop framed in the center of the room's only window.

He couldn't deny that she was attractive. Automatically he compared her with the one woman whom he'd always felt had set the standard for women. Laurel Miller was about the same height as Kendra, but any similarity ended right there. Kendra was softer and rounder and infinitely more sensible, wearing her long golden brown hair in a fat, flat braid that lay against the back of her head and trailed down over her shoulders. She'd never have considered Laurel Miller's short, sassy cut or that sexy, tailored dress, for that matter. He let his gaze slide down the length of Laurel Miller's long, slender legs and couldn't help thinking that if, by some wild, implausible chance she was ever to become his, he'd want that hem lowered a good three or four inches, minimum. Still, she did look good. What was it about high heels that made a woman look so...*womanly?*

The bus arrived before he could castigate himself for asking such a question even in the privacy of his own mind. It was only when the door opened and she stepped up inside that he realized she was actually traveling by bus. Creeps, hadn't she come out of the divorce with even a car? He scribbled another note on his pad, and then another and another... Frowning, he put the pencil down. At the very least, he was looking at gross dereliction of duty here. Even Danny Hardacre ought to have been able to make

a case for actually needing private transportation in a city where the public sort was next to nonexistent. Come to think of it, Kennison was usually more careful than this. Was the old thief getting careless in his declining years?

He shook his head, searching for some clue as to what was going on here, only to have her breathless, husky question explode inside his head again. *"Edward White, will you marry me?"*

He pushed a hand over his face, shaking off a small, very private thrill. What a stupid idea! Well, at least she'd rated him higher than Hardacre. Him she'd turned down. Not that it mattered. It didn't matter in the least. It wasn't even really flattering, considering Danny Hardacre. All that mattered was the case and whether or not he could win it.

That thought firmly in mind, he reached down and pulled out the bottom drawer of his desk, extracting a thick, zippered, leather case, which he placed squarely in the center of his desk blotter. Sliding open the zipper, he flipped back the top and clicked open the small computer inside. Next he extracted a smaller case and took out an external modem, which he plugged into the computer before hooking into the telephone. Finally he pulled up the two sections of the keyboard and fitted them together; his big hands just couldn't manage those standard notebook boards. In short order, he had tapped into a private line and was asking permission to look around. Some time elapsed before permission was granted, but then he rubbed his hands together in glee. Fingers poised over the keyboard, he smiled at the blinking cursor on the screen.

"Get ready, Kennison," he muttered. "Here I come."

A few seconds later, he had tapped into the correct probate court, and moments after that, he was making another list on his legal pad. Just one break was all he needed, just one little slipup on Kennison's part. And something told him that he just might get it. Laurel Miller he would worry about later.

"She's here!"

"Hey, Laurel's here!"

Laurel smiled and waved as she whipped around the end of the

diner counter and made for the back to change her clothes. "Hi ya, Carl. How's your mom doing?"

"She smiled today, Miss Laurel," the shy middle-aged man called from his usual seat in the corner booth. "I think she knew who I was."

"That's great!" Laurel called, pushing through the swinging metal doors. Carl's mother was pushing a hundred and clinging tenuously to life in the bed of a local nursing home. Carl visited her faithfully every day, then stopped in the diner for lunch on his way home. Never having married and already retired, he had plenty of time on his hands, time he liked to use to help others. Laurel was terribly fond of the fellow, and the feeling was mutual, as it was with many of the diner's customers.

She was sliding into her uniform when Fancy entered the room, her too black hair piled high on top of her head, pencils sticking out of the brittle, netted mass.

"So? How'd it go?"

Laurel sighed and willed the tremble from her voice. "I'm not sure. I think I found the right man for the job, but I'm not sure he'll take the case."

"He didn't turn you down flat, then?"

"No."

"Well, that's progress, isn't it?"

"I suppose." Laurel traded her heels for cheap athletic shoes and turned her back so Fancy could zip her up.

"Kennison didn't faze him?"

"No."

"You gotta admit, that's good, then."

"True again," Laurel agreed, wrapping the ends of her apron around her waist and tying them. She reached for the small, paper hat, stepped over in front of the mirror and pinned it on. She hated the hat. It looked like the sort that nurses had once worn, except that it was banded with garish colors and stamped front and back with the name of the diner. Fancy flatly refused to wear hers, but the hair net was no improvement as far as Laurel was concerned. She concentrated on getting the hat straight, avoiding Fancy's heavily silvered eyes, not that it helped.

"You didn't tell him about the baby."

"No, of course not," Laurel replied mildly.

"There's something more, though," Fancy pronounced ominously, "something you're not telling me, and it's got you worried."

Laurel rolled back her eyes. It would be useless to deny it. Fancy had the scent and would bug her until she told. According to Fancy it was a sixth sense she'd developed during her days as a stripper because of the married men who had hit on her. She'd learned to identify them with one look, and they were the only kind Fancy would date. The single guys, she said, always wanted to change you, make you into something you weren't, and what Fancy had been back then was an "exotic dancer." Showbiz, or so she said, was in her blood. Laurel didn't know about her blood, but she knew about her heart: it was as big as all outdoors. She couldn't have asked for a better friend.

Laurel folded her arms and put her back to the mirror. "I think I blew it."

"Oh, that's plain silly," Fancy retorted dismissively. "You've got that pitch down to a science by now."

Laurel shook her head and dropped her gaze. "I asked him to marry me."

"*What?*" Fancy's horror was second only to her own. Laurel stared at the toes of her nylon shoes while Fancy gaped at the top of her head. "Y-you asked that man to marry you, that Edward White?"

Laurel nodded miserably. "At the moment, it just seemed the only thing to do. It would certainly guarantee that he'd get his fee."

Fancy let loose a few of her more colorful phrases, but then she came right back to the meat of the issue. "You didn't ask any of them others, did you?"

"No, of course not."

"It was Danny that gave you the idea, wasn't it? That sorry excuse for a...person with something between the legs."

Laurel smiled. She couldn't help it, knowing as she did what Fancy thought of the man, though Fancy would have choked before she'd have called him such. Laurel shook her head. "I can't blame this on Danny or anyone else. It was a stupid idea. I

thought of the community property thing, and somehow it just seemed like the only guarantee I could give him, so..."

Fancy's silvered lids elongated, drawing her eyes into slits and blocking them with the heavy fringe of store-bought lashes. "He turned you down, did he, this White?"

Laurel averted her eyes and said evasively, "It was an unbelievably stupid suggestion."

"But one you didn't make no one else," Fancy pointed out shrewdly. "He something to see, is he, this White?"

Laurel swallowed. "H-how do you mean?"

"You know perfectly well what I mean," Fancy retorted, her hands on her hips. "I know you, honey, and inheritance or no inheritance, he'd have to flip your switch before you'd consider, let alone propose, even a marriage of convenience. You learned your lesson too well with muscle man Bryce."

Laurel thinned her lips in a grimace. "Don't remind me."

Fancy tapped her toe. "You're attracted to this guy."

Laurel closed her eyes in embarrassment. "That isn't why I suggested marriage," she defended weakly.

"No?"

"No. I told you, it was the only way I could think of to guarantee his fee."

"The only guarantee is that you'd be legally hitched," Fancy pointed out. "What if you didn't win your case? Ever think of that?"

Laurel gulped. "N-no, actually."

"Well, you were thinking of something," Fancy prodded.

Laurel searched for the answer to that and couldn't find it. "I—I don't know what I was thinking."

"I gotta see this man!" Fancy drawled.

Laurel opened her mouth to beg her friend and co-worker not to pursue that ambition, but Shorty stuck his head through the door just then.

"Hey, I got orders up out here!" he chided in his Spanish-accented English. He was the only totally bald Mexican Laurel had ever known and not short at all. The nickname came from his position as short-order cook, not his stature.

"Hold your horses!" Fancy barked at the same moment Laurel called, "Sorry!"

Fancy made a face that clearly stated the matter would not be dropped permanently, whirled and pushed through the doors. Laurel was thankful for the reprieve. She bent and lifted one foot at a time to tie her shoes. What *had* she been thinking to propose marriage to Edward White? Had she really expected him to agree? And why had he kissed her? More questions, always more questions, but this time she wasn't sure she wanted to know the answers.

Edward pecked feverishly at his computer. He'd promised himself that he wasn't going to do this today. He was not going to devote any more time to following this electronic trail. He was going to sit and wait for some of the other feelers he'd put out to produce some sort of feedback. He had other cases to work on, after all, *legitimate* cases, cases for which people had paid him cold, hard cash. It was just so frustrating, though. He'd found definite proof that at least three of the charities to which Laurel's grandmother had left money were fakes, but he hadn't been able to tie Abelard Kennison to any of them. The total funds involved added up to less than three hundred thousand dollars, a mere pittance compared to the original forty million. The old girl had really strained herself giving one tenth of the whole sum to her only living relative.

Then again, what he knew of Laurel Heffington Miller did not exactly inspire confidence. He could hardly believe that she had waltzed in here and proposed marriage to him! Still, what he knew of Abelard Kennison was ten times more damning. If anyone had been victimized here, it was surely Laurel Miller. The kiss he was not going to think about, period.

The speaker phone buzzed. Without taking his eyes off the screen, Edward reached out and hit the appropriate button. "Yeah?"

"Williams is on the phone for you, sir."

That got his eyes off the screen. "Great!" He rubbed his hands together, punched another button and picked up the telephone receiver, kicking back in his chair. "That was quick."

"You sounded urgent the other day" came the drawling male voice.

"What do you have?" Edward asked noncommittally.

"A list of names, all of them elderly clients whose estates were handled by our boy Abe, all deceased, all cared for at the end by a practical nurse named—are you ready?—Bryce Miller."

Edward sat straight up in his chair. "Bingo."

"Thought you'd like that."

"How'd you come by such an interesting, and comprehensive, piece of information?"

"Hey, now," objected the other man good-naturedly. "Do I ask you trade secrets?"

Edward chuckled. "Okay, okay. Fax the list to my private line, and thanks."

"My pleasure. Anything else I can do for you?"

"Stay on the charity trail. There's got to be a Kennison connection somewhere."

"Will do."

Edward hung up the phone, well pleased. Moments later, the fax machine on the far left-hand corner of his desk began to whine. Edward leaned back and linked his hands behind his head, grinning as the machine spat out the single sheet of paper. The paper in hand, Edward studied the list of names, committing each one to memory. Then he carefully stored the paper away inside a metal box with a combination. He placed the box inside a locked desk drawer. Tossing and catching the key, he decided it was time to call on Bryce Miller.

A pale, achingly thin girl wearing an ill fitting maid's uniform answered the door.

"Who are you?"

Edward pulled a business card from his coat pocket and handed it to the girl. "I'd like to see Mr. Miller, please."

Without so much as another glance, the girl turned and bellowed down the hall, "Bryce, some shyster wants to see ya!" She flipped her hand over her shoulder, an apparent signal for Edward to come in, and promptly disappeared behind a swinging door. Edward was just about to follow when a blond man with

bulging biceps stepped into the hall from another door farther down the way.

Bryce Miller was of medium height with short, flat-topped, golden blond hair. Attired in chinos and a blue tank top obviously chosen for bringing out a similar color in his eyes and showing off muscle, he looked Edward up and down before saying dismissively, "I already have a lawyer."

Edward took an instant dislike to him. "Don't you mean 'employer'?" he suggested pleasantly.

Miller slanted grayish blue eyes and presented his perfect profile, surgically enhanced, if Edward was any judge. "What's your beef?"

"No beef," Edward answered with an easy shrug, "but I'm not soliciting business, either. My name's Edward White, and I'm here on behalf of...your ex-wife." He'd almost said *a client*.

Miller's entire demeanor changed. A flicker of apprehension came first, then a very studied composure, a definite softening. "How is Laurel?" he asked with a genuine note of interest to mark the low, tender tone.

"Well enough."

Miller made a great show of relief and switched abruptly to a sort of forced bonhomie. "I'm so glad. Come in and have a seat, won't you?"

"Don't mind if I do." Edward followed him into what had once been a splendid study or library. The oak shelves were empty of books now, however, and except for two low-backed, overstuffed easy chairs upholstered in a heavy flowered damask, the furniture had been replaced with weight machines and workout equipment. A Federal-style butler's cart bearing crystal decanters and glasses sat to one side of a clean, redbrick fireplace. Miller walked over to it, unstoppered a decanter and poured a full measure of bright red liquid into a glass. "Cranberry juice," he said, holding it aloft. "Good for the kidneys. Would you like one?"

"No thanks."

Miller nodded at one of the chairs, and Edward made himself comfortable, long legs crossed. Miller took the other, perching on

the edge, legs spread and elbows balanced upon knees. He looked Edward over again, then slugged back a long draught of juice.

"Where is Laurel? I haven't seen her since she moved out of the last apartment."

It came out entirely too casually but with just the right touch of concern. Edward smiled to himself. He was pretty good, considering his IQ had to come in somewhere below that of a poodle. "Mr. Miller, I came here—"

"I don't care!" Miller declared, coming to his feet.

"Excuse me?"

Miller walked back to the butler's cart and refilled his glass. "Whatever it is," he said over his shoulder, "I don't care." He turned to face Edward again, feet braced apart as if he dared Edward not to believe what he had to say. "I still love her, and I know she still loves me. If we could just talk, the two of us, alone, I'm certain we could patch things up."

Edward lowered his gaze. "I'll tell my...*Ms*. Miller, that you're interested in a private meeting, though I'd say it's a little late, considering that the divorce is final."

"I don't care about that, either," Miller vowed. "All I care about is her."

"Oh, then you won't mind signing over her fortune," Edward said smoothly, "and the house, of course."

Anger flashed across Miller's face, but then he put on an expression of misery. "I can't," he said sadly and pushed his free hand over his hair, not disturbing so much as a lock of it.

Edward wanted desperately to tell him that he wasn't buying his act, but he knew that would be counterproductive. Instead, he brought both hands together in his lap and made himself smile with understanding. "And why is that?"

Miller registered surprise so patently false that Edward felt the urge to slap him. "Don't you know?" Miller whispered.

Edward clenched his hands into fists and forced disinterest into his voice. "Know what?"

An impressive parade of emotions fixed themselves to his face one after the other, first indecision, then sadness and resignation, followed by grim determination. "No, I won't embarrass Laurel like that. She's too precious to me, despite her, ah, *problems*."

He made a sudden, impassioned plea. "Please, Mr. White, if you could just give me an address or a telephone number, I know we could work this out."

For some reason, the very idea of Laurel "working out" anything with this muscle-bound bozo made Edward's stomach turn. He didn't realize that he was clenching his teeth until he unlocked them to speak. "As I said, I'll mention your request to Laurel, but I warn you that she does not appear to want to work out anything, Mr. Miller, except access to her inheritance."

Miller moved quickly across the room and dropped down onto the edge of his chair again. "I know I could make her remember how good it was between us before she got this notion into her head that I'm some kind of enemy. I blame that on her divorce lawyer," he said bitterly.

"Daniel Hardacre has much to answer for," Edward stated noncommittally.

"If you won't tell me how to contact her," Bryce pleaded, "then just ask her to come and see me. Please. And tell her that I love her, that I can't stop thinking about her, that it's lonely in our bed at night...."

Spurred by sudden images of Laurel and this walking muscle wrapped around each other, Edward shot to his feet. "I..." He cleared his throat. "I, um, must again state my, that is, Laurel's position. She wants her home back and control of her inheritance."

"That's not going to happen," Miller said flatly, and Edward had the unassailable sense that he had just heard the truth for the first time since he'd walked in here.

"I see. Well, I was afraid that would be your position," Edward said, bluffing for all he was worth. "I had hoped that it wouldn't come to litigation, and you understand, of course, the obligation to try to settle the matter outside of court. That being impossible, however, I'll be on my way. I'll let myself out. Thank you for the time."

He didn't wait for Miller to speak or anything else, just walked out the same way he'd come in and hurried down the elaborately manicured path to the big, boxy, luxury sedan parked at the apex of the broad circular drive. He was mad at himself by the time

he got there. What the hell was wrong with him anyway? He'd nearly blown it. He'd all but declared himself the attorney of record, and what a pretty fix that would have been. What was it about this case that made him want to leap right in? He wanted to see Kennison go down, yes, but he'd wanted that for years. No, in all honesty, he had to admit—to himself, if no one else—that what compelled him was Laurel Miller herself, but he couldn't for the life of him understand why.

Oh, she was attractive, no doubt about that, but he saw and dealt with attractive women every day. He didn't find himself assaulted with visions of them with other men or wanting to throttle those other men. Mostly he didn't think about those other women at all. Then again, no other woman had ever proposed marriage to him within moments of making his acquaintance.

Oh, if he'd let himself, he supposed he would still think of Kendra in that vein. He had intended to marry her, after all, but that had been before Parker had chosen her as the wife meant to ensure his guardianship of his orphaned infant niece. And to think that as Parker's attorney it had been his own idea! It wasn't supposed to have been a real marriage at all, but it certainly had become that, and only the fact that both Kendra and Parker were happy together made the situation at all palatable. Maybe it was that marriage-of-convenience scheme that drew him to Laurel Miller. Maybe he could identify with her moment of madness because he'd experienced a similar one himself. Yes, that had to be it, that and the chance to put Kennison away once and for all. But that's all it was. That's all it could be.

Wasn't it?

Chapter Three

Laurel groaned, slipped her foot free of her shoe and flexed her toes. It had been a long day, but at seven-thirty they only had a half hour to go before they could lock the doors. With any luck, they'd be out of here in another hour, so long as no one walked in that door and ordered a hot meal, forcing Shorty to fire up the grill again. Laurel stretched her arm across the bar counter and laid her head upon it, pulling the offending paper hat free with her other hand.

Next to her, Fancy snapped the tiny elastic band on her hair net and chomped her gum. "What a day," she moaned.

"Hey, Fancy," Old Plug shouted, rousing from his nap in the booth nearest the door. "Did I ask you to marry me?"

Without blinking so much as an eyelash, Fancy shouted back, "Yeah, Plug."

"Are you gonna do it?"

Laurel giggled into the bend of her elbow, and Fancy kicked her with a sideways swing of her foot, saying loudly, "Naw, honey, I can't—not this month. I ain't got a free day for weeks."

"Oh," Plug said with no obvious emotion. "Okay."

Laurel giggled again.

"Will you shush!" Fancy hissed in her ear.

"I can't help it. I think it's sweet, the way he never gives up."

"You wouldn't think it was so funny if he was after you all the time."

"You're his dream," Laurel pointed out.

Fancy snorted inelegantly, snapped her gum and said, "You know, the sad thing is, I remember him from the good old days as well as he remembers me, and he was quite a man back then. Nothing special, but he had all his hair and all his teeth and he was kind of shy with women. If he liked the bottle a little too much, well, which one of them didn't? Who'd have thought he'd turn out this way, living on the street, drinking away his life?"

"It is sad," Laurel agreed softly. "Doesn't he have any family or anyone to take care of him?"

"Oh, they've tried," Fancy said. "They hunt him up and take him home, dry him out, get him to see a doctor. He goes along for a few days, and then he just disappears again. It's like the streets just call to him, poor soul."

"He sure is taken with you," Laurel pointed out wryly.

"Aw, I just remind him of better times."

"I guess."

Several seconds passed in blessed silence. A couple got up from the center booth, tossed some bills on the table and moved toward the door.

"Y'all come back!" Fancy called to them. They raised hands in acknowledgment. Fancy pulled a nickel from her apron pocket and slapped it onto the counter in front of Laurel. "I'll flip you. Loser cleans the table."

"Split the tip?" Laurel asked.

Fancy dropped a hand negatively. "Honey, if you clean that table, it's all yours."

Laurel would rather have cut off her nose than clean that table, but she needed the money. Old Plug wasn't the only one whose life had taken an uncertain turn. If anyone had told her even a year ago that she'd be scrubbing tables for loose change, she'd have laughed in that one's face. A Heffington clearing tables? Preposterous! Only, it wasn't, of course. With a sigh, she reached

down to yank loose the ties of her shoe and slip it back on. While she was bent over, tying them, Fancy groaned and muttered out of the side of her mouth. "Oh, no."

"Darn," Laurel muttered, realizing from Fancy's exclamation and the soft tinkle of bells that a new customer had come in. She looked up quickly to see which table the customer would take and her heart stopped. "Oh, my word, it's him!"

"Who?"

"*Him.* Edward White, the attorney."

Fancy eyed him boldly. "Mercy me, he's a big one, ain't he?"

Laurel didn't answer. She couldn't. What if he'd come to tell her that he wouldn't take her case? She gulped. Fancy gave her a little shove. "Well, go on. I'll clean that table. You find out what he's got to say."

Laurel nodded and hurried around the counter, patting her hair down with her hands. She licked her lips as he caught sight of her and turned, looking rather awkward there in the small diner in his baggy, expensive suit. Laurel put out her hand as she approached. "Mr. White." Her voice sounded breathless and small.

"Ms., uh...I can't call you Laurel if you go on calling me Mr. White," he said almost reluctantly.

She smiled, hoping this was a good sign. Why would he care what she called him in the future if no future relationship existed? "Edward, then? Or Ed?"

He shrugged. "Either one. Um, can we talk?"

"A-all right. Why don't we sit down?" She indicated a booth in the center of the long row opposite the counter. Edward White nodded and stepped to the side, lifting a hand to assist her as she slipped into place. Only after she was seated did he place his briefcase on the table and slide in across from her. Knowing that Fancy was watching, Laurel glanced over her shoulder and saw Fancy lift an eyebrow as if to say that she was impressed. *And you don't know the half of it,* Laurel thought. That kiss she had kept entirely to herself.

"Well?" she asked, both impatient and reluctant to hear his decision.

He didn't look at her, just took out a legal pad and a cheap ink pen and wrote the date at the top of the page. "I find it a good

practice to make notes during consultation. Is that all right with you?'' he asked mildly.

It wasn't quite what she'd expected, but that didn't matter. She nodded. ''Certainly.''

He still didn't look up at her. Pen poised over the paper, he asked, ''Is there any chance you'll reconcile with your ex-husband?''

The question was so unexpected, so unlikely that she couldn't quite believe she'd heard him correctly. ''What?'' It came out almost as a laugh.

He began repeating himself slowly. ''Is there any chance that you will reconcile with your ex—''

''No! And I can't believe you're even asking!''

He looked up at her then, doubt evident in his eyes. ''You're sure?''

Laurel sat back and folded her arms. ''Let me guess. You talked to Bryce, and he declared his undying love and begged you to convince me to take him back.''

Edward rolled the pen into the palm of his hand, closing his fist around it so that only the tip and the round blue stopper in the other end showed. ''Something like that.''

Laurel shook her head, disappointed in a way that she hadn't expected. ''I can't believe you bought into his act. He tells everyone that he's desperately in love with me. He begs them to tell him where I am or to get me to talk to him. Then in private he threatens me. He tells me how lucky I am that he'd have me to begin with and that if I knew what was good for me, I'd just shut up and accept the fact that I'm a dismal failure.''

Edward White's pale blue eyes had gone narrow. ''He threatens you?''

She had to backtrack, blinking rapidly as her own words replayed in her ears. Threats. She sighed. ''He likes to remind me how easily he could break my bones if he chose to.''

''That son of a—'' He bit off the rest of it, took a deep breath and said, ''He's threatened to 'break your bones'?''

She shrugged, torn between pleasure at his obvious concern for her and discomfort with the subject at hand. ''I'm not really sure he'd do it,'' she admitted. ''Not anymore.''

His hands folded into fists beneath his elbows. *Huge* fists. "He's hurt you before?"

She dropped her gaze so that he couldn't see how she coveted the strength in that pair of fists. A man with fists like that could kill a woman—or protect her from every danger. She sensed that for Edward White only the latter would be an option, and she found a certain comfort in that. "He's only hit me a couple times," she said, "and when Kennison found out, they argued about it. I couldn't hear anything they were saying because they locked me out of the room, but they were shouting, and it was obvious that Kennison was enraged because of it. Afterward, Bryce apologized and promised not to do it again, but when Kennison left, he said one day he'd give me everything I had coming and Kennison wouldn't say a word. I'm pretty sure it's a bluff, but he uses every opportunity to remind me what he can do."

"When was the last time he threatened you?"

"Immediately after the divorce was granted."

"What did you do?"

"I moved."

He muttered something under his breath and lifted a hand to push his hair off his forehead. It fell forward again immediately and he batted it impatiently out of his eyes.

"You know," Laurel said lightly, "you wouldn't have to do that if you got a good haircut."

His dark brows drew together. "What's wrong with my haircut?"

Her answer was confident, for this was one thing about which she knew a great deal. "Well, for one thing it's out of style."

He made a face. "I don't have time to worry about what's in style and what isn't."

"Of course you don't," she agreed smoothly. "That's what your hairstylist is for. He or she should keep on top of the latest styles and be able to suggest one that's right for you."

"I don't have a stylist," he grumbled. "I use a good old-fashioned barber—when I have the time."

"Ummm." She wouldn't say that it showed. She didn't have to. After a few silent moments during which frustration got the

better of him, he thrust his hand through his hair again and sent her a glower that seemed to signal some kind of surrender.

"Okay, okay, in detail, what sort of hairstyle should I be wearing?"

She smiled, warming to the subject. "Well, it should be shorter, definitely shorter, especially on the sides."

"I hope you're not talking about one of those buzz cuts."

She laughed. "Hardly. But it should be short enough that it needs trimming every week to two weeks to keep it in shape. And the top should be no longer than an inch at the crown, graduating to maybe two inches right in front. Then you just spritz a little dollop of mousse in your palm—and you just kind of shape it right here like this." Reaching across the table, she demonstrated by raking her fingers through the hair at the top of his forehead. His thick caramel brown hair was roughly textured, almost springy to the touch, yet without a hint of curl. She pulled her hand away. "Actually, you might not need the mousse. Just comb it up and let it dry or blow it that direction with a gun-type dryer."

"I'll, um, remember that," he said, avoiding her gaze and patting down his hair where she had ruffled it. He opened his briefcase and stowed away the pad and pen, saying, "Listen, about Miller... He tried to get me to tell him where you lived, but I didn't. Not that it matters, really, because if he truly wanted to know where to find you, he could easily enough. Trust me on this."

"All right," she said. "So what should I do? Move again?"

He shook his head. "No, that's temporary protection at best. I'll have a talk with Kennison, let him know that Miller's straining at the leash. Abe's too smart not to reel him in. But if he makes another one of these threats, we're going to the police. Understand?"

She was genuinely surprised. "I thought the police could only get involved if he actually followed through."

He lifted one shoulder in a noncommittal shrug. "Technically, there's not much they can do, but keeping them apprised of his threats serves several purposes. One, if the worst does happen and he actually follows through, the authorities will tend to act more quickly and take the situation more seriously than if it comes to

them out of the blue. Also, we may have to build a case for harassment later, and complaints to the police could be a very powerful tool for our use. In essence, we're documenting his abuse through a fairly impeachable source. Plus, once he knows he's been reported, he might back off. Just the threat of prosecution might be all the protection you need.''

She nodded. ''I understand.''

''Good. Now this doesn't mean that you shouldn't take routine precautions to protect yourself. Just don't move without telling me first. Okay?''

''Does this mean that you're taking my case?'' she asked finally.

He immediately began hedging. ''I didn't say that. I'm still investigating. Once I'm reasonably assured of success... Well, let's cross that bridge when we come to it, shall we?''

She nodded, disappointed in spite of the good advice she'd just received—and given. He closed his briefcase again, this time with every indication of leaving. Suddenly she didn't want him to go. ''Can I get your anything? A cup of coffee? A sandwich?''

He shook his head, glancing at his wristwatch. ''No, thanks. I have an appointment downtown in a few minutes.''

''All work and no play,'' she began, reciting Parker Sugarman's words, then wisely cutting them off.

Edward lifted a brow censoriously as he slid out of his side of the booth. ''Well, if I'm working long hours, then so are you.''

''Yes, but I have to,'' she pointed out. ''I have to support my—m-myself.''

''And I don't?'' he retorted, completely missing her little slip of the tongue.

''But you make so much more money than I do,'' she argued lamely, sorry she'd ever broached the matter.

''Not in this case, I don't,'' he pointed out wryly. ''Not yet and maybe not at all.''

''I see,'' she said quietly, embarrassed by the obvious. To her surprise, he immediately took pity on her.

''Hey, I didn't mean anything by that.''

''Of course not,'' she said blithely. ''After all, I did offer to...'' She swallowed the reference to marriage at the last moment.

"That is, I—I'm very grateful for the time you've given me, and I—I hope it won't be for nothing."

He smiled—sort of. It could have been an uncertain grimace. "No problem." He got quickly to his feet, saying, "You know to call me immediately if you hear from Bryce, don't you?"

"Yes."

"Fine. I'll be in touch." With that he left her, shouldering his way through interior and exterior doors to the parking lot.

She rose wearily, uncertain whether she was relieved or just exhausted. It was no surprise when Fancy appeared at her elbow.

"So what'd he say?"

Laurel was suddenly too weary to relate the details. "Suffice it to say, maybe I didn't blow it after all."

"Yeah?" Fancy gushed. "He's gonna take the case?"

"Well, at least he hasn't said no yet," Laurel told her dryly.

Fancy waggled her hand-drawn brows. "Maybe that marriage proposal wasn't such a bad idea, after all."

Laurel could only smile wanly and shake her head, weary to her bones.

"Listen," Fancy said, taking pity on her. "You go on home to that little boy. I can close here by myself. I'll make Plug help."

Laurel laughed at the very idea, but she was just too tired to argue. "Thanks, Fancy. I owe you." It wasn't the first time.

Kennison greeted Edward like a fond uncle.

"Edward, my boy, how good to see you again!"

Edward clapped a palm heartily against Kennison's soft, pale one and pumped his arm enthusiastically, fighting a grin as the older man fought against showing pain at the fierceness of his grip. After several seconds, Edward took pity and released him.

"Have a seat, won't you?"

Edward waited until the tall, dignified, silver-haired man lowered himself into the imposing chair behind his desk before filling a much smaller one in front of it.

"Now," Kennison said, every inch the elder statesman, "how may I help you?"

Using the nickname that he knew Kennison hated, Edward smiled and got right to the point. "Well, Abe, I'm after some

information. A young woman named Laurel Heffington Miller came to see me the other day. It seems she's in a rather odd position. Somehow, her *ex*-husband managed to gain control of every one of her assets during their divorce, and naturally she'd like them back.''

Kennison spread his hands, not quite able to suppress a smile of such smugness that Edward had to physically restrain himself from removing it. ''I realize how it must look,'' he said smoothly, ''but Mr. Miller really does have his wife's—''

''*Ex*-wife's.''

''Ex-wife's best interests at heart.''

''And would you care to explain those 'best interests' to me?''

Kennison's lips quirked. Edward had the unmistakable impression that he was enjoying himself. ''Well, I'm not sure I can do that. It's unethical, you know, to betray a client's confidence.''

''She's not your client,'' Edward pointed out succinctly.

Kennison pursed his lips. ''True. All right, then. It certainly can't hurt Mr. Miller's position.'' He made a great display of composing himself and choosing his words, as if he hadn't been bursting to blab this from the moment Ed had mentioned Laurel's name. Finally he took a deep breath. ''Poor Bryce really has no other choice. Mrs. Miller, she isn't...responsible.''

''Responsible,'' Edward repeated, waiting for the rest and knowing that he wasn't going to like hearing it.

''Frankly,'' said Kennison, ''she's unstable.''

''Oh, really?'' Edward smiled and shook his head, playing it as if for a jury. ''Funny, she seemed stable enough to me.'' *Or did she?*

Kennison's smile brimmed with pity. ''That's because you aren't acquainted with her history.''

''Oh, that's right,'' Ed said, as if only then remembering. ''You represented her grandmother, didn't you?''

''I did.'' He bounced the tip of one finger against his chin contemplatively, as if deciding how much to tell. ''I always felt rather sorry for young Laurel,'' he finally said. ''Virdel Heffington was an autocratic, stubborn old woman to whom consequence was everything. Her mother, Virginia, was the daughter of a Louisiana shrimper, but Delbert, her father, had some pretensions to

greatness. It was rumored, but never substantiated, that he was a direct descendant of Sam Houston, and that was reason enough in his mind to gain his daughter entry into the homes of the finest families in the state. I understand that she was rather brash and obvious, but she was also very beautiful, and eventually she made herself a good marriage."

"To Mason Heffington."

"Correct. And as with so many pretenders, she became more protective of her social position than the true elite. She produced the requisite heir, then set about making herself the queen of Dallas society. That was her work, promoting the Heffington name, sustaining the aura of Texas 'royalty' with which she cloaked herself. I think she came to believe her own press, as it were."

"And how did this affect Laurel?" Edward prodded, more than a little interested in the tale. Moreover, he sensed that every word of it, so far, was fact.

Kennison spread his patrician, manicured hands. "In every possible way. Virdel, whose name was a combination of both her parents, controlled every aspect of her granddaughter's life. Laurel's father was only too willing to relinquish his daughter to her direction. It freed him to travel the globe in search of entertainment. Her mother was a biddable, appallingly stupid woman who repeatedly succumbed to her husband's expectations and demands. And Laurel, like everyone else, fell far short of her grandmother's standards, something I'm sure Virdel never let her forget. It was an unhealthy situation. It should come as no surprise that Laurel developed certain, er, abnormal behaviors."

Like asking virtual strangers to marry her, said an alarmist voice inside Edward's mind. He shifted uncomfortably, dreading what was yet to come but resigned to it. Since his interview with Bryce Miller, he had suspected what tack Kennison was prepared to take in order to retain control of the Heffington millions, but he needed confirmation. More than that, he required a peek at the opposition's ammunition. "What 'abnormal behaviors' would those be?" he asked, never doubting that Kennison could and would tell him.

"Oh, there was a small matter of pretending to be kidnapped and ransomed."

Edward felt as if he'd been sucker punched. "K-kidnapped?"

"Pretending to be kidnapped," Kennison repeated. His expression was solemn, but those cold, predatory, blue-black eyes gleamed with unseemly delight. He was loving this, so much that he stretched the moment as long as possible. Finally he faked a dismal sigh and carried on. "Mmm, she was about fourteen, going to a fancy boarding school. You know the kind. Apparently she wasn't getting on well, but Virdel refused to allow her to come home. So she wrote a phony ransom note and disappeared. I don't think she knows herself whether she intended to take the money and run or play the heroine and rescue it and herself. Either way, she was thwarted. Virdel refused to pay the ransom."

Kennison chuckled, and Edward wanted to rip his throat out. The kid had obviously been begging for some sort of proof that her grandmother valued her, and Virdel Heffington had simply refused to give it. Edward felt a shadow of the pain that Laurel must have felt. Still, to pretend to be kidnapped... It wasn't a very *rational* scheme. He swallowed his anger and dismay. "What happened?"

"After a few days, the custodian at the school found her hiding out in the basement. Virdel was called. She had Laurel sent to a pricey hospital that specialized in dealing with problem teens."

Damn. Now that could blow a hole in any case, a forced stay in a hospital. Maybe Virdel Heffington had had too much pride to allow them to admit her granddaughter as a mental case. For Laurel's sake, Edward hoped so. Keeping his fisted hands out of sight, he adopted a casual tone. "And did they make a diagnosis at the time?"

Kennison pursed his lips. "I don't know. I only know that after she returned to school, she faked—or imagined—several illnesses. After some time, Virdel sent her to yet another hospital for a complete medical workup. They found nothing wrong physically, but the doctors recommended intense counseling. She went to a private institution, what we once would have called a posh sanitorium. She earned her high school equivalency degree during that period. She also tried to elope with a groundskeeper seven

years her senior, but Virdel tracked them down somehow, and he quietly disappeared for a few thousand dollars.''

Edward felt a burning in the back of his throat and swallowed it away, only to have it return immediately. He cleared his throat, as composed outwardly as it was possible to be. "And then?"

"And then," Kennison said smoothly, "Virdel brought her granddaughter home, where she became a source of constant battle between her and Mason. Unfortunately, a year or two later, Mason Heffington was declared incompetent and Virdel seized complete control of the Heffington millions. There is a family history, you see, of mental instability.''

His smirk nearly sent Edward out of his chair and over the desk to put his fist in Kennison's face. Only one thing stopped him—the fact that Kennison was very likely right. Edward recalled now the rumors that had circulated about Mason Heffington. It was said first that he had died but the family was keeping it quiet to prevent panic from investors in several public companies in which Heffington held large shares. Later, the speculation was that Heffington had suffered some sort of debilitating ailment, a stroke perhaps. Whatever the cause, Mason Heffington had never again appeared in public until the viewing of the body prior to his funeral. Edward knew in his heart that even if Virdel had kept it quiet, a record existed somewhere that would prove Mason Heffington had been legally declared mentally incompetent, and that could only bode ill for Laurel.

Edward felt as if he'd had his feet swept out from under him, but he had scrambled for purchase on shifting ground before. He relaxed and reached for the hypothesis that would frame his next comment or question. As always, his training paid off. He looked Abelard Kennison straight in the eye. "Well, it's been an interesting history lesson, but an unfair divorce settlement is an unfair divorce settlement.''

The smile that curved Kennison's mouth was downright reptilian. "I'm afraid you have been misinformed, dear boy. It was not my client who outlined the divorce agreement. It was Laurel herself. You see, Mr. Miller did not wish to divorce his wife. She offered him, through her attorney, of course, everything her grandmother left in her direct care—the house, the furnishings,

the cars... It almost seems an *irrational* act, does it not? But it certainly demonstrated the depth of her commitment to parting ways with her husband. Bryce felt that the only thing he could do was allow her the freedom she wanted while keeping the Heffington estate together for her eventual return. It is his belief, his ardent desire, that she will return to him.''

''So he's merely protecting her interests,'' Edward clarified sarcastically.

Abelard Kennison bowed his silver head. ''Until she comes to her senses and returns to him.''

''And to prove it,'' Edward surmised, ''you would draw into question her mental stability, with Miller declaring loudly from the witness stand that he adores the ground she walks on.''

Kennison said nothing, but he looked like the cat that ate the canary, and his eyes were declaring, *''Gotcha!''*

As loath as he was to do it, Edward allowed his dismay and confusion to show. Let Kennison think he had won whether he had or not. Edward still hadn't made a decision about representing Laurel Miller, and he wasn't going to until he had settled some of the questions rocketing around in his mind. But if it came to it, he meant to give Kennison the fight of his life.

Stretching as if waking from a short nap, Ed got to his feet. ''Well, thanks for the info, anyway.''

Kennison rose in one suave movement, began a practiced tug at the vest of his three-piece suit and halted with a pained glance at his hand. ''My pleasure,'' he said, leaving some doubt as to his veracity. ''Feel free to call on me again any time I may be of service. But if I might be allowed an opinion and if you have any influence with our dear Laurel, you really should encourage her to go back to her husband. It's for her best, believe me.''

Edward contented himself with a small, wry smile. ''Oh, I doubt that,'' he said lightly. ''I've met Bryce Miller.'' He then added, ''And by the way, if he ever makes another threat against Laurel or attempts to carry out those he's already made, I'll see him behind bars if I have to cage him myself.'' With that he took his leave, wishing he'd never laid eyes on Laurel Heffington Miller.

Chapter Four

It was the height of the lunch hour, and she had a dozen things to do, but she reminded herself that beggars cannot be choosers and smiled down at him, her hands reaching for order pad and pencil from sheer habit. Besides, he had cut his hair, and the results were all she'd hoped they would be.

"Well, well, Counselor, don't you look sharp today!"

"Hello, Laurel," Edward said, a hand self-consciously sweeping over his expertly cut hair. "You don't think it's a little too trendy?"

She bent at the waist slightly, bringing her eyes on a more even par with his face and turned her head to and fro. His face looked leaner, the bone structure more pronounced, those pale blue eyes somehow more commanding. In addition, his upper lip was clearly visible, now merely framed by the thick, dark brush rather than obscured by it. "Oh, no," she said at last, "I think it's wonderful. I like the trim of your mustache, too."

He seemed to relax, smiling broadly. "Yeah, me, too. I wasn't sure at first, but the stylist insisted, and I figured, what the heck, in for a penny, in for a pound."

"You made a wise choice."

"Thanks."

For a moment, each of them seemed to search for something else to say, but then Laurel remembered the pad and pencil in her hand and snapped to.

"Lunch or business?"

He glanced around him, slid his briefcase up onto the tabletop and said, "Business, if you have the time."

Glancing at the trio of workmen standing expectantly just inside the door, Laurel leaned forward and softly asked, "Would you mind moving to the counter? The boss doesn't like us to tie up the booths during the lunch rush."

"Oh. Sure. No problem." Getting to his feet and gathering his briefcase to his side at the same time, he stepped over to the counter and wedged himself between the seat and the bar.

"Those seats are too close," Laurel whispered apologetically, watching him pivot sideways in order to find space for his legs. "It's just so cramped in here."

"It *is* a diner," he reminded her mildly.

She nodded, bit her lip and indicated the three workmen who slid into the booth just vacated by Edward. "I've got to get this. Sorry."

"I understand." He deposited the briefcase on the counter in front of him, clicked it open and removed the ubiquitous yellow legal pad and ink pen.

Laurel quickly took orders for two chicken-finger baskets and a patty melt, poured three cups of coffee and refilled a fourth, then delivered a plate of onion rings for Fancy before scurrying back behind the counter to clear off the place next to Edward and slide him a glass of water.

"You sure you won't have something to eat?"

He shook his head. "No, thanks. I've already had lunch. I will have a cola, though."

"Great!" She pulled him a tall glass of soda from the dispenser and set it in front of him, taking great pleasure in telling him that it was on the house, which literally meant on her. He smiled slightly and took a drink, failing to quite meet her gaze.

"I, um, have some questions I need to ask you."

She shrugged. "Okay. Go ahead."

Edward uncapped the pen and poised it over the paper. "Is it true that your grandfather was ruled incompetent."

Laurel nodded. "Yes, unfortunately, he was. Why do you ask?"

He drew the number *1* on the yellow paper and drew a circle around it. Next to it, he wrote the words *grandfather—yes*. Then he laid down the pen and spread his hands. "I want you to tell me about it."

Laurel shifted her weight. "Well, the doctors felt that he had a series of small strokes and they affected his mind. I always figured that he just sort of wore down, you know?"

"No," Edward rumbled, his gaze on the notes he was making. "I don't know. That's why I asked you to tell me."

Laurel sighed and went on. "Okay, well, a few months after my father died, my grandfather resigned from the boards of several companies on which he sat. Then he created three trusts—one for me, one for my grandmother and one for charitable concerns. My grandmother disagreed with this 'division of the wealth,' as she called it. She claimed it was unsound financial planning. So Grandfather released management of her trust to her, and he spent his time administering my trust and the Heffington Charitable Fund. From that day on, he and Grandmother led very separate lives. She simply could not forgive him for 'abdicating his leadership in the business community'—again, her words. The changes began then—nothing much at first, just irritability and forgetfulness.

"Anyway, to make a long story short, I first noticed a really big change in Grandfather when I returned from Europe. I lived there for a few months after my first two years in college. The thing was, he couldn't seem to pay attention anymore. His mind wandered, when he was awake, that is."

"So what you're saying is that his mental condition had deteriorated," Edward clarified.

"Exactly, and even when he was making sense, he didn't seem to trust anyone anymore. I mean, for example, after I came back from Europe, I went to Grandfather and asked for enough money to go back to college. I'd had a semester in England, and then

I'd laid out a semester, working in France. Actually, it's the only time I've ever been able to do what I went to college to do.''

"Which was?"

"Fashion designing."

He looked up at that, the light of understanding in his eyes. "Of course, now back to Grandfather."

"Oh, right. So I asked for the money, and he did the strangest thing," she mused, thinking. "He started digging money out of hiding places around his room, some from a box in his closet, some from drawers and pockets of his clothes. He'd even stuffed money into the drapery valances over the windows. It was wild. He came up with *thousands* of dollars, and he made me promise never to tell Grandmother or his doctors where I'd gotten it. I remember that it gave me chills at the time." She grimaced. "I didn't tell her anything, but she knew. Somehow she always knew. I didn't see either of them for several weeks. Then the police contacted me. She had accused me of stealing the money, they said. Then she contacted me herself and said that if I came back home and returned the money, she'd let it drop. I went home. Grandfather was a wreck. His mind was completely gone. He was confined to a wheelchair. I don't know why, but he was too weak to walk. I managed to get my degree anyway, for all the good that it did me, and I've been paying off the loans ever since. That's pretty much the whole story."

She watched him make a question mark at the end of a sentence. "All right," he said, pecking spots on the paper with the tip of the pen. "Now I have to ask—"

"Laurel? Honey, could you..."

Laurel glanced at Fancy who, arms laden with lunches to be delivered, indicated several more waiting on the windowsill between the kitchen and the back counter space. Laurel nodded, slipped Edward an apologetic look and hurried to make herself useful. After delivering a trio of lunches, pouring a half gallon of coffee and dishing out coconut cream pie, she was back. "Sorry."

"Never mind," Edward began, only to be interrupted again, this time by the tinkling of the doorbell.

"It's my turn," Laurel told him apologetically. He sipped cola and pretended patience, while she raced around taking orders,

refilling cups and making change at the register. By the time she returned, he was checking his watch and glowering.

"Sorry," she said again. He waved her apology away with a movement of his hand. "Go ahead, ask your question," she urged.

He tried to drain a final drop of cola from a glass containing nothing but ice, put it down with a clunk and bluntly asked, "Did you pretend to be kidnapped?"

She closed her eyes. Shame and embarrassment washed over her in a cold wave. She had hoped that humiliating mistake was behind her, but she had believed that before. She took a deep breath. "Yes." It came out even and subdued, much to her surprise. Taking heart, she went on. "I was fourteen. She sent me to a boarding school in Minnesota while Grandfather was out of town dedicating some new wing at a hospital in my father's name. I was utterly miserable. I wanted to go home. I wanted her to want me home. I wanted to know that she cared, that she loved me." Laurel blinked away the tears that had gathered in her eyes and chuckled at the irony of it. "She never even told Grandfather about the phony ransom note I sent. I got a one-word reply, written in her own hand. 'No.'"

He said something under his breath, but she was too preoccupied, too caught in the old misery to notice. "Ah, well." She sighed. "Water under the bridge."

"Not," Edward told her solemnly, "if someone wanted to use it against you."

She opened her mouth to ask him what he meant by that but suddenly felt a presence at her elbow. She looked to the side and encountered Fancy, who was snapping her chewing gum, a predatory gleam in her eye as she surveyed Edward White.

"Laurel honey, ain't you gonna introduce us now that things have slowed down a mite?"

Fancy's smile displayed a fresh coat of bright red lipstick, and she had removed her hair net. Old Plug was staring over her shoulder. A quick glance in the direction of the kitchen showed Shorty's bald pate poking through the order window, head cocked as if trying to catch every word.

Laurel rolled her eyes. "Uh, Edward White, I'd like you to meet Fancy Bright and—"

"Maybe you heard of me," Fancy said in her most ingratiating voice, thrusting an arm across the counter.

Edward seemed flustered. "Uh, no, I don't think so."

"I used to be a dancer," Fancy went on. "Well, it was some years ago, but I had quite a reputation around here, if I do say so myself. They billed me as Queen of the Exotic Dancers."

Edward's mouth dropped open and quickly snapped shut again as he jerked his hand up to grasp Fancy's, which he shook and released again in the space of a heartbeat. Laurel had to bite back a groan. Then Fancy jerked a thumb over her shoulder, a hip thrown out as a prop for her free hand.

"This here is Old Plug," she said. "And over yonder, that's Shorty." She poked Edward in the shoulder with a bloodred nail as thick as lumber and whispered loud enough for the whole place to hear, "Did ye ever see a bald Mex'can before?"

Edward paused in the middle of nodding at Shorty, shocked speechless. "Uh... Well... Uh..."

Not to be ignored, Plug pushed forward and offered a dirty hand to Edward, who looked at it, then to his credit, shook it without obvious reaction. Unfortunately, Plug was not so wise. He elbowed Laurel, saying, "I asked Fancy t' marry me. Did you know?" He went on without giving her a chance to answer. "He the one you asked?"

Laurel heard Edward White's teeth clack together, and her face bloomed red with color.

"Plug!" Fancy scolded.

"Don't feel bad, honey," he said to Laurel, patting her head. "Fancy here, she turned me down, too." He went on to address Edward. "Now, I'm just an old drunk," he said, "and Fancy, she's just an old stripper—uh, pardon me, exotic dancer. But our little Laurel, now she's class stuff, the very best. Ain't she, Fancy?"

"The very best," Fancy confirmed, "a real class act."

"Th-that's just Fancy's way of talkin'," Plug clarified. "Wouldn't want you gettin' the wrong idea, see, cause Laurel,

now, she never took off her clothes in front of nobody. Did you, Laurel?''

"Plug!"

"Well, she never," Plug insisted, glaring at Fancy. Then his brow wrinkled and he turned to Laurel. "Did you, Laurel?''

"Uh, no, Plug, I never did," Laurel said, placing her arm about his shoulders and turning him away, hoping to send him back to his booth. No such luck.

"Well, it's a good thing," he told her kindly, ignoring the shove Fancy gave his shoulder. "You couldn't have outdone Fancy here nohow. They didn't call her the queen for nothing."

Fancy suddenly preened. "Now, Plug, you don't know that. Laurel could be even better than me if she set her mind to it."

"Oh, no!" Laurel exclaimed. "Never!"

Edward White had given up trying to keep his mouth closed and just let it hang open. Laurel cringed inwardly, but then she stopped herself. These were her friends. No matter what else they might be, they were that, and she wasn't at all certain that she could say it of anyone else, certainly not those snooty girls she'd gone to school with and not the debutantes and society matrons with whom her grandmother had tried to surround her. She smiled at Plug and Fancy. "Thanks for coming over, guys," she said, "but this is a business meeting, so if you don't mind..."

Fancy, at least, caught on. "Oh, sure! We ain't staying or nothing. We just, you know, we can't help wondering what he said."

"Is he gonna get your money back?" Plug asked excitedly.

Laurel glanced at Edward, who was staring at her like he couldn't believe his ears. "Uh, we haven't gotten that far yet," she muttered, wondering if they ever would now.

"This really isn't the place for a business meeting," Edward said brusquely. Tossing the pad and pen into his briefcase, he wrenched himself out of his seat and stood. "Why don't we meet on your off time? We can discuss this then."

Her off time. Laurel thought of Barry, of the long hours he spent at the sitter's on a daily basis. How could she leave him there any longer? Mrs. Martinez wouldn't mind, but Laurel herself couldn't bear to be parted from the little scamp longer than absolutely necessary, and their evenings together were all too

short as it was on this shift. She looked to Fancy for help and received nothing more than a shrug as Fancy beat a hasty retreat, herding Plug before her. Laurel licked her lips, thinking quickly.

"Um, I get a dinner hour on this shift. How would that be? I—I could meet you somewhere."

He thought that over, tugging at the cuffs of his sleeves. "Okay. Where do you want to meet?"

Laurel tried to think, but not a single place came to mind. "Uh, um, w-well, I could just come to your office."

He shook his head and slid a hand into his pants pocket to jingle his change. "That'll take too much time. We wouldn't have fifteen minutes to work."

"Well, we'll just meet here, then."

He slid a quelling look in the direction Fancy and Plug had taken and lifted a dark brow. "I think not."

Laurel shot an apologetic glance at the others, then hurried around the counter to seize Edward White by the arm and tug him toward the door. "Listen," she said beneath her breath, "they don't mean to interrupt. They're just concerned for me."

"That's obvious," he said, teeth never parting. "Nevertheless, the problem remains." He pushed through the interior door and pulled her into the small foyer with him, crowding his big body into a corner with two newspaper vending machines and a trash can. "I have some rather sensitive questions to ask you, and I'd just as soon do it with at least a minimum of privacy."

"I just can't think of a private place to meet."

"Well, I can't talk to you with every oddball in Dallas looking on!"

"They're not oddballs!" she said defensively, then immediately capitulated. "Oh, all right, they are, but that doesn't keep them from being my friends."

"Why am I not surprised?" he muttered.

Laurel knew she was blowing it. "Listen," she said, determined to make him understand, "they care about me. Maybe that doesn't mean anything to you because you have parents and friends who love you, but they're all I have. Plug is crazy as a loon, and Shorty, well, he isn't short, and Fancy..." She threw up her arms. "Fancy is just *Fancy*. What else can I say? But

whoever and whatever they are, they think I'm fine. They don't care if I am a Heffington or that I wait tables or if I...propose to a strange man just because I think I can trust him!'' she blurted out. ''They care about *me,* and that's worth more than I can tell you, so if that's the excuse you need to back out of this, then you just go ahead.''

She turned away, looking out over the jumble of skyline that closed in the little diner, one hand pressed against the glass. ''There's got to be someone out there who'll help me,'' she told herself. She heard a sound like shoe leather against cement and suddenly felt Edward White at her back.

''I never said I wouldn't help you. I just said this wasn't the place to talk.''

Laurel closed her eyes, unaware that her face was reflected clearly in the thick glass enclosing them. ''Where would you like to meet?''

''How about this,'' Edward said, looking out over the same skyline that held her. ''Say you work through your dinner hour, then take off an hour early, go home and change, and meet me at...oh, how about The Blue Plate? You know that place?''

She frowned. ''Yes.'' She knew the exclusive dinner club in the West End of downtown Dallas only too well. It was one of Bryce's favorite places. He had, in fact, taken her there on their very first date, and it hadn't bothered him at all that she had had to pay the tab. Yes, she knew The Blue Plate, and she'd as soon set foot in there again as in a snake pit, but she wasn't going to tell Edward White that any more than she was going to work through her dinner hour so she could spend two hours getting through an overpriced meal she couldn't begin to afford anymore, while the baby-sitter was wracking up overtime.

He seemed to take her simple affirmative answer as agreement to his plan. ''Shall I pick you up, or would you prefer to meet there?''

''Oh, definitely meet there,'' she told him, turning away.

''What time should I expect you?''

She answered carefully. ''I couldn't possibly get there before eight.''

''Eight it is.''

"I may not be able to get away," she hedged.

"All right, we'll make it eight-thirty," he said, "but I warn you, if I don't eat by nine I turn into a bear."

"Well, I'll see that you eat before nine, then," she returned lightly, fully meaning it.

He nodded as if uncommonly pleased with himself and moved to the outer door, where he paused and asked, "Do you suppose she knew from the beginning that the note was a phony?"

Surprised that he even cared to know but not doubting of whom or what he spoke, she took a deep breath. "I don't know for sure. I asked her once. She said that anyone who knew anything about the Heffingtons would have asked for a great deal more money than the imaginary kidnappers had—and anyone who knew anything about me wouldn't have bothered to ask at all."

Edward cast her a look over his shoulder. It said everything and nothing at all, that look. After a moment, he turned away. "I'll see you at The Blue Plate."

She said nothing, did nothing until he had pushed out into the parking lot and gotten into his car. Only then did she turn and go back inside, regretting what she must do but understanding that she had no choice. She had a previous commitment, and she couldn't very well ask an eleven-month-old to understand why he had been supplanted by an older man.

Edward sucked the last of his Scotch from the ice cube, then shifted it with his tongue to the side of his mouth and bit through it. The cold pierced his mouth. He wondered if he ought to order another drink, decided against it and glanced once more at his wristwatch. Eight thirty-five. So she was five minutes late. Why did he have this uncanny feeling that she wasn't going to show? He shook his head, telling himself that he was being silly. It was to her benefit to show. She needed his help. She wouldn't miss a business meeting. So why did he feel as if he'd coerced her? And why did this feel like a *date*? Why did he feel as though he was being stood up? He shook his head, and the flip phone in his breast pocket trilled.

Glowering, he plucked it out and shook it open. The press of

a button sent a short, thin, metal antennae up from one corner of the black plastic case. Another turned on the speaker.

"Edward White."

"It's me."

Yes, of course it was. He congratulated himself on intuition. "What's going on, Laurel?" He could hear her nervousness in her voice.

"Um, I must have missed the bus," she said. Street noises and some sort of low pattering punctuated by a baby's whiny cry filled the background.

"Where are you calling from?"

"The pay phone at the bus stop."

"What's that noise?"

After a long silence, she said, "It's raining."

He flashed on a sudden picture of her standing wet and bedraggled, alone in the night. "I'll come get you. What's the address?"

"There's no shelter here," she said into the phone. "I can't stand around, I'll be drenched. We'll just have to reschedule."

"I'll meet you at your apartment."

"No! I—I mean, I wouldn't want to inconvenience you. You're probably starved by now."

He looked ruefully at the basket of pretzels he'd just decimated and said into the phone, "I'll hold a while longer."

After a long silence, she reluctantly capitulated. "A-all right. Give me a few minutes."

"See you soon," he promised, his spirits unaccountably lighter. Folding up the phone, he tucked it away and slid off the bar stool, flipping bills onto the counter. The bartender thanked him with a small salute, and Edward turned to make his way out the door.

Precisely eighteen minutes later, he eased the sedan into a narrow parking space between a flatbed truck loaded with construction equipment and a low-rider with a fringe-embellished interior, not exactly run-of-the-mill transportation. Getting out of the car, he turned up his collar and took stock of the buildings in the quadrangle that surrounded the crowded parking area. Though three decades old or more, they seemed well maintained. Still, the aging autos parked at curbside and the bare dirt where grass

should have been marked the place as lower-income housing. Quite a comedown for a Heffington.

Popping open an umbrella, he located the correct building and strode swiftly toward it, avoiding the puddles that collected in depressions in the paving. Determining the correct entrance, he climbed the exposed stairs in the open center of a triple quad of apartments. It was quite a climb to the third floor, and his footsteps rang loudly against the steel-encased concrete steps. Given that fact and the movement of curtains and shutters, a man didn't have to be too observant to realize that his presence was being noted by the occupants of every apartment. Upon attaining the upper deck, he shook out the umbrella and closed it before following the landing around to the correct apartment.

The umbrella fitted beneath one arm, he rapped sharply on the metal, hollow core door. The sound echoed down the stairwell and bounced off the metal doors of the other apartments opening onto it. Hearing a baby cry, Edward wondered how anyone got any sleep around here, not to mention maintained a bit of privacy. Several long minutes passed before a bathrobed Laurel opened the door and almost instantly disappeared again, allowing him entrance into a dark, claustrophobically small area about a yard square in size.

"Come on in," she called as she moved into a dimly lit room. "I'm sorry I don't have anything for you to sit on, but we'll be on our way as soon as Fancy gets here."

He closed the door and followed her into the half-light of what was apparently the only actual room of an extremely small efficiency apartment. The kitchen consisted of a two-burner stove, a sink and a tiny refrigerator built into about five feet of cabinet in one corner. A metal percolator coffeepot sat on one burner of the stove and a single cup and saucer on the cabinet top. Clothing hung all around him from hangers hooked over the end edge of the wall cabinet *and* the open door of what was obviously the bathroom—from which the majority of the light came—and the door of a closet so full that it could not be closed, *and* the drapery rod over the window. Folded clothing was piled in neat stacks inside clearly labeled cardboard boxes against one wall, and shoes were lined up side by side along another. A small air mattress

and a pillow covered with a single folded blanket lay on the bare floor. But none of this was what caught his attention.

What caught and held his attention was the small crib parked beneath the lip of the counter that separated the supposed living area from the tiny kitchen—and the red-haired imp that stared at him from enormous golden brown eyes, a plastic pacifier bobbing busily in a plump, pink mouth. The imp shook the side of the crib, rattling it much like a monkey would rattle the bars of its cage. Edward cocked his head, trying to make sense of this engaging little creature. Vibrant hair standing practically on end, puggish nose wrinkling in curiosity, fat, minuscule fists gripping the edge of the crib, the little person launched into a series of rattling, deep knee bends, spat the pacifier on the floor and emitted a stream of shrill gibberish that ended with short arms being thrust demandingly into the air. Soberly, Laurel plucked him out of the enclosed bed and swung him up onto her hip, hitching up the hem of her white terry-cloth robe to expose a length of black tights encasing a slender thigh.

"This is Barry," she said. The baby got a more thorough introduction. "Barry, this is Mr. White. He's a very nice man, so you be good and impress him."

Barry responded by pursing his lips and blowing spit into the air. Laurel immediately clamped a hand over his mouth, which reduced Barry to the kind of infectious giggles only very young children can produce. Edward suddenly flashed on a vision of Darla Sugarman throwing her little self backward in her father's arms, confident that he would not let her hit the floor and laughing with toddler glee. He saw most clearly the look of utter adoration that had softened Parker's lady-killer face. He looked at Laurel Miller, and a shiver snaked up his spine. Before he could make sense of that or even follow it to a sensible, coherent thought, the door burst open at his back and Fancy blew into the room in a whirl of uniform, hair net and pungent perfume.

She scooted right by him and snatched Barry from Laurel's arms. "Hello, little darlin'. I'm here!" She spun an ingratiating smile on Edward. "I'm so sorry I held y'all up, but you can go on now!" She flitted about the room, gathering baby goods and flashing Laurel meaningful glances.

Laurel swept a hand through her damp hair and smiled wanly, her face set in an oddly blank expression. Loaded with gear and baby, Fancy blew kisses and flew from the room. Barry for his part looked thoroughly confused, two fingers thrust into his furiously working mouth. The door closed behind them, leaving an unnatural silence in their wake.

"I'll only be a minute," Laurel promised lightly and disappeared into the bathroom. Edward found a bare spot along the wall and leaned against it, arms folded across his middle. A hair dryer whirred beyond the bathroom door. Edward rubbed his mustache and wondered how often Laurel baby-sat for Fancy. Often enough, apparently, to warrant leaving the crib in place and a few baby things in the way. Strange, he'd been under the impression that the two women usually worked together on the same shift. And come to think of it, Fancy was awfully *old* to have a kid that young. Maybe it was her grandchild.

Edward's eyes narrowed. He framed a question in his mind, nothing too probing or obvious. When the hair dryer cut off, he asked it. "Who's Barry's regular baby-sitter?" It seemed to him that she hesitated, but he couldn't be sure without seeing her face.

"Her name is Libby Martinez. She lives in this building, number 117. The apartment opens onto a fenced play area, not that Barry goes out much yet, but the Martinez children enjoy it."

Well, that explained a good deal. He started to ask if she often stopped by and picked up the baby early for Fancy, but the next instant she opened the door and walked out of the bathroom. Edward's mouth went dry, and every thought in his head disappeared.

Nearly every square inch of her was covered and yet nearly every square inch was exposed by the tights and the little black dress that she wore—emphasis on the word *little*. Beginning well above mid-thigh and made of some sort of weighty black knit, it was every bit as form hugging as the opaque hose encasing her long, slender legs. And though the dress included long, tight sleeves and a wide collar banding her throat, the square cutouts at the shoulders and across the chest and back exposed plenty of pale, smooth skin. Her hair had been slicked straight back except for a few individual locks of hair framing a face almost devoid

of makeup, and yet what she wore added drama and depth to an already arresting face—a sweep of violet in the creases of her eyelids, dark cherry pink on those wide, full lips, maybe a touch of smoky gray brow pencil. He wasn't quite sure. He only knew that she was breathtaking.

Smiling, she walked to the wall and stuck her feet into black leather shoes with long, squared-off toes and big gold buckles, the medium-high heels shaped like flanges. They were perhaps the ugliest shoes he'd ever seen, and come to think of it, he'd seen a lot of ugly shoes lately. Yet, on her they looked *right*. It all did—the tiny black and gold balls nestled against her earlobes, the shiny gold, hooded raincoat that she belted at the waist and the small, round, black suede handbag that hung from her shoulder by a long gold chain.

"Ready."

He had to clear his throat before he could find his voice and even then it was gravelly and thick. "Great." He faked a cough. "Let's go. I'm starving."

She followed him out the door and locked it with her key, then led the way down the stairs. At the top of the stairwell, he opened the umbrella and afterward kept close, sheltering them both from the rain that dwindled to a steady mist, telling himself that her raincoat was too pretty to get wet.

"I hope I don't ruin my shoes," she said above the sounds of their footsteps, obviously trying to make conversation. He didn't reply simply because he couldn't seem to wrap his mind around any words. "I have a thing about shoes," she went on. "Used to, when I found the perfect shoes for a certain ensemble, I just had to have them. Now I can't afford them, so I try to take especially good care of what I already have."

"Ah," he said, congratulating himself on his brilliant repartee. She was obviously too spellbound by his brilliance to chance another try at mundane conversation. He couldn't blame her.

They came to the curb and looked out over a virtual sea of black asphalt standing in as much as two inches of water in the lowest places. He thought of her shoes and, irrationally, the matching handbag. A sensible, cohesive plan burst into his thoughts. Without preamble he thrust the umbrella into her hand,

bent and swept her up into his arms. She gave a small, truncated yelp. Her free arm landed behind his neck and across his shoulders. She was a light, comfortable weight. Liking the feel of her in his arms, he stepped off the curb.

The umbrella wobbled precariously overhead. "What are you—" She had it figured out before the sentence ended. "I didn't mean..." The umbrella stabilized, the steady rain again sounding a measured pitty-pat against its taut shield. "They're only shoes, Edward."

He smiled to himself and, looking straight ahead, said, "I like them."

She lifted a slender leg and pointed her toe, eying the subject of discussion. "Really? I would think you'd hate them."

He looked at her then and as a result waded through a deep area that he could have just as easily gone around. "Why would you think that?"

"Well, because you're not quite the fashionable sort."

"I'm not," he admitted. "I just don't have the knack, but I admire those who do." He realized suddenly that he meant it. She gave him a look that seemed to ask if his head hurt. He wouldn't have been surprised if she'd laid a hand across his brow in order to check his temperature. She knew him better than he'd realized, and for some reason that made him smile. "Maybe you can give me some tips later."

She cocked her pretty head. "You'd like that?"

"Why not? You were right about the haircut."

He might have given her roses, so wide was her smile. She looked over his head with proprietary smugness. "I was at that."

He laughed, feeling absurdly lighthearted, and set her on her feet. She tugged a skirt that couldn't have wrinkled unless the skin beneath it did. "Thank you, Sir White."

"My pleasure."

Bowing at the waist, he unlocked the passenger side door and opened it. She handed him the umbrella, smoothed that skirt that fit like second skin over her nicely rounded bottom, turned slightly and sat down on the edge of the seat. He watched as she drew her legs in after her, pivoted gracefully on the seat and planted her feet. His pulse was racing as he hurried around to the

driver's door and awkwardly got into place, fighting the umbrella and a sudden gust of wind that blew rain into his face. Impatient, he tossed the closed umbrella into the back seat, only to have it open again with a *fhwup,* one of the spine tips poking him in the back of the head. Twisting in his seat, he made a grab for the handle and missed.

"Let me," Laurel said, humor in her voice. Releasing the safety belt that she had just buckled, she twisted fully in the seat until she was resting on her knees, her back to the windshield. Her firm, delicious little bottom presented itself as she bent over the back of the seat and grappled with the stubborn umbrella. Edward closed his eyes and gulped, but he couldn't keep them closed. His hands had fashioned new grips in the steering wheel before she had twisted back into her seat, tugged at that damnably short skirt again and began rebuckling her belt.

He jammed the keys into the ignition, rumbled a thank-you and concentrated his entire being on getting the car out of the parking lot and into moving traffic, telling himself over and over again that this was business—and that she was nothing whatsoever like Kendra Sugarman, not at all the sort of woman to interest him.

Chapter Five

Laurel stared through the windshield and clasped her hands together in her lap. He liked her. She had seen it in his eyes when she'd stepped out in this dress, had felt it in the gallantry with which he'd swept her off her feet and the tension he'd radiated when she'd so stupidly decided that she could better wrestle that umbrella than he could. She had felt—*felt*—his hands on her backside, the way they would slide up her thighs and beneath her skirt to cup her. She shivered with the thought of it. He really liked her, and just the idea of it made her heart do funny things. But she couldn't afford an erratic heartbeat.

What had happened this evening, him insisting on coming to her apartment and then showing up before Fancy had a chance to get there, proved how unlikely she was to get through this without him knowing. And once he knew everything, once he understood all about Barry, he wouldn't like her anymore. No matter how hard he'd gripped that steering wheel tonight, he wouldn't see her with anything but contempt once he knew. It wouldn't matter that she had no choice. A man like him, an honest man with only honestly held intentions would never understand

how she could do what she was doing, and he would never forgive her for using him to do it. But she had no choice. For Barry's sake—and for her own; she wouldn't lie to herself about that—she really had no choice.

The thought of Barry with Fancy made guilt rise up. She gulped it down and said to Edward White, "I can't be out late tonight."

He didn't look at her, just nodded and answered, "Sure. We both work tomorrow."

And Barry will go to the sitter, she thought. She wondered how she could pay for dinner. Maybe a simple salad, a glass of water. She mentally counted again the one-dollar bills folded away inside her purse. A tiny voice in the back of her mind suggested, *Maybe this is really a date.*

Was it her imagination or did he slow down the car? She glanced at him, and he sped up again. She made herself relax.

He said, "Technically, I suppose we're both working now. At least I am."

She felt a crushing sense of disappointment. But that wouldn't do. Oh, no, that wouldn't do. She smiled. "Technically."

He shifted in his seat, one arm draped over the steering wheel in a pose of relaxation. What made him nervous, she wondered. Was it her or was it something on his mind?

"I had a meeting with Abelard Kennison."

Something on his mind. She turned her head to look out the side window, not wanting to chance that he could see her foolishness on her face. "I see."

He made her wait a moment before he came out with it. "Kennison's going to claim that you're incompetent."

Why was she surprised? For the same reason that her skin turned cold and her stomach turned over. The fear was so strong that it swelled inside her, threatening to burst free. She made herself breathe deeply and calmly.

After some time, Edward said, "He told me about the sanitorium."

"Sanitorium?"

"The hospital, um, after the *kidnapping.*"

She shook her head. "He called it a sanitorium? It was a hos-

pital, and after that a reform school, a private reform school for wayward teenagers with funds.''

His glance was enigmatic. "Tell me about the hospital."

She shrugged and watched out the windshield. "They did some tests, brought in a psychiatrist. He said there was nothing wrong with me that a little counseling couldn't cure. Problem was, he wanted to give the counseling to Grandmother. She had me moved at once and threatened to see his license revoked. He tried to have me removed from her control. My grandmother inferred that I had seduced him. He lost his position at the hospital, but not, thank God, his license to practice. A judge barred him from any contact with me. I went to the reform school."

"And ran away with a groundskeeper," Edward said softly.

She laughed, but she wanted to cry. She lifted her chin. "He was twenty-four," she said, "tall and very handsome. He'd taken advantage of several girls there, but I didn't know that until afterward. All I knew was that he said he loved me and that he'd take me away from there. I hadn't seen or heard from my grandparents in nearly two years. I found out later that my grandfather didn't even know where I was, hadn't known all along. He thought I was happily ensconced in the boarding school and spending holidays with my many imaginary friends. Derek—that was his name—he took me to a motel. Then he told me that he had arrangements to make so we could be married as quickly as possible. He kissed me, and he left. I never saw him again."

Edward pushed a hand over his face. "Ah, let me guess. He called your grandmother and offered to tell her where she could find you—for a fee."

She nodded wryly. "Grandmother wasn't going to pay him at first, but it turns out that Derek was a reporter for a tabloid and he'd located Dr. Murray."

"The psychiatrist."

She nodded again. "Now you know the whole story."

"Not quite," he said softly.

She looked at him then, at the light that slashed through the window across the strong lines of his lower lip, jaw and chin.

"Did you love him?" he asked.

"Yes," she answered without blinking, "him and Dr. Murray,

a lab technician at the hospital, the older brother of a casual
friend, a history teacher, a Paris designer, a classmate who turned
out to be gay, anyone who showed me the least attention since I
was about thirteen. Now, did any of them love me? No, of course
not.''

He was irritated enough to snipe at her. ''Did you propose
marriage to any of them?''

''Each and every one,'' she lied.

He huffed as if she'd insulted him, so she turned away. How
could she insult him? How could she dare? She wanted to laugh.
Instead, she cried, the tears clinging precariously to her lashes
until the sheer will to survive stubbornly dried and locked them
away. She would endure this evening and return to the world she
had built—was building—for herself and Barry. Just let them try
to stop her. Just let them try.

They caused a sensation. Edward looked around the opulent
room and noted the heads that turned in their direction, the hands
that came up to cover whispering mouths. He mentally chastised
himself for not expecting it. She was Laurel Heffington Miller.
He should have realized that showing up here with a man other
than Bryce at her side would make the grapevine hum. He began
to stare them down, until he realized that Laurel had no intention
of acknowledging the interest their appearance generated. She
held her head up and strode gracefully through the dining tables,
her shoulders squared, her hips gently swaying. He felt a burst of
pride, realized the stupidity of that, and occupied himself by looking with a new eye at their surroundings.

The chrome tables were covered with heavy, starched table
linens, a layer of crimson topped by a layer of white, gold napkins
folded like small crowns and placed among heavy brass charger
plates cradling carefully contrived combinations of expensive
china, tall crystal goblets and graceful flutes etched and carved in
intricate patterns, heavy gold and silver flatware, fresh flowers in
unusual vases and bowls, tall white tapers flickering with tiny
flames sheltered behind gleaming globes. Scattered among the
tables and chairs upholstered in plush crimson velvet were lush,
strategically situated plants in huge brass pots and a number of

large statuary, most of it modern art and none of it blocking the view of the glass dance floor, which allowed the true exhibitionists among them to gyrate over an enormous well of deep blue water that flowed and undulated around a fanciful garden of white stone carved in fanciful shapes, steps that led nowhere, arches covering nothing, columns tumbled about enormous bones and fake coral. He saw again the beauty of the place, the imaginative brilliance of its decor, a perfect play place for those who could afford it. He'd never felt really comfortable here, but the food was excellent and many of his clients expected to be wined and dined at the most "in" places. For the first time, he saw it as a nest of vipers.

The maître d' stopped at a table in the midst of things and pulled out a chair for the lady.

"Thank you, Wallace," she said, folding herself elegantly into the chair.

He bobbed his head in a deferential bow, spreading a look from her to Edward. "Mrs. Miller," he said, "Mr. White. Welcome and enjoy."

A waiter appeared, menus bound in crimson leather in one hand, water pitcher in the other. A beverage cart followed at his heels. "Cinnamon coffee for Mrs. Miller, Scottish ale for Mr. White?"

"Thank you, Benjamin."

"If I may say so, ma'am, so glad to see you again."

"Yes, It's been a while. Forgive me for not knowing, are you married yet?"

"Six weeks now."

"And the wedding was everything your fiancée had hoped for?"

"Everything."

"I'm so glad."

"Thank you, ma'am." He looked at Edward, his manner everything proper. "Just signal when you're ready to order."

Edward opened his menu. As usual, it contained only four entrées. He was torn between the sea bass and the prime rib, assuming that Laurel would choose either the prairie hen or pasta with

clams for their smaller portions. But when he closed his menu, he knew that she had never even opened hers.

"Aren't you hungry?"

"Not really, but I know you are. Let's go ahead and order."

He barely lifted a brow before the waiter was there again, hands clasped behind his back.

"I'll have the prime rib."

"Very good, sir. How would you like the potato?"

"Baked."

"Garlic butter and the Edam dressing?"

"You never forget a patron's preference, do you, Benny?"

"I try not to. And what can I bring you, ma'am?"

Laurel touched the tips of the fingers of one hand to her throat. "Does the chef still make that lovely little green salad with Gorgonzola?"

"Yes, ma'am."

"I'll have that with a touch of lemon and a dark grain roll."

"Very good, ma'am." But Benjamin's very blank face did not conceal his surprise.

Edward knew instantly what was going on. He sent a stern look at the waiter. "Ms. Miller will have the range hen with her salad," he told the waiter, "and the pasta, I think, or... You'll know her preferences better than I do."

Laurel reached to touch his wrist discreetly. "Really, I'm not very hungry."

He cut her an impatient glance and looked back to the waiter. "Make it quick, Ben, I'm starving here."

"At once, sir." The waiter smiled with satisfaction and backed away.

Laurel frowned. "I wish you hadn't done that."

He smoothed the napkin across his lap. "Did you think I'd make you buy your own dinner?"

Laurel smoothed her own napkin. "It isn't a date."

Edward lifted an eyebrow at that. "I'll expense it." She said nothing. He looked again around the room. "Do you know that couple at the second table over?"

"Yes."

"Smile. They're heading this way."

Laurel smiled and returned the effusive greeting, letting her cheeks be kissed at and her fingers squeezed. "You look marvelous. Divorce must agree with you."

"Definitely. Allow me to introduce Edward White."

It was the beginning of a parade. By the time the entrée arrived, Edward had met half a dozen new faces whose only interest in him concerned how he'd wound up with Laurel Miller nee Heffington on his arm. He sensed beneath the broad smiles and gushing greetings an avid desire to know the latest dirt on the haughty Heffington's only living heir. For the first time, he understood what Laurel's divorce had cost her—not just the money and her home, but the position she had given up in exchange for her freedom. And then Tyler May arrived.

He was fairly harmless looking, wan and reed thin with hair black as night and dark brown eyes that moved languidly behind lenses framed in silver. His teeth were too large but perfectly straight and white as snow, his features thin, his Adam's apple prominent. He wore pale blue and black beneath a pearl gray suede jacket and somehow managed to look as though he wore a fortune. Tyler looked down his nose at Edward following an introduction that just missed the graciousness of those previous and extended a slender hand so smooth that it bordered on reptilian. "I don't believe I've had the pleasure," he said, dismissing Edward as unimportant. "Honestly, Laurel, you're a sight for sore eyes. Where have you been keeping yourself?" His thin lips quirked into a smile that positively dripped venom.

Edward, who had released Tyler's hand almost the same instant in which he had touched it, felt an immediate spurt of annoyance.

"Oh, I've been around," Laurel said lightly.

"Around where?" Tyler prodded. "I gather even Bryce doesn't know where you're keeping yourself. Tell me, how did it happen that Bryce got the house?"

The color drained from Laurel's face, but she relaxed back into her chair and smiled secretively up at the slime. Edward knew that she had a perfectly civil, uninformative answer all prepared for the jerk, but Edward didn't let her deliver it.

"Miller didn't get the house," he said smoothly, "and he's not going to."

She looked squarely into Edward's eyes, silently pleading for him to say no more. Tyler frowned on Edward then turned his damning gaze back to Laurel. "I thought the divorce was all settled."

"You thought wrong," Edward told him.

Tyler May lifted both brows. "Oooh. And I thought we'd missed all the fun."

Laurel lowered her eyes, then lifted them again. They were sad but resigned. "Say hello to your mother for me, Tyler."

He smiled dazzlingly. "Oh, I will. But tell me, darling, is it true that the dear departed Virdel was so scandalized by certain behaviors of yours that she left the monies to that nobody Bryce?"

Laurel's smile would have withered plants if any had been in the line of fire. "How absurd. These things get sticky, that's all. You should know." She leaned forward, her eyes speaking volumes at Edward. "Tyler's been through a number of failed relationships. His poor mama has despaired of him ever marrying."

Edward understood exactly what she was telling him. "Well, the marriage laws in Texas are narrow," he said mildly.

Laurel looked at Tyler, who was clearly fuming. "Edward's an attorney," she explained sweetly.

"Oh?" Tyler said cattily. "Do I smell a nasty court battle? Wouldn't Virdel love that!"

"What you smell," Edward said, firmly banishing notions of any lawsuits connected with him, "is a prime rib headed my way. Now if you don't mind, I'd like to have my date to myself for some part of this evening."

Laurel gasped but when Edward looked at her, she seemed perfectly composed. Deliberately, he covered her hand with his where it lay against the table linen and curled his fingers around it possessively. Tyler's mouth turned down in a frown as he swept Laurel with an assessing gaze.

"I'll tell Mother you asked after her."

Laurel's smile was dazzling. "Do that." Dismissively she turned her gaze back to Edward, and the warmth there rocked

him back into his chair. Stunned, he was barely aware of Tyler May flouncing off. Benjamin exchanging his empty plate for one filled with sizzling beef made him turn away from that grateful gaze. Guilt stole his appetite. She thought he'd done that for her. She thought he'd pretended to be her date as an act of kindness toward her, when he'd only been protecting himself from being associated with a case he wasn't yet certain he wanted to pursue. He gulped.

"Uh, I shouldn't have said that."

"It's all right," she told him, concentrating on her roasted hen.

He didn't say anything else, just forced himself to eat with a gusto he no longer possessed. When he finally chanced a look up, he found her staring longingly at the dance floor, where couples now swayed and glided to a gentle tune. He set his jaw, knowing that she wanted to dance and that it would be the greatest folly to do so. Determinedly he pushed aside his plate and fished a small notebook and an ink pen from a pocket.

"I do have some questions."

Her smile faded. "All right."

He tapped the pen on the notebook page. "You, um, spoke about attending college."

"Yes."

"Did you earn a degree?"

"I did."

Here it was, another glaring inconsistency. He put down the pen and linked his fingers together over the pad. "How is it then," he asked softly, "that you're waiting tables in a diner? Fashion designing not your thing, after all?"

Something flashed in her bright eyes. Something dangerous. She smoothed her form-hugging skirt. "Do you like my dress?"

He blinked in surprise, his gaze falling involuntarily to her lap and traveling the length of her skirt down her slender legs—but not far down. He felt a curious flutter in his chest. "Very much," he admitted hoarsely, "but it's a little, ah…" He gulped, his gaze going again to her legs then zipping back up again to fasten on her eyes. The dismay he saw there shocked him.

"What?" she insisted, voice shaking. "My dress is what?"

"Well, it's a little..." He searched for the right word and settled lamely for "Little."

Abruptly she shot to her feet, hands smoothing fabric that already fit like second skin. "It's a perfect fit!" she exclaimed. "Perfect!"

"Shh!" Edward hushed her, embarrassed by a very public display of a very fine— His breath quickened. "Sit down!" he hissed.

She seemed not to have heard him as she twisted about, showing him her backside. He closed his eyes, biting back a groan, then abruptly opened them again to sweep the room. If they had been the object of curiosity before, they were now the center of attention.

"Everyone's staring!" he said through his teeth and made a grab for her wrist, intending to pull her back down into her chair. To his mortification, she spun away. An instant later, she was preening, literally, for the whole room. A man across the way— a man old enough to know better by Edward's estimation, a rather dignified, middle-aged man, in fact, with sleek silver hair—inclined his head in silent acknowledgment of Laurel's antics and, incredibly, lifted his hands to applaud. Suddenly the room rippled with applause. Laurel shot him a smug glance over one shoulder and sank into a half-bow, half-curtsy, her back to Edward. He watched the hem of her skirt rise up the backs of her thighs and nearly had a heart attack.

Unthinkingly, he lurched to his feet, one hand clamping around her upper arm to spin her around to face him. Stunned, she yanked back. He instantly yanked her forward again. No match for his strength, she landed against his chest with a "Hut!" of expelled breath. He clamped his arms around her to prevent her from bouncing off again and falling to the floor. For one eternal moment, they stood there, locked together, trapped in one another's eyes, bodies pressed together in tingling awareness. He forgot that they were standing in the middle of a crowded restaurant, forgot that this was business, that she was not the sort of woman who appealed to him. She moaned a low, husky "Oh-oh."

His gaze shifted to her mouth, a wide, luscious, perfect, pink mouth with the promise of a hot little tongue inside. He bent his

head. She lifted her chin. He felt the warm, humid caress of her breath. He could almost taste her, almost feel her. The tap on his shoulder came as a rude interruption. Eyes narrowed, he swiveled his head and impaled poor Benjamin, who swallowed visibly and in a quavering voice swept him back to reality.

"Will that be all, sir, or will you be wanting..." His troubled gaze flicked to Laurel, and he croaked, "Dessert?"

Embarrassment surged from deep in Edward's chest, forcing its way up his throat and face to burst through the top of his head, anger following in its wake, hot, volatile, unruly. "That will be all," he rumbled, holding Laurel with one hand and snatching up his notebook with the other.

"Perhaps you'd prefer to settle up later?" Benjamin whispered helpfully.

Edward growled assent and propelled Laurel toward the door, vaguely aware that she snatched her purse from the arm of her chair at the last possible instant and, at one point, dug in her heels. He literally shoved her through the door onto the covered walkway. The car waited at the curb, motor running, both front doors open. The valet hurried forward, and Edward slapped a bill into his palm, aware only by the young man's gleeful expression that he'd overtipped outrageously. He didn't care. All he wanted was out of there. It was not to be.

As he attempted to hand Laurel into the car, she suddenly hauled up short, threw out both arms and screamed at him. "Stop!"

He turned an incredulous glare on her. "Just get in the car!"

"No!" She had the effrontery to return his glare with fire of her own, one slender hip thrust out to provide a perch for her hand. "What is wrong with you?" she demanded.

He thought his eyes would pop out of his head. *"Me?"* He poked himself in the chest with a forefinger, then stabbed it at her. *"You* were the one making a spectacle of yourself in—"

"A spectacle!"

"Well, what would you call it?"

She gasped, and he thought he saw a flicker of hurt in her eyes, but then the fire came roaring back and she was shouting at him again. "You insulted my dress!"

The urge to shake her was so great that he spun away from her, clenching his hands and thrusting them to his sides as he turned back. "All I said was that it's too tight and too short!" he argued, trying for—but not entirely achieving—a reasonable tone.

She stuck her chin out pugnaciously and leaned forward at the waist, both hands on her hips. "Well, no one else seemed to think so!"

"Oh, come on!" he shot back. "Every man in the place was drooling! Tongues were hanging out all over the room!"

She straightened and took a step forward, eyes narrowing. "Is that so?"

"You damned well know it!" he shouted, only belatedly realizing that she had lowered her own voice. Something strange swept through him. He grabbed instinctively for the remnants of his outrage. "That dress is so t-tight, you might as well be—" He didn't say it, for he had a sudden vision of her standing there bare to the skin, and what his imagination showed him was the folly of the very thought. All at once he wanted desperately to put hands on her again, to haul her up against him and lock his arms around her. When she took another step forward, he shuddered with the effort to keep his hands at his sides.

She brought her face up next to his and fixed him with a hot-eyed stare. "This dress," she purred ferociously, "is a perfect fit. I know because I designed and made it!"

He capitulated utterly, much more concerned now with tearing his gaze from her mouth. "You're absolutely right," he said quickly. "It's a perfect fit. *Please* get in the car."

She stepped back, squared her shoulders with a nod and whirled away to slide herself neatly onto the seat. The valet rushed forward to shut her door, and Edward let him, stalking around the front of the car to put himself behind the steering wheel. He forced himself to pull away from the curb circumspectly, to ease into the stream of traffic moving along the downtown street. The rain had stopped, but he failed to notice, just as he failed to notice the irony of the silence that filled the car. Now that they had no audience, they found nothing to say to one another, nothing to shout about. Troubled by his own poor behavior, Edward soon

left off trying to puzzle out hers. What had possessed him to yell at her? What was he thinking? He flashed on that kiss in his office, and suddenly he knew too well what he had been thinking. He had been thinking that every male in the place was looking at Laurel Miller with the same lust as he had—was. Dear God. A thrumming began in his belly and climbed up into his throat, concentrating in the hollow above his sternum.

At one point she folded her arms and muttered to her window something about him sticking to what he knew and letting her do likewise. He ignored her, too shaken to chance a clarification. The car wheeled into a space in the parking lot. He hadn't even set the gear before she had her belt off and her door open.

"Thank you so much for dinner," she snipped. "Good night!"

He clamped a hand on her shoulder. "Wait!"

For an instant she remained tense, but then she melted back against the upholstery and swiveled her head around to look at him. "What?"

Heaven help him, she wasn't going to make it easy. He meant to take his hand away; instead, he slid it around to the nape of her neck. "I'm sorry," he told her softly. "I don't know what happened. I—I just..." He pushed his free hand through his hair in frustration.

Clucking her tongue, she eased around and reached up a hand. "You've messed it up," she said softly.

He mumbled another apology, not giving a fig whether his hair was mussed or not. "We didn't get anything done," he muttered.

She folded her arms and said quietly, "You asked why I'm waiting tables. Well, I'll tell you. It isn't because I can't design. It's the cold hand of my grandmother reaching out from the grave."

"Your grandmother." He choked out the words.

"My grandmother," she said, "and Bryce."

He put a hand to his forehead, feeling a vague ache starting between his eyes. "How? Why?"

"Why? Because fashion designing is frivolous. Anything that makes you look better and feel better about yourself is frivolous, according to my grandmother's edict. The only thing in which we can take pride is our heritage, our standing on the social ladder."

The ache moved to the vicinity of his heart. "Why did you let her discourage you?" he asked gently.

She shook her head sadly. "I didn't. Even after she effectively had me barred from all the better schools. But then she just used her influence to bar me from every decent design house on the continent." She made a disgusted sound in the back of her throat and added, "I couldn't get a job as a salesclerk by the time she finished with me."

"And Bryce naturally followed her lead," he concluded.

"The hand that controls the Heffington millions," Laurel said bitterly, "as few as they are now, controls the Heffington heir."

Edward sighed and twisted around to face her, one arm draped over the steering wheel, the other laying across her shoulder. "I didn't know," he said. "I'm sorry."

She had the grace to add her own apology to his. "Me, too."

His hand found the nape of her neck again. He could feel the blood throbbing in his veins, thick and hot. "You, um, seem to know your stuff," he said, more for something to say than anything else. "Maybe, uh, you could give me some pointers. The haircut seems to have worked, after all."

She smiled and laid her head back against his arm. "Let's see now. I don't think you need so much help, really."

He smiled at that. "No?"

She shook her head. "All you need is the attention of a good tailor."

"Mmm-hmm." God, she had glorious eyes, bright as emeralds and tilted exotically at the outer edges, her long lashes curling back.

She sat up straight and began tugging at his jacket, taking up big handfuls of it. He sucked in his gut, fire jolting through him. "Look," she was saying, "you don't need all this room. You have broad shoulders and a big chest, but your middle's flat and your waist is relatively small." She brushed and patted her hands over him in demonstration.

"Oh." He was strangling. His lungs locked. His body stirring and hardening.

"What you need to start with is a well-tailored double-breasted suit," she was saying. "Black, of course, and brown would look

good with your coloring.'' She ran her eyes over him. It was like a physical caress. ''Tan would be good,'' she went on, ''and olive.''

''O-olive.''

''Oh, and cream. Yes, definitely cream.''

He wasn't certain but he thought he repeated that, too. He couldn't be sure, what with wondering how his arm came to be around her waist when he had draped it, pointedly, across the steering wheel.

''T-try a monochrome color scheme,'' she said, sounding breathless, ''and a-accent with another. F-for instance, c-cream shirt and jacket and slacks—the pleated kind—and wear them long.''

''Wear them long,'' he mumbled, compelled to bend his head so that his breath warmed her ear. A lovely little ear, neat and trim and... He had never before seen a perfectly delicious ear.

''S-so they break at the top of your foot.'' She sighed.

''The top of my foot,'' he whispered, feeling his breath flow back to him from the perfect shell of her ear. She shivered, so he pulled her closer for warmth.

''A different color tie,'' she rambled, ''or a vest—brown tweed, maybe. They make shirts without collars, you know, so you don't necessarily need—'' She seemed to lose the next word and closed her eyes.

Her jaw beckoned, and he allowed his mouth to glide around it to her chin. She let her head fall back again, leaving him to contemplate the smooth column of her throat or the short trip to her mouth.

The trip was so short that he didn't even know he'd taken it until he felt her lips meld with his. She was hot and liquid and sweet, curling into him, melting against him, her arm coming up to hook around his neck. She moaned, and he breathed in the sound with something very like triumph swelling within him. His hands moved over her, registering her shape and the firm, supple softness that comprised it. That damned dress didn't give an inch, and he wanted skin. Oh, how he wanted skin.

He leaned back into the corner, wedging himself against the steering wheel and the door, pulling her on top of him. She

wrapped both arms around his neck and ground her mouth against his. He went up in flames, his hands skimming down to the hem of her dress and up again over that luscious rump and tiny waist to... Skin. Bare, cool, silky skin. Her breasts against his chest were both fuller and heavier than he'd judged. Her hips lay perfectly in the cradle of his, pressing her soft belly against his hard... He ravaged her mouth and began trying to figure out how to do this. She was so slender, that he'd have to lift her legs up and drape them over his hips to fit himself between them. And these clothes had to give. Briefly he considered the mechanics involved in ripping apart her tights, then his mind whirled on to making room by yanking the steering column out of the dashboard and kicking open the door at the end of this too-short seat. His hands fortunately found something with which he could easily deal, the clasp in the band of her bra.

It parted with a flick of his fingers, and immediately he felt through their clothes the added warmth of her unbound breasts. His body leapt, and he moved his hands to her hips to press down the need to put himself inside her. It occurred to him dimly, desperately, that never before had he felt such intense need. He felt close to tears, very close to losing all control. He thrust against her and in the same moment stuck his tongue deeply into her mouth. And then she changed everything.

She reared up, one hand planted squarely in the middle of his chest, and slapped him. Hard.

Chapter Six

As shocked by what she'd done as he was, Laurel scrambled for the door, ignoring where her knees and elbows landed as she moved across his big body.

"Ow! Oof!"

She yanked open the door and lurched out onto the parking lot, sinking her precious shoes in a puddle of rainwater.

"Laurel, wait!"

But why should she wait? The damage was already done. Why should she stay and let him rub her nose in it? What was wrong with her anyway? Letting him kiss her like that again, getting so carried away that he thought it perfectly permissible to start undressing her in a parked car! Oh, God, if only she hadn't proposed marriage to him! Blushing to the roots of her hair, she ran across the parking lot, no longer caring that her feet were soaked.

"Laurel!"

She gasped, whirling to see that he'd come after her. "Go away, Edward!"

"No, wait!"

But she couldn't. She just wanted this whole horrible night to

end. "Good night, Edward!" She turned and ran as quickly as her squishy shoes would allow. He caught up with her at the bottom of the stairwell, his big hand closing around her upper arm. This was becoming a habit with him, a bad habit. "Take your hands off me!"

He released her instantly. "I'm sorry. I just wanted to..." He lifted one hand. "You forgot your purse."

She snatched it away from him, snapped "Thank you" and backed up a step.

"Laurel," he said, "I really *am* sorry."

She turned her face away, too embarrassed to look at him. "I'm the one who's sorry. I—I was a fool to think..." No, she wouldn't get into that stupid marriage proposal. How could she have thought even for a moment that she could pull off something like a marriage of convenience with this man? She shook her head, wanting desperately to get away. Following sheer instinct, she hurried up the stairs.

He came after her. "Laurel, please can't we talk about this? I—I didn't mean to... That is, I don't even know how it happened."

"No!" she called down to him. It came out more of a question that she'd intended, a product of her confusion and embarrassment. She stopped and jerked around on the step to face him, intending to tell him that it wasn't his fault, that she didn't blame him, that she just wanted him to go away.

He looked up at her and exclaimed, "Hell, you're not even my type!"

Abject humiliation flooded her. Her heart dropped to the soles of her feet. Hurt unlike anything she'd ever felt before hit her, knocking the breath out of her, slapping tears into her eyes. She grabbed the handrail, mouth opening to release an exclamation that no sound could adequately communicate. She turned and began to run up the stairs again, only to break the heel off one shoe two steps later. Bawling in frustration, she yanked it off and threw it over her shoulder.

"Ow!"

She whirled awkwardly, nearly tumbling headfirst down the stairwell. He glared up at her, her destroyed shoe in his hand. She

saw the anger in his eyes and welcomed it, her own leaping up to meet his. How dare he be angry? She was the one humiliated, insulted, manhandled! She yanked off the other shoe and threw it at him with all her might. It glanced off the top of his head. "Ow! Stop that!" He clamped a hand over the spot, glaring up at her, but she knew darned well that it hadn't really hurt. A head that hard could take anything thrown at it!

"Drop dead, Edward White!"

She flung herself up those stairs, only the soles of her tights between her and the cement steps. Behind her he yelled, "You perverse little loon!"

"Shut up!"

"I will not, not until you calm down and listen to me!"

"Never! Not in a mil—" She broke off at the landing of her floor. Fancy was pacing there, bouncing a weakly wailing Barry on her hip.

"Thank God!" She rushed forward and practically threw Barry into Laurel's arms. "You've got to help me. He won't stop crying! I've tried everything I can think of, he just won't hush! I didn't know what else to do. I tried Mrs. Martinez, but she's not home, and—" She was looking at Laurel's feet. "Where are your shoes?"

Edward came bounding up behind her then, just in time to say, "I have them. She threw them at me."

Fancy reeled back in surprise. "Threw them at you?" She glanced at Laurel's flushed face, even though Laurel tried to hide it from her by bending her head and crooning to Barry, who snuggled against her, snuffling and rubbing his teary eyes wearily. Fancy immediately rounded on Ed. "What the hell'd you do to her?"

"Me?" he yelped defensively. "She's the one who made a scene in the middle of the best supper club in town! And then she...she let..." His words seemed to dwindle away with his anger. He glanced guiltily at Laurel and, both her shoes held in the crook of one arm, pushed a hand through his hair. She stared accusingly at the top of his head. Exasperatedly, he combed it back into place with short, fierce tugs of his fingers, then glared at her as if to say, "There! Satisfied?"

Unwilling to allow the softening that was beginning in the vicinity of her heart, she turned her head away. Concentrating once more on the baby, she put a hand to his forehead. It was warm. "I think he has fever!" she said to Fancy.

"Oooh," Fancy whined, "I was afraid of that, but it ain't my fault! I'm just not mama material."

Laurel shot a concerned look at Edward, saying, "It's okay. We'll, um, figure out what to do." She targeted the door to her apartment and headed toward it, Barry rubbing his face against her shoulder as she fumbled in her purse for her keys. Fancy glared at Edward and followed. Laurel's shoes in hand, he came right behind her.

"Listen," he was saying, "if you need some help, I have a friend you could ask."

"I think we can manage," Laurel muttered, balancing Barry on her hip and getting the key into the lock.

"We can manage," Fancy affirmed sharply.

"I'm just trying to help," Edward pointed out entirely too mildly.

Laurel shoved the door open and turned on him. "I'm not incompetent, Edward! You think just because I haven't given birth I can't possibly know how to take care of a child?"

"I didn't say that. As a matter of fact, Kendra's little girl is adopted. It's just that Kendra's been at it quite a while, and on top of that, she's a pediatric nurse. She knows what she's doing." He looked at Fancy, his implication clear. "She's an excellent mother."

"Well, bully for her," Fancy said, bristling. "Laurel's an—"

"Intelligent woman!" Laurel interjected quickly. "Intelligent enough to take care of a little fever, thank you very much."

"Fine," he said testily. "Like I said, I was just trying to help, and of all the mothers I know, Kendra Sugarman is not just the best, she's the most helpful and—"

"Sugarman!" Laurel exclaimed. "Parker's wife?"

He momentarily gaped at her, taken completely off guard, and then a shield came down behind his eyes. "That's right."

She was the one, the one Edward had wanted to marry, the one he had loved, maybe still did love. He certainly was not

above bragging about her, and for some reason that hurt more than Laurel could fathom. Not his type. Not the type he could love and respect, just the type he could undress in the front seat of his car!

"Go away, Edward," she said, her voice shaking despite her best effort at control. He stared at her dumbly, as if English was a foreign language or she was a creature from another planet. "Go away, Edward!" she screamed, helpless against the tears that rolled down her cheeks.

He stared a moment longer, and then he nodded and thrust her shoes at her, gaze averted in confusion. It was Fancy who took the shoes, Fancy who guided Laurel into the apartment and stood guard at the door, watching until he retreated into the stairwell, his quick footsteps echoing into the silence as curtains and blinds twitched back into place, and it was Fancy who pronounced the final, unprintable and most appropriate conclusion to the whole miserable episode.

Edward waited with his hands in his pockets, jiggling change and shifting his weight from foot to foot. It was after eleven, too late to be dropping by, but he didn't know where else to go or what else to do. He felt as wound-up as an eight-day clock and as confused as a soap opera plot. He needed a sounding board and trustworthy advice. What he needed, he told himself, was the woman he couldn't have and the friend he wouldn't give up. He needed the pain with which he had learned to live, the friendship he had learned to treasure and the combined wisdom he couldn't deny—and he needed it *now*.

By the time the door opened, he was in such a state that common little civilities like greetings were beyond him. He swept by Parker, ignoring the fact that his good friend wore nothing but partially zipped jeans, and got right to the point by exclaiming, "I must be out of my mind!" He threw up his hands. "What am I talking about? *She's* the one out of her mind!"

"She?" Parker queried, half turning in order to do up his jeans and run a hand through his damp hair.

"Don't play stupid," Edward snapped. Pointing a finger at his

best friend in all the world, he added, "You did this to me, you worm, insisting I take that...that *loony-tune* into my office."

"Ah." Parker folded his arms in satisfied understanding. "The delectable Ms. Heffington Miller."

Edward's brows furrowed and his eyes darkened tellingly at that. "Do I have to remind you that you're a married man?"

Parker smiled smugly. "No. My wife was doing that rather nicely just before you leaned on the bell—in the tub, I might add. Kendra, that is, not you. Nice haircut, by the way."

Edward grimaced. "Don't talk to me about my hair."

What was it with him? Parker was the most appearance-conscious, sex-addicted man he'd ever known, and he just never changed, not even after all this time being married to the sweetest little woman alive. He tried not to think about what Kendra might have been doing in the bathtub to remind her husband of something that he ought not to be able to forget. Disgusted, Ed turned and left the entry, tramping down the steps to the living room then crossing over and stoically trudging up more steps to the austere, spotless kitchen. After taking off his coat and loosening his tie, he pulled out a chair from beneath the small table there and sat down.

Parker skipped lightly up the steps and came to stand at the counter, the heels of his palms braced against the edge of the slate countertop. "To what do I owe the honor, old buddy? I haven't seen you this worked up since you wandered in and caught me making love to my own wife in the living room."

Edward glowered from sheer habit, but oddly enough the reminder of that particular past folly did not produce the same lurching pain as usual. He attributed it to his state of mind. Maybe he was losing it. God knew a female like Laurel Miller could drive a guy right over the edge. Now Kendra was a different case. Kendra was a quiet, restful kind of woman. You could almost forget that she was around. As if conjured from mere thought, the quiet female in question laid a welcoming hand on his shoulder.

"Hi, Ed. What's up? Ooh, nice haircut."

"Uh, don't talk to him about his hair," Parker quipped.

He glowered and smoothed his hair self-consciously as Kendra

glided across the room to stand at her husband's side. She wore a sensible flowered robe zipped all the way to the chin and had combed her long, wet hair straight back over a towel draped around her shoulders shawl fashion.

"What shall we talk about, then?" she asked brightly. Edward felt greatly mollified.

"It's this case I've been working on," he grumbled.

Kendra smiled knowingly at her husband, saying, "Why don't I brew us up a pot of herbal tea while you tell us all about it?"

Parker looked at Ed and quietly added, "I'll get the whiskey."

Ed nodded agreement. Adding a strong dose of liquor was the only way he could get Kendra's herbal tea down, but he wasn't about to tell her that. Half an hour later he was sipping his second cup, feeling as mellow as it was possible to get in his state of mind, and doling out his story.

"Anyway, there wasn't a chair to sit on, a table to eat from, not so much as a radio—just an air mattress on the floor and clothing everywhere. Clothing and shoes. She must have a hundred pairs lining the walls." He shook his head.

"No furniture at all?" Kendra asked over the top of her cup.

He started to say no, then shrugged. "Well, there was a crib," he allowed, "and like a little dresser thing."

"A baby bed?" Parker queried, balancing himself on the back legs of his chair.

"Apparently, she baby-sits for this friend of hers, and let me tell you, this is one for the books. The dame must be fifty if she's a day, dyed black hair, false eyelashes out to here, makeup for six. She's some kind of reformed stripper. Name's Fancy Bright." He shook his head over the contrived name.

The front legs of Parker's chair hit the floor. "No kidding? I mean, *the* Fancy Bright?"

Edward frowned. "Don't tell me you know this broad."

"Know her?" Parker hooted. "Hell, I spent my entire puberty sneaking in to see her. She's a legend, man, an artist."

"An *artist!*" Ed snorted. "She's an old has-been stripper."

"What I want to know," Kendra interjected pragmatically, "is what she's doing with a baby at her age."

Ed rubbed a hand over his face. "Yeah, I wondered about that,

too, but it's Laurel who concerns me. Honest to God, I have to wonder if she's playing with a full deck. Kennison says she's not, and he's got some pretty powerful ammunition. And after everything that's happened..." He chugged tea and set the mug down with an audible crack. Kendra reached for the teapot while Parker uncapped the whiskey.

"Just what is *everything*, Ed?" Kendra asked. "I mean, those other things happened when she was a kid, right?"

"Yeah," Parker put in, "what's happened to get you all stirred up?"

Edward ran his fingertip around the edge of his mug, saying, "Well, for one thing, that very first day, the day you pushed me into a consultation with her, she asked me to marry her."

"She *what?*" It came in chorus, but it was Parker who added the refrain of laughter, tipping his head back and howling so that Kendra scolded him, fearing he'd wake Darla, who was arguably the most remarkable three-year-old in history, thanks entirely, Edward was sure, to Kendra's skills as a mother.

It was just those skills that had brought Parker and Kendra together in the first place. After the deaths of her parents, Parker's brother and sister-in-law, Parker had needed Kendra to help him keep his niece with him. A custody battle waged by a sister of Darla's mother had prompted Parker to find a wife quickly in order to cement his claims to Darla. A good friend and a pediatric nurse, Kendra had seemed the logical choice, especially since she had broken off her engagement to Edward some weeks earlier. Much to Edward's dismay, what had begun as a marriage of convenience involving the two people closest to him had become a great romance and a marriage in truth. The pair had adopted Darla as their own and turned themselves into a real family, which meant, of course, that Kendra was lost to him forever, no matter that he never had and probably never would love another woman. Somehow, though, over time, he'd grown accustomed to the idea. It was something about which the three of them never spoke.

Predictably, Kendra was shocked by Laurel's abrupt marriage proposal. Just as predictably, Parker was more willing to give her the benefit of the doubt. "Actually," he said, when the whole

tale of the proposal had been told, "it's a pretty sound solution to the problem."

"Don't be stupid," Edward growled. "Who in his right mind would marry someone he wasn't in love with and didn't intend to stay married to?"

Parker grinned at Kendra. "Worked for me."

Kendra smacked him lightly on the shoulder with the flat of her hand. "It did not. We were already in love, we just didn't know it."

"Look," Edward cut in irritably, "it's not just the marriage proposal. I took her to The Blue Plate tonight—"

Parker whistled.

"And she made a huge scene in front of everyone," he went on, ignoring Parker pointedly.

Kendra frowned. "What do you mean?"

Edward grimaced. He really didn't want to get into this, now that he thought about it. He waved a hand dismissively. "Aw, it was about this dress she was wearing."

"What about it?" Parker wanted to know.

Ed tried to shrug it off. "It was too short and too tight."

"Sounds perfect to me," Parker quipped, winking at his wife.

Kendra rolled her eyes. "You would think so."

"Oh, come on, you're not as conservative anymore as you pretend."

"I don't pretend," she replied mildly.

Parker smirked at Ed. "Yeah, right. Like she ever wears that Mother Hubbard robe except when you or her dad are around— and like you don't know she's stark naked beneath it."

Edward nearly swallowed his cup along with the tea he was sipping.

"Parker!" Kendra scolded, but the flame red of her face told Ed that Parker had spoken the truth, and the very idea of Kendra naked made him uncomfortable. It was kind of like picturing his mother naked; it just wasn't respectful. *But you got your face slapped for trying to strip Laurel naked in the front seat of your car,* whispered a perverse little voice inside his head. Resolutely, Edward shoved both thoughts away, snapping, "Can we stick to the point here?"

Parker ran his tongue around the inside of his mouth, poking lumps in both cheeks. "Right," he said, "and the point is?"

"The point is, what am I going to do about Laurel? If Kennison's right and she's inherited her grandfather's emotional instability, I don't have a prayer of winning this case in court."

"And if he's wrong," Parker mused, "and you drop the case for *fear* of losing in court, Laurel can kiss her inheritance goodbye."

"You think I don't know that?" Edward retorted. "Why do you think I'm asking for advice?"

Kendra shook her head thoughtfully. "It's not our opinions that you need," she said. "What you need is a professional opinion."

"A shrink, you mean?"

"A psychiatrist, yes."

"Oh, swell, so I just tell her I won't pursue the case unless some Freud clone gives her a passing grade in sanity? I can't do that! You don't know this woman and what she's been through. I mean, her parents couldn't be bothered with her, and her grandmother had all the warmth of an ice cube, and that's putting it mildly. Her grandfather was a nut case. Her husband rips her off for several mil and the only home she's ever known. She's locked out of her chosen profession and reduced to waiting tables in a diner with a retired stripper for a running buddy, living in a shabby walk-up furnished with a pile of shoes and an air mattress, and on top of it all you want me to tell her she has to see a shrink and get his stamp of approval? I don't think so." He shook his head, firm but stymied. "God, what am I going to do?"

Parker grinned. "You could always marry her. Not even psychoanalysis gives you insight into another human being like marriage does."

"Oh, that's very funny," Edward said sarcastically. "Just the kind of solution I might have expected from you." He meant it to be pithy. It wasn't. He put his head in his hands, elbows on the tabletop. "Oh, it's impossible. I can't find a solution because there isn't one."

"Maybe there is," Kendra said thoughtfully, eyes narrowing. "Yes, I think it just might work."

Edward looked at Parker, hoping for some insight into this

possible solution of Kendra's, but Parker just shook his head, shrugging. Finally he took pity on Edward and gripped Kendra's hand where it lay next to her teacup. "Come on, honey. Let's hear this plan of yours. Ed's biting his nails over here."

Kendra sat forward suddenly, targeting Ed with her gaze. "Are you on friendly enough terms with the woman to invite her to a private dinner?"

Edward stroked his mustache consideringly. He'd already invited "the woman" out to dinner and that had ended in unmitigated disaster, the scope and particulars of which he had no intention of divulging. Would she go out with him again? Would a heartfelt apology and an honest explanation have any influence? On the other hand, what the hell was an honest explanation for what had happened in the front seat of that car? He rubbed a hand over his face, suddenly exhausted, and sighed. "I don't know."

He missed the look shared by Parker and his wife, missed the slight lift of a brow, the biting of a full lower lip, the thoughtful decisiveness with which Kendra pressed him.

"Listen, you've got to bring this Laurel Miller here to dinner."

"Here?" Edward echoed in surprise.

"That's right. We're having a dinner party, and I'm going to invite a certain friend of mine from the hospital."

Parker snapped his fingers. "David Greenlea! You brilliant little schemer you."

Edward cocked his head. David Greenlea? Why did that sound familiar? A picture flashed before Edward's mind's eye—a lean, longish face wearing a perpetual smile and golden blond curls blowing about broad, tan shoulders. Suddenly the picture bled into a scenario, and he frowned. "You're not talking about that kooky guy I found sleeping on your living room floor back about five years ago, are you?"

"David's not kooky," Kendra said, laughing. "He never was. You just thought so because he used to wear his hair long, and he only slept on my living room floor for a night or two."

"You never did explain that," Edward reminded her, conveniently forgetting that she hadn't been obligated to do so.

Kendra complied with an airy wave of her hand. "It was no big deal. His residency and his apartment lease ended at about

the same time. He wanted to take a trip out West to visit relatives before establishing his practice here, but you know how relentlessly they work residents. He needed someplace to rest up before he started driving.''

"So you just naturally booked him into the Kendra motel," Edward scoffed, shaking his head.

Parker winked at his wife, grinning, and said, "David himself tells me that he slept around the clock for two solid days and was so sore when he got up off that floor, he could hardly walk.''

Edward grunted noncommittally, unconvinced and yet as certain as ever that Kendra never had and never would indulge in anything the least "improper." But that was beside the point. "So what's any of this got to do with Laurel?''

"Think about it," Kendra instructed. "David is a psychiatrist...and a friend. " When it didn't immediately click together in Edward's mind, Kendra rolled her eyes. "He owes me a favor, Edward." When that didn't penetrate, she threw up her hands in exasperation. "Oh, for pity's sake! You don't want to ask her to submit to a formal psychiatric evaluation, so you invite her here. We invite David. Then we just let the two of them alone together and afterward David can tell you in private what he thinks.''

For a moment, Edward could only marvel—and disapprove— that Kendra had devised such a plan all on her own. But then he began to see the benefits of it. Laurel would never have to know. He'd have a professional opinion. He could make a reasonable, unemotional decision about the case.

"It won't be the same as a thorough evaluation," Kendra was saying, "but I'll tell David everything you've told us, and if we leave them alone long enough, that ought to at least give him some idea about her stability.''

Edward was beginning to see flaws in the plan now. How did he know that he could trust David Greenlea? Would it be fair to stake Laurel's future—and that's what he'd be doing—on a dinner party conversation? On the other hand, what option did he have? He couldn't trust his own judgment where Laurel Miller was concerned. He understood that much now. He shook himself in confusion, ordering his thoughts.

"Ken, I respect your judgment," he said, "but how do I know I can trust Greenlea?"

"I trust him," she said simply.

"The hospital trusts him," Parker added, "enough to make him acting chief of psychiatry when the old chief left unexpectedly earlier this year."

Not bad five years out of residency, Edward privately admitted, but the lawyer in him pressed for hidden weakness. "Why acting chief? Why not just chief of psychiatry?"

Kendra laughed. "He's a junior staffer, Ed. Can you imagine how many senior staffers would resign if they picked him as permanent head of the department? I mean, everybody knows he deserves it, but those other doctors have families to support and careers to foster. The official line is that David got the, quote, thankless, unquote, job as acting chief because he has no family."

"No family?"

"No immediate family," Parker clarified. "No one to make demands on his time."

"He's never married," Kendra explained further. "I think he'd like to. Guess he just never met the right woman. Anyway, the last chief was a widower with grown children, and he said he quit because the job took too much time and energy. I think he was just getting on in years, you know? Didn't have the energy to keep up things anymore. But it gave the hospital board a good excuse to tap David for the interim. I expect their search for a permanent chief to go very slowly."

"Yeah," Parker added, "David might be the senior staffer by the time they officially decide that they just can't do any better than him."

Edward was hung up on the notion that blond, good-looking David Greenlea was not married. "Hasn't he got anyone?" he asked. "You know, a fiancée, a girlfriend?"

"Not that I'm aware of," Kendra said.

For some reason that he couldn't quite pinpoint, Edward didn't feel comfortable with that. He scratched his chin and said, "He's not gay, is he?"

Parker and Kendra looked at one another and burst out laugh-

ing. After a moment, Parker cleared his throat. "Definitely not gay."

Kendra leaned forward to foster an air of confidentiality. "Actually, he had a torrid affair with a nurse on my floor last year. Everyone was talking about it. I don't know what happened, but there was an audit and some things came up missing. It could be coincidence, but soon after the nurse in question was escorted out of the building by security, and we've not seen her since. I asked David if he ever saw her, and he said that he didn't but that it was too painful to go into further. And that was that."

"Personally, I feel sorry for the guy," Parker said. "If he did find out that his lover was a thief, that had to be pretty hard to take."

Edward nodded. "It doesn't say much for his judgment, though, does it?"

"On the contrary," Kendra said. "Rumor has it that he turned her in."

Edward lifted his eyebrows at that. A man with that much integrity might indeed have a difficult time in the romance department. His gaze strayed to Kendra. A man with high standards seemed to have an extremely narrow field from which to choose. But none of that mattered, really. The only relevant question was whether or not David Greenlea could truly help him make a decision about Laurel's case. Finally, he had to admit that there were no hard and fast answers, and he was left with that one tricky source of judgment: his instinct. And instinct told him that he couldn't trust himself to see Laurel clearly. He wasn't sure why; he wasn't even certain that he wanted to know why. He shook his head, telling himself that he was getting off track again. Once more, he missed a shared look of deep speculation between his friends.

"Okay," he said on sigh. "Let's see if we can make it happen."

Kendra glanced innocently at Parker and then fixed her gaze on the tea in her cup as she sipped from it. Edward picked up on the silent signal this time, however. He just didn't know what it meant. Thankfully, Parker seemed to be trying to let him in on it with his next words.

"Think two weeks will give you the time to turn her up sweet enough for this?"

Edward remembered the slap and the argument that followed. For an instant, he wondered if Parker had somehow divined... But no, that was nonsense. No one but he and Laurel could know about those two kisses. So, the only thing he had to worry about was whether or not he could convince Laurel to forgive his previous actions and trust him enough to join him for dinner with friends.

"Two weeks," he agreed, wondering if two months would do it.

"Make that two weeks from Sunday," Kendra said, showing them both who had the final say around here.

Parker chuckled. "Two weeks from Sunday then."

Two weeks and three days, Edward told himself, to accomplish the impossible.

Chapter Seven

Laurel balanced the five-gallon, plastic water bucket on her hip and stepped carefully onto the small metal stool. With her left hand, she lifted away the lid of the coffeemaker, while her right held the bucket against her hip. Slowly she laid aside the lid and shifted the bucket into both hands. Just as she lifted the sloshing three gallons of water, Fancy's elbow slammed into her ribs.

"Oof!" Water splashed onto the front of Laurel's uniform. She swayed wildly, hugging the plastic bucket and wetting her arms. One foot slipped off the stool. "Oh-oh-oh!" She stepped down and back hard, sloshing water all down her front again.

"Will you stop that!" Fancy hissed, oblivious to the fact that she had caused the mess.

"I didn't do anything, Fancy!" Laurel hissed back. "You nearly made me fall!"

"He's here!" Fancy whispered hoarsely, grasping her by the shoulders. Immediately diverted, she peered over the top of Laurel's head. "Oh my gawd, is he looking sharp or what?"

Laurel glanced over her shoulder, more concerned with her wet, limp uniform than whoever had come into the diner. She did a

double take, at first disbelieving. There stood Edward White, his new haircut perfectly combed, his tall, powerful frame shown off to heart-stopping advantage in a double-breasted suit of roughly textured olive green silk. His shirt was a shade lighter, and his tie a smartly patterned combination of light and dark with a touch of vibrant blue, just enough to bring out the color of his eyes. She couldn't have chosen better for him herself and felt a spurt of pride that he'd so obviously taken her advice to heart. Pain and shame quickly overwhelmed that one tiny spurt. She turned away.

"I don't want to see him."

"Now, honey," Fancy crooned, calming her, "you know he's your best hope."

Laurel shook her head, whispering, "I can't see him, Fancy. I'm so embarrassed."

"Well, I don't see what you've got to be embarrassed about," Fancy told her, the gleam in her eye saying only too obviously that she knew full well she hadn't gotten the entire story behind that battle royal late last week. "Now you hold up your head and you go over there and you tell that big hunk of man you'll forgive him if he still wants to take your case." She took the water bucket out of Laurel's arms, balanced it on one hip and waved her off with a flick of a wrist. "Go on now. Won't do no good to try to hide back here. He's already seen you anyway."

Laurel turned with heavy dread, knowing that Fancy was right. He stood just where she'd last seen him, looking terribly uncertain. Gulping, Laurel rubbed at her soaked uniform with a kitchen towel as she moved reluctantly around the counter to the narrow aisle between bar stools and booths. Edward stood his ground, moving neither forward nor back. Not until she got within a yard of him did his gaze drop pointedly to the huge wet spots on her uniform. Laurel cringed inwardly. "It's, um, just water."

He nodded solemnly. "I saw what happened. You can blame me. Fancy was obviously as shocked to see me here as you are."

She didn't know what to say to that, so she just stood there like a lump, twisting the kitchen towel in her hands. After a long, awkward moment, he put on a patently false smile and said too

jovially, "What do you think? The tailor said you have a good eye. He, um, wondered if you might be interested in a job."

She couldn't tell if he was serious or not, so she merely shrugged. "I—I don't know. I have friends here."

He nodded and looked away. "Um, could we sit down for a minute?"

She immediately slid into an empty booth. It was the slow part of the afternoon, too late for lunch, too early for coffee breaks. He unbuttoned his suit coat and slid in opposite her. He seemed uncertain how to begin. Pricked by the awkwardness, Laurel launched into small talk. "You had lunch? I've got a tuna melt going to waste back there. Some guy got beeped and ran out without it. It's paid for."

He didn't even look at her, just laid his big hands atop the table and stared at them. "I don't quite know how to apologize to you," he said softly. "I've never done anything like that before." He raised an agonized gaze to hers. "I don't know what came over me. I'm not usually so... That is, I've never tried to undress a reluctant woman in a car before."

"I wasn't reluctant."

He looked suddenly as if she'd slapped him. Again. Laurel sighed and tried to find the words. "I know, I know." She leaned forward, lowering her voice. "I didn't slap you because I was unwilling and frightened you would force yourself on me. I did it because I was frightened by how quickly it happened, how quickly I let it happen."

He blinked at that, and then she watched the struggle of emotions mirrored upon his face: surprise, relief, confusion, even a trace of pleasure. "You seemed so angry," he said finally.

"I was angry," she said, "but at myself as much as you, and I was also embarrassed." She couldn't say that and hold his gaze, especially considering what she had to be embarrassed about. She had let him begin taking her clothes off her! More than that, she had considered helping him do it. She'd behaved like some lovesick schoolgirl, like that needy teenager who'd convinced herself once before that an unattainable man loved and wanted her. She shook her head, feeling the quick burn of color in her cheeks again. "It was as much my fault as yours."

"No, I took advantage," he argued softly. "It won't happen again."

"Truly?"

"I swear it won't."

She attempted a smile and teasingly said, "Too bad."

His gaze zipped up to snag hers. "What did you say?"

She almost groaned aloud. She had obviously shocked him again. "Never mind. I just... I, um, ought to be getting back to work. Was there something else?"

He seemed to need a moment to compose himself. Then suddenly he began fishing in his pocket for a notepad and pen. "Yes, I wanted to ask you, first of all, if you're aware that your ex has worked in a similar situation with Kennison before?"

She frowned. "You mean, did I know that Kennison had used Bryce as a kind of caretaker/nurse before?"

"Yes, exactly."

She shrugged. "Of course. It was on the basis of that work and Kennison's recommendation that Grandmother hired Bryce."

He seemed deflated by that bit of news. "Humph. I see. Well, we might as well look into the possibility of any wrongdoing on those previous jobs, anyway. Also, I wanted to know the name of the doctor who championed you, the one who lost his job after he suggested your grandmother might be the one in need of counseling."

Distractedly, she gave him what he wanted. "That would be Eugene Iverson."

He wrote that down. "Would you know where I could find him if need be?"

If need be. Her heart lurched hopefully. "Er, I think I heard he'd moved to Illinois, but that was a long time ago."

Edward nodded. "Fine. That's fine." He stowed the small notebook and pen. "I'll let you get back to work now, but we'll talk again soon, if that's okay with you."

She nodded dazedly. "Does that mean you're still considering my case?"

He busied himself straightening his suit jacket. "Of course I'm still considering your case. Why wouldn't I?"

A feeling of such gratitude overwhelmed her that she reacted

without thinking. She reached across the table and clasped his hand in hers. "Thank you. Oh, thank you."

He seemed terribly uncomfortable. He all but shook her off. "There's no reason for you to thank me. I haven't done anything yet."

"But you have! You let me into your office. You heard me out. You didn't turn me down flat like everyone else, not even after I... Well, you know. And then you started an investigation, and you took me to dinner, and you even put Tyler May in his place, and you pretended to be my date." Her heart was beating very hard, and she knew that she was taking a stupid step that could never lead her where she wanted to go, but she said it anyway. "And you kissed me and made me feel desirable and—"

He rumbled something that sounded shockingly like a foul word, and Laurel blanched, knowing she'd gone too far. She instantly began backtracking, trying to find the right path.

"A-and after all that nonsense, y-you're still willing to try to help. I think that deserves a little gratitude."

He made an impatient gesture and began sliding out of his seat. "Just forget that crap, will you? I don't need your—" He stopped, closed his eyes and seemed to decide to take a different tack. "I'll be in touch. Okay?"

"Sure. Great."

"Okay. Well..." He smoothed his suit coat into place and buttoned it. "Take it easy."

She watched him turn and walk out, his steps barely restrained. Sighing, she told herself that it had been a very near thing. She'd almost blown it—again. He couldn't get out of there fast enough, but he'd said he'd be back, and she believed him. Oh, yes, she believed him. If only she didn't have to lie to him about Barry, if only she could go back to that night in his car with truth between them. But it couldn't be, and she was courting a broken heart by hoping that it could. And so she was courting a broken heart.

Edward grimaced at his image in the mirror. The small, duskyskinned tailor fluttered around him like an annoying insect, tugging here, checking there. At last, murmuring joyful little sounds

of approval, he backed away, turning his head this way and that, as if judging a work of art. Edward swore silently that if the fop kissed the tips of his fingers again in that stupid dramatic gesture of praise, he was going to knock him on his skinny tush. Seeing the look on Edward's face reflected in the mirror, the effusive haberdasher tempered his enthusiasm, assuming a supercilious air, nose turned up, mouth pursed.

"I believe we are finished. Now about the brown. How would Monday be for the final fitting?"

Edward bounced a glare off the mirror. "No way. We've done this three times already. Just send the other two suits by messenger."

"But Mr. White—"

"I'm sure they'll be fine," Edward insisted, stripping an ivory-and-burgundy-striped tie from a knob on the wall and looping it about his neck.

"Very well." The tailor sighed unhappily. "You may expect them Tuesday. Will there be anything else?"

"Not just now," Edward muttered, his chin tilted up while he swiftly and expertly knotted his tie. Finished, he backed up a step or two, smoothed a hand down his chest and admitted guiltily that he had never looked better. The summer weight, cream linen suit felt and looked as natural as breathing on him. He hardly recognized that man in the mirror. Had a new haircut, a mustache trim and a few words of wisdom concerning his wardrobe really made all this difference? He no longer looked like a bear freshly awakened from hibernation. Everyone noticed. Friends around town had taken to complimenting him. Some asked if he'd slimmed down, and it irritated him to know that he'd kept himself in shape all these years and not a soul had noticed outside the gym until he'd moved into longer, narrowly tailored suits in monochrome color schemes. Suddenly, women were coming on to him. Even his secretary had taken to batting her eyelashes at him lately, which appalled him in a way he couldn't quite define and made him grind his teeth together to keep from saying something rude. Worse yet was the way Parker and Kendra carried on about his "new look." Only they had an inkling that it was due to Laurel's influence, and the knowing looks they gave each other

made him very uncomfortable. He wasn't uncomfortable enough to go back to his old baggy ways, however. He'd started this as a way to "turn up Laurel sweet," as Parker had put it, and it had worked out far better than he'd anticipated—too well, perhaps.

The grimacing tailor brought him the jeans and sweatshirt he'd worn in, now neatly hung and bagged. Giving his tie a final straightening, Edward tossed the bag over his arm and left the shop. He was painfully aware of heads turning as he strode down the sidewalk toward his car, painfully aware and secretly, embarrassingly pleased. He felt both vain as a peacock and smugly satisfied. For as long as he could remember, he had been serious, responsible, dull Edward—hard-nosed attorney, lonely guy, the antithesis of good buddy Parker, the movie-star handsome, creative, exciting lady-killer. Edward coveted his solid reputation, but he was beginning to understand that there was more to him than the stolid, plodding lawyer with the closely held temper. Why shouldn't everyone else understand that, too?

Besides, this new way of dressing was much easier to organize and sustain. That was the beauty of it. He picked out one color and put it on, then accessorized with whatever came to hand. The sophistication of it was in the cut of the clothing. He'd never realized what a difference that could make. And he had Laurel to thank for it.

Laurel. When he thought of the coming meeting with her, his stomach cramped and knotted, not because he feared he would be unsuccessful but because he knew he would not. It was getting harder and harder to figure himself out these days. Shaking his head, he hung the bag of clothing over the back seat of his car and got in the front. Distractedly, he started the engine and backed out of the parking space. A glance at his watch told him that he was going to be a few minutes late picking up Laurel. He could only hope that she wouldn't be put out. Two or three minutes shouldn't make any difference, but he couldn't be sure with her.

In fact, all he knew for certain about Laurel was that he had led her on shamefully. She thought he was interested in her romantically. That much had become glaringly apparent over the past week. And now he had to invite her to dinner with friends, just as if they were a normal couple getting to know one another

better. She would go, that slightly worshipful gratitude shining in her bright green eyes, and he would know what a sham it was, what a duplicitous, nefarious scheme. But how else could he make a sound decision? It was, after all, for her own good. He had that much figured pretty well.

Either way, he was pledged to use whatever came out of this "evaluation" for her benefit. If Greenlea pronounced her mentally fit, Edward would start building a case in earnest to support that diagnosis and wrest control of her home and inheritance from Kennison and his ape Miller. If the opposite should occur, then Edward intended to see that she got whatever help she needed.

As for the supposed budding romance, he would simply explain that formally taking on her case made a personal relationship unethical. On the other hand, he imagined that refusing her case would dampen her own enthusiasm for the romance. If it did not, well, he'd cross that bridge when he got to it. Meanwhile, he had little option beyond letting her draw her own conclusions. He couldn't discourage her embarrassingly obvious interest and get her to that damned dinner party at the same time. And so he had arranged to give her a ride home from work this evening.

He didn't know why he was so nervous or why he felt compelled to turn up again in another new suit. It, of course, had nothing to do with the way her eyes had lit up the last two times he'd gone to the diner, first to apologize and then merely to chat and cement his position. She had told him then about her marriage, and he had heard in her voice the desperation with which she had strived to win the approval and love of her grandmother, her only remaining relative, by marrying the man of her grandmother's choice. Edward thought over all she had told him as he negotiated traffic, hoping to make up those few lost minutes.

According to her, Bryce had seemed an ally, a kind if not overly demonstrative man with a fondness for elderly people and a great deal of patience. If he had pandered too much to her grandmother's wishes, he had also demonstrated some ability to talk sense to her and a penchant to defend Laurel against her grandmother's unreasonableness. In that way, Bryce had seemed a godsend, and she had convinced herself that she was in love

with him, though in retrospect she'd had to say that it was a marriage built more on hope than love.

Hope. Edward squirmed uncomfortably in his seat. Wasn't that what Laurel was living on now, the hope that he would, and could, help her? Well, it was his hope, too. That's why he was doing this, after all, in order to understand how best to help her. It wouldn't turn out as it had before. He was not Bryce Miller, and this situation was nothing at all like her marriage. Nothing.

He remembered how she had told him that not long after the wedding Bryce's supposed kindness had deteriorated into mere tolerance. At the same time, he was gradually becoming not her champion but her grandmother's. As Virdel Heffington's health had deteriorated, her attacks against Laurel had become more vitriolic and Laurel's husband had become colder and colder. He began to criticize her every move, her appearance, her ideas, even the sound of her voice. Worse, every detail of their marriage had apparently been discussed with her grandmother, who openly condemned her and blurted intimate episodes to others.

Laurel had begun to think of ending her marriage even before her grandmother's death, but she had stupidly sought counsel from Kennison, who had assured her that Bryce loved her, that only his great compassion for Virdel's physical suffering due to debilitating arthritis, diabetes and vascular disease caused him to side with the old woman and humor her. Kennison had pleaded with Laurel to bide her time, to wait. He convinced her that she could not know the strengths or weaknesses of her marriage until her grandmother's influence was removed and she and Bryce had some time alone together. To Laurel, that sounded horribly like waiting for her grandmother's death, but Kennison promised to encourage Bryce to find other work. Bryce had agreed to look for other employment, but Laurel eventually realized that he had no intention of leaving Virdel's case. Still, she had stayed, for Bryce's much younger sister, Avon, had come to live with them and Laurel had apparently felt some responsibility toward the girl.

By the time Virdel Heffington had succumbed to her physical ailments, Laurel had known in her heart that her marriage was a mistake that could only be rectified by divorce, but she had wanted to give Bryce every opportunity to change her mind. She

had suggested counseling for the two of them. Bryce had laughed in her face, presented her with her grandmother's will and informed her that their marriage would continue on his terms or she would find herself homeless and penniless. Shortly thereafter, eighteen-year-old Avon Miller had moved away, Laurel had filed for divorce and Bryce had made good on his threat. Laurel had spent almost the last two years desperately trying to convince one attorney after another to help her wrest control of her inheritance from her ex-husband.

Edward had only her word that she had not proposed marriage to any other lawyer as a means by which to secure his fees, and that bothered him. He didn't want to take her case, see it go public and learn then that half of his contemporaries were laughing at him. Ultimately, all any attorney had to recommend him was his professional reputation, and Edward felt justified in protecting his. He had risked that reputation once by revealing his complicity in the Sugarmans' marriage of convenience during the custody fight for baby Darla. He had suffered no professional repercussions from that, but he'd endured the teasing of his contemporaries for months afterward. He didn't want to go through that again. If, therefore, he was being overly cautious in this case, he felt that was understandable. If this secret evaluation of Laurel was to his benefit as well as to hers, that wasn't so bad, was it?

He was honest enough to realize that he was justifying what he was about to do, and on the heels of that honesty came a deep, soul-shaking guilt that so distracted him, he almost ran a red light. Slamming on the brakes, he told himself aloud just what he thought of himself. And then he told himself silently that he couldn't go through with it. Immediately relief swamped him. He tightened both hands on the steering wheel and pulled a deep breath. All right, no dinner party. So what was his next step, then?

The first option seemed to be to refuse the case, but then he thought about how disappointed Laurel would be and how inadequate her living conditions were and he rejected that notion. Besides, that would mean that Abelard Kennison had won again. Okay, so refusing the case outright wasn't an option. What did that leave? Simply put, he could just take the case as it stood now and hope for the best. He already had an investigator looking for

Dr. Eugene Iverson, Laurel's psychiatrist back in her teens. If he could find him, surely he could persuade Iverson to testify on Laurel's behalf. Surely he could counter the incidents Kennison was bound to cite in order to prove a history of incompetence on her part. But what if Iverson refused to testify? What if Laurel's version of events was not quite correct? What if Iverson was dead or something? Worse, what if Iverson could only testify that Laurel's state of mind had been as scattered and incompetent at Kennison alleged? No, he had to know. One way or another, he had to know for certain with what he was dealing.

So he would have to ask—insist—that Laurel go in for formal psychiatric evaluation. Yes, that was by far the better way. If it should upset her—and he had little hope that it wouldn't—well, it was still for the best. Wasn't it? His mind sent him a sudden picture of Laurel with her face ravaged by disillusionment, tears standing in her vibrant eyes, her lower lip trembling with the prelude to a sob.

He recoiled physically. Damn and blast! How could he put her through that? No matter how he phrased it, she was going to take it as a condemnation. If only so much evidence hadn't piled up against her. He went over it all again mentally.

She had asked him to marry her within a quarter hour of laying eyes on him—and the old him, at that. She'd married before in order to win her grandmother's approval when any sane person would have realized the futility of that. She was a former debutante from a well-known, socially prominent family whose new best friend was a former stripper past her heyday. She lived in a cheap apartment furnished with clothing and shoes after having grown up in the lap of luxury. She'd once faked a kidnapping, been confined to hospitals and sanitariums and eloped with the first man to pay her the least attention. She'd built a romance out of a couple harmless kisses and an apology. And then there was that scene at The Blue Plate...and that slap...and the family history.... He knew what he was going to do, what he'd intended to do all along.

He pulled up in the diner parking lot to find Laurel waiting on him out front. A smile split her pretty face, and she waved enthusiastically. Why had he thought she'd be upset with him just

for being a few minutes late? He smiled back, feeling oddly lightened and leaned over to open the passenger door for her. She jumped in and grabbed her seat belt.

"Hi!"

"Sorry I'm late," he said. "I had to stop by the tailor's and pick up a new suit of clothes, and it just took longer than I figured."

She had already scoped out the cream-colored linen and abandoned her seat belt to twist up onto one knee and finger his lapel. "Wow! Man, you are taking this new look to the limit. I love the tie!" She sank back into place, looking him over appreciatively. "You've really developed some style. Heck, I'd say you've got this thing down cold." Her smile became flirtatious. "I think I must have the best-looking lawyer in Texas."

He felt absurdly pleased with the compliment. "Aw, shucks, ma'am. I owe it all to a funny little snob of a tailor and my own personal fashion consultant."

She laughed with unrestrained delight, and he caught himself winking at her. Grinning like an idiot, he backed out and moved once more into the stream of traffic. For the moment, he just wanted to enjoy her company. Why were all his other acquaintances, with the exception of the Sugarmans, of course, so deadly dull?

They drove in companionable silence for some time before Laurel broke it by saying, "It's sweet of you to do this."

"No problem."

"The bus takes over an hour, so it's like getting an extra forty-five minutes for myself."

"You need a car of your own," he said, "and a different job."

She smiled wanly. "I'll have those things when I get control of my own inheritance. Plus, I'll have my home back."

He didn't say anything to that. What could he say when she was so obviously counting on him to help her achieve those things? When they pulled into the apartment complex, she sent him a nervous glance and said, "You don't have to come up."

He parked the car and killed the engine, saying, "I need to talk to you about something."

He looked around him. The sun had set. Soon it would be

getting dark. The last time they'd sat together out here in the dark, he'd gotten his face slapped. He reached for the door handle. "I'll, um, walk you up."

She opened her mouth to do the polite thing, no doubt wanting to tell him that it wouldn't be necessary, but he let her know that he wasn't going to be put off, by getting out of the car and coming around to her side to open the door for her. She gave him a rather lame smile as he assisted her. Was she thinking about that night, too? He put his hands into his pockets and strolled toward the building, giving her plenty of time to fall in beside him. She twisted her hands together nervously, and he felt a pang of guilt, but he made himself walk on. He had to settle this.

They started up the stairs. He noticed that she glanced almost longingly at a door on the ground floor, but before he could even wonder what that might mean, the door opened and a pleasant-faced Mexican woman in her mid-thirties appeared, baby Barry on her hip, small brown faces appearing from behind her legs and hips.

"Laurel, you are home early tonight!"

Laurel halted, shot an enigmatic look at Edward and started back down the way they'd come. "Hello, Mrs. Martinez, children."

Barry reached out for her as she drew near, and she eagerly lifted him out of Mrs. Martinez's arms. "Hello, sunshine. How are you, hmm?"

"He certainly knows and likes you," Edward said, coming to stand at her side.

"But of course, he knows—" Mrs. Martinez began, but Laurel cut her off.

"Oh, I'm sorry! How rude of me not to introduce you," she said. "Edward, this is Libby Martinez. She's Barry's baby-sitter. Mrs. Martinez, this is Edward White, my, er, attorney."

Libby Martinez nodded pleasantly. Edward extended his hand, and she placed hers in it for a friendly shake. "Nice to meet you."

"So nice to meet you, Mr. White." She indicated the little ones clustered around her. "These are my children." She rattled off five Spanish names, none of which Edward really caught.

"My goodness!" he exclaimed. "You certainly have plenty of experience."

"Oh, Mrs. Martinez is a wonderful mother and sitter," Laurel said; then, turning to Mrs. Martinez, she added, "I'm sure you'd like a few minutes off, though, so I'll just take this guy upstairs. Okay?"

Mrs. Martinez nodded happily and reached into her apron pocket. "You'll need this. I know you don't have any more extras in your apartment." She held out a bright yellow pacifier.

Barry comically opened his mouth for it, then leaned forward and clamped it between his four front teeth. The children all laughed and commented between themselves in Spanish. Edward laughed, too, and ruffled the boy's neon bright head, leaving his hair sticking up even worse than usual. Barry grinned around the pacifier, showing his four good teeth and one or two others that had barely broken the gum line.

Laurel tickled his tummy and attempted to take the pacifier from his mouth. "You silly boy! You don't want that nasty old thing anymore, do you?" But Barry bit down and hung on.

Edward chuckled. "I think we can safely say that he does, indeed, want the pacifier, don't you, guy?" Barry grinned and gibbered baby talk without ever relinquishing his hold on the pacifier nipple. He really was a cute little guy. Edward could see why Laurel was so fond of him. He wondered again how Fancy had come to have a kid like this. Or was it that he belonged to a mutual friend of hers and Laurel's? He wasn't completely straight on that yet. Not that it was high on his priority list at the moment.

Laurel said goodbye to Mrs. Martinez and her brood and began the climb again, this time with Barry on her hip. Edward wondered if the baby wasn't too much of a load for her, but she shook her head when he offered to take him. She seemed awfully tense, and he decided a little small talk might put her at ease about the conversation they were about to have, whatever it turned out to be.

"Mrs. Martinez seems like a good choice for a sitter."

"Oh, she is," Laurel assured him.

"How did Fancy come to choose a sitter in your building? Or does Fancy live here, too?"

Laurel shook her head. "No, Fancy lives a couple blocks west of here. I, um, actually found Mrs. Martinez. We sort of take care of him together."

"Ah. That explains why you sure seem fond of the little guy."

Her face went all soft, and she shifted the boy in her arms to hug him to her. "Oh, yes. I couldn't love him more if I'd given birth to him myself."

Edward nodded, uncertain why that bothered him. "Um, where did you say his mother was?"

Her expression abruptly closed. "I don't know. No one knows."

"Someone must," he replied.

She shook her head. "No one around here does. His, ah, birth mother knew she could trust her friend to take care of him, so she left him and disappeared. She was too young to make a good mother herself, and a little selfish, if you know what I mean."

"I can imagine," he said. "What surprises me is that child welfare would go along with the arrangement. I mean, I wouldn't think Fancy is exactly their idea of a proper foster mother."

Laurel shot him a scathing glare. "You don't know what you're talking about," she told him coolly.

He bowed his head. Would he never learn not to insult her friends? She was wrong about his not knowing the workings of the child welfare system, though, not that he was going to tell her that. He said, "Sorry. I didn't mean to be insulting, honestly."

For some reason, her face look utterly bleak, but she said, "I know you didn't."

They reached the landing and walked along it, Laurel fishing in her purse for her key. "Here, let me," Edward said when she'd found it. She turned it over and he bent to unlock the door. As he straightened again, Barry reached out and snagged his lapel. Edward laughed. "Like the new threads, do you, pal? Me, too."

Laurel carefully pried loose the plump little fingers while Barry gibbered around his pacifier and Edward pushed open the door. They went inside. The place was dark as a tomb. Laurel switched on a light, but it didn't help much. Edward leaned a shoulder against the wall and waited for his eyes to adjust while he listened

to her move around the room, depositing the baby in the crib and getting herself a glass of water.

"Want a drink? I've got some canned soda."

"No, thanks."

She stepped out of her shoes and wiggled her toes, sighing.

"Tough work, being on your feet all day," he commented, and she nodded.

"Yeah, well, I'm sure lawyering is tough sometimes, too."

Man, she didn't know the half of it, and now was not the time to tell her. He shifted his position against the wall, thinking about her and this dark, too-small apartment. He was all too aware that she was counting on him to help her get out of here. If only he knew what to do about that. Laurel might have been reading his mind, for she cocked her head suddenly and said, "You wanted to talk to me?"

He cleared his throat. "Uh, yeah, I was...I was wondering if you'd like to go to dinner with me on Sunday?"

She didn't look at all surprised by the invitation, but oddly she glanced at the baby. "I don't know...."

He found himself hastening to convince her. "Listen, the Sugarmans have invited us and some other friends to dinner. I thought it would be a good chance for everyone to get to know one another. They really are my best friends, and you're my—" He swallowed the word he'd nearly said. Choking on it, he coughed and cleared his throat. What was wrong with him? Had he really nearly said the word *girlfriend?* Good grief! She was much more client than...and she wasn't even really a client! He licked his lips and stammered, "Or-ordinarily I h-hate dinner parties, but I thought if you would go with me, it—it wouldn't... That is, I wouldn't mind..."

She was smiling so he shut up, a finger creeping up to tug at his collar, which seemed awfully tight suddenly. "Sunday?" she said. "Well, maybe I can make it."

He felt an almost overwhelming relief, which in itself was absurd. "You won't regret it," he said. "Parker and Kendra have some interesting friends."

"Yes, I know," she told him, her smile leaving little doubt that

she was alluding to him. He felt lower than an earthworm, and suddenly he wanted out of there.

He rattled off something about picking her up and answered a question about appropriate dress while heading for the door. She followed him out, thanking him for the ride and watching as he hurried along the landing toward the stairs. The last thing he heard before she'd closed the apartment door was Barry shrieking for his absent mother, whoever she was.

Chapter Eight

She wore white leggings with lace around the ankles and a lace-edged tank top beneath a long, lightweight, frock coat of periwinkle blue with push-up sleeves and extreme lapels, deeply notched and top-stitched with white plastic lacings. Her shoes, with their thick platform soles and blunt, rounded toes matched the shiny plastic lacing, as well as the narrow band with its long, flat bow on the side that she wore to hold her bangs back off her forehead. She was as nervous as a songbird in a room full of cats.

When Edward's fist landed on her hollow metal door, she started just as if she hadn't heard his heavy treads coming up the stairs and along the landing. She knew instantly that she should have dressed more conservatively, maybe a tailored pantsuit and a silk blouse. Desperately, she glanced around the room, as if she had time to change before she had to open that door.

"Laurel?" He was trying to be quiet, but his big voice boomed along the stairwell, and everyone in the building was bound to be home on a lazy Sunday evening.

She hurried to let him in, her first words being, "I have to change!"

He moved inside as she did, leaving the door open behind him so that the early-evening light softened the darkness of the apartment. He leaned a shoulder against the wall and said, ''What's wrong with what you're wearing?''

She fully turned to face him. ''Really? It's all right?'' And then she forgot the question as her startled gaze traveled over him.

He wore a soft, loose, collarless shirt of natural ivory silk that draped his powerful torso in graceful, clinging lines, the narrow cuffs at his wrists keeping the slightly blousy, overlong sleeves from falling down over his hands. The matching, generously pleated slacks were long enough to very nearly puddle atop the supple pierced leather slippers on his otherwise bare feet. It was a look she had known he could wear, but who'd have thought to see big, tough, uncompromising, all male Edward White in soft pastels? Heavens, he looked as though he could don armor and go jousting. How had he come to this all on his own? She felt as proud as a parent whose dearest hopes for a difficult child have just been realized.

''Edward, you look great,'' she said, a touch of awe in her voice.

''Thanks.'' He shrugged and said, ''I thought this was one time I didn't have to be, you know, buttoned down, but jeans didn't seem quite right, either.''

''Well, this is perfect,'' she said, lifting a hand bemusedly.

He smiled, his gaze snagging and holding hers. ''You're looking pretty perfect yourself.''

''Yeah?''

''Oh, yeah.''

She fought down a blush of pleasure and began buttoning her coat. ''Maybe we should just go, then. I wouldn't want to be late. Oh, and I'd like to get in early, if we can.''

He nodded understanding. ''Work tomorrow.''

And Barry, she answered silently, resisting the urge to toss a glance at the baby's crib in the corner. As usual, thoughts of Barry stuck with a baby-sitter again—in this case, Fancy—dampened some of Laurel's enthusiasm for the evening. She remembered with aching clarity the discussion she'd had with Fancy when the

older woman had come for Barry. Fancy had been insistent that Laurel was going to have to tell Edward about the boy.

"You can't go on pretending you're just a helpful friend pitching in occasionally," she had argued.

Laurel had admitted that Fancy was right. "I know. I never expected things to develop this way, though. I never dreamed that he'd, well, *like* me."

Fancy had shaken her head. "Girl, why is it you can't see what you've got to offer a man? 'Course he likes you. Any man in his right mind would. And I've got the feeling old Eddie boy is more often in his right mind than the average feller."

Laurel had smiled at that. "All the more reason I can't let him find out about Barry."

"You honestly think this cute little tyke is going to make that big a difference?"

"I don't know," Laurel had been forced to say. "I feared at first that Barry's circumstances might keep Edward from taking my case. I have enough strikes against me there. And I can't risk Bryce finding out about him—that hasn't changed. So I kept quiet, and now I'm afraid that keeping the truth about Barry from Edward will cost me more than I ever realized. I don't know what to do."

Fancy had sighed and said warningly, "I wouldn't want to be in your shoes if he found out from somebody else. You stand to lose not just a possible lover but, more importantly, a lawyer, too. You're gonna have to decide which relationship is most important and do what's necessary to protect it."

Laurel hadn't been sure then and wasn't sure now which relationship might mean the most to her in the long run. She knew intellectually that securing his aid in gaining control of her inheritance ought to rate highest, for Barry if not for herself, but somehow she couldn't convince her heart of that. And she hadn't even been on a real date with the man yet! Today would change that, though, and she couldn't help wondering if the significance of that had struck him as deeply as it had her. Certainly the way that he was looking at her seemed to say that he attached some significance to the occasion. But of course he did! He was taking her to meet his friends, his very best friends, one of them a

woman with whom he'd been in love. Oh, dear, what if Kendra Sugarman hated her on sight?

She tried to put that possibility out of mind as Edward escorted her out of the apartment complex to the car and drove her leisurely toward the Park Cities. He talked about Parker and Kendra as he drove, telling her about Parker's former life-style, his career as an architect and his transformation from playboy to proud dad and househusband. He spoke of Kendra as a "soft touch" who had originally married Parker in order to help him secure custody of his orphaned niece, her reputation as a pediatric nurse making her the best prospect around for the job. She was, according to Edward, an amazing mother to her adopted daughter and the miracle worker who had transformed Parker into model mate and parent. Laurel couldn't help wondering if he wasn't still a little in love with the woman and if *she* was going to hate *Kendra* on sight because of it.

She loved the house on sight, a fact that seemed to surprise Edward, who informed her that the reformed Georgian facade done up in fawn brown and creamy white was Parker's current pride and joy. "He can't keep his hands off," Edward said. "He's constantly redesigning and remodeling."

"How exciting!" was her reply.

He shrugged and got out of the car. She waited like the lady into which her grandmother had bullied her for him to come around and open her door. She was trembling when he took her hand and led her along the landscaped walk to the front door tucked away behind two immense columns. When Parker opened the door in answer to their knock, she saw that the columns were part of a theme carried throughout the house.

To her surprise, Parker greeted her with a kiss on the cheek and an effusive welcome. Then he stepped back in awe of Edward's fashionable splendor and demanded to know where he was getting his clothes these days. When he heard the name of his own tailor, he vowed to have a talk with the "disloyal little twit."

"He didn't show me those things when I was there last."

A lovely, wholesome young woman with long golden brown hair hanging in a single plait down the center of her back carried a tray of appetizers into the sunken living area. She placed them

on a glass coffee table between two cream-colored sofas, announcing, "Your tailor has a new favorite, I see."

She popped a tiny cracker into her mouth, dusted off her hands and moved forward with confident, businesslike steps. "Hello, I'm Kendra." She held out her palm and Laurel timidly slid her own against it.

"Laurel."

"Yes, I know. I've been dying to meet you." Her smile seemed guileless and gay, even mischievous when she turned it on Edward. "Quit loitering in the entry, you big galoot, and find her a comfortable seat."

Edward rolled his eyes. "Do you bully those poor kids at the hospital this way?"

"Nope, just their parents" came the quick reply. Then she turned and led the way down into the living area.

Laurel took her time, looking around her with great appreciation. The place was spotless, despite the pale shades of the cream, white and tan furnishings that stood out against the burnt almond walls. The place was more like a showroom than a house, with columns flanking the sunken area and art objects on pedestals scattered among exotic pot plants and the occasional painting on an easel. But here and there were the small oddities that made it a home—a framed photo, a tiny pair of Mary Jane shoes, a baby blue sweater, a doll-size cup and saucer. Kendra pointed out the shoes, sweater and toys to Parker, saying, "Your daughter still has not picked up her things."

"I'll take care of it," Parker replied good-naturedly, continuing across the sunken floor and up a quartet of stairs to a door in the end wall. He opened that door and called into the room beyond. "Darla, Uncle Eddie and Ms. Miller are here."

"Uncle Eddie?" Laurel whispered to him, her brows raised.

He gave her a murderous look, then turned his attention to the adorable munchkin with dark hair caught up in twin ponytails who shot through the door, down the steps and across the room to throw herself against Edward's legs, climb them, crawl over his lap and raise up on her knees to choke him with a fierce hug. Not content with crushing his larynx, she covered his face with noisy kisses. He pulled her legs out from under her so that she

fell across his lap, tickled her until she couldn't kiss him anymore, then kissed her back. "Come here, brat!" he said, scooping her up to stand her on her feet on the couch. "I want you to meet someone. This is Laurel."

Laurel smiled. "Hello."

"Hello." Darla cocked her little head, dark eyes blatantly sizing up this newcomer and bent forward to press her small hands against Laurel's cheeks. "You're pretty," she said matter-of-factly.

Laurel's smile became laughter. She covered Darla's hands with her own. "Thank you! So are you."

"I know," Darla said with that same confidence with which she seemed to do everything else. Belatedly she added, "Thanks you," and pulled her hands free, slid down onto her bottom, flopped over and wiggled off the couch. Running toward Kendra she said, "Mommy, can I have a drink?"

Parker intercepted her, saying, "Not until you've picked up after yourself, little miss." He pointed out the offending items.

She covered her little mouth in a silent "oops," giggled and ran to do as told, gathering up the items in her chubby arms and bolting down the open hallway to disappear through an open doorway at its end.

"Oh, my," Laurel said, seeing what she was in for a couple years down the road.

Kendra laughed. "She does everything at full throttle these days. I get tired just watching her."

"And I get tired running after her," Parker put in, sitting down on the arm of the sofa where his wife had taken a seat, opposite Laurel.

"He loves every minute of it," Kendra confided wryly.

"Every second," Parker amended, and the couple traded an intimate smile of complete harmony. A lump of pure envy formed in Laurel's throat, and she groped blindly for Edward's hand before she even realized what she was doing. To her joy, his strong fingers closed over hers and pulled her hand onto his thigh, the action seemingly as instinctual as her own. Suddenly there were tears in her eyes, her heart leaping in her chest. She had to laugh and blink away the tears, drawing everyone's attention. Knowing

she had to explain herself, she said the obvious. "Darla is just adorable. You're obviously doing something right."

The Sugarmans turned their smiles on for her, and Edward squeezed her hand between his own and his thigh. She felt herself beaming with intense delight and surging hope. The doorbell rang, breaking the spell and sending Kendra Sugarman to her feet.

"That must be David," she announced gaily, and just like that, Edward set aside Laurel's hand and, it seemed to her, edged away.

Hope deflated and delight waned, but Laurel charged up her smile as Kendra led into the room a handsome blond in chinos and a blue polo shirt worn beneath a tweedy brown sport coat. Minus the gold-rimmed glasses, he was the type one expected to find on a beach in California with a surgically enhanced bikini model draped over his arm. He pushed his longish, sun-streaked hair off his forehead and targeted her with a frank, vividly blue gaze as Laurel introduced him.

"Dr. David Greenlea, allow me to introduce Laurel Miller."

His smile was utterly charming as he leaned down, offering her his hand and said, "Just David, please."

"All right, and I'm Laurel."

"Pleased to meet you, Laurel."

Kendra placed a hand on his arm, turning his attention. "You remember Edward, I'm sure."

The sparkle in David's inhumanly blue eyes took on a mischievous glint. Laurel wondered if the glasses were calculated to blunt their effect. "Edward," he said and slung his head in Parker's direction. "You've been hanging around this clotheshorse over here too long, I see." He stuck out his hand. "Good to see you again."

Edward practiced his grip on David's much leaner hand. "Looks like you've cleaned up your act some, too. Ponytail's gone."

David laughed and retrieved his hand, wiggling it to start the blood flowing again. "I've still got the jeans with the holes in them," he said cheekily, "but I promised Ken I'd be on my best behavior tonight."

Kendra laughed and said, "Thank you very much." To Laurel she added, "The holes are in the seat."

"The holes *are* the seat," Parker quipped. "We've cataloged every pair of David's underwear."

"He favors boxers with cartoon prints," Kendra teased.

"I never have figured out what they've got against ducks," he said to Laurel, and she laughed, liking him immensely.

Kendra released him and went off to play hostess, saying, "I'll get the drinks."

Disappointingly, Edward got up and followed her out of the room, mumbling that he'd help her. David picked a spot next to Laurel and stretched out an arm along the back of the sofa, blatant appreciation showing through the lenses of his glasses as he looked her over. "You look familiar to me," he said.

Laurel shrugged, but Parker said, "I thought that, too, at first. Maybe we've seen her on the society pages or at a fund-raiser, possibly."

"Oh, my," David said, grinning, "are you someone we'd have seen on the society pages or at a fund-raiser?"

Feeling uncomfortable, Laurel looked away. "I doubt it."

Parker spoke up again. "She's being modest. You see here before you, David, my friend, the one, the only, Heffington heir."

"Good God!" David exclaimed. "You must be Virdel's grand-daughter!"

Laurel blanched and softly admitted, "Yes."

"She left over a million dollars to our program!" he went on.

Laurel forced a wan smile. "Did she?"

David cupped a hand against the back of his head and said baldly, "What a distasteful old snob she was."

Laurel looked up in shock, certain she couldn't have heard what she'd thought she'd heard. "I beg your pardon?"

But David was not the least undone. He went on as smoothly as if he were reciting poetry. "She tried to derail my appointment on the grounds that I was too young and, as she put it, my family heritage is 'disappointingly unremarkable.' I believe I told her that my unremarkable family was at least intelligent enough to practice basic civilities in public."

Laurel's mouth fell open. "You didn't!"

"Why not?" He shrugged and went on. "She drew herself up

in her wheelchair and demanded, 'Young man, are you insinu-
ating that I am rude?'"

Laurel groaned, imagining the scene that must have ensued and
what he must think of *her* based upon it. "I'm sure she didn't
know what she was saying. Her health was very poor and…"

David chuckled and said, "She was a pathetic shell of a woman
with the heart of a tyrant, and I told her so. Pleasantly, of course."
He tossed off that last with an insouciant grin and a nod.

Laurel's mouth was hanging open again. He shut it by chucking
her under the chin and confessed, "It's a bald-faced lie. I only
wanted to say those things."

Which meant, of course, that Virdel had not had the opportunity to lash him with her saber-edged tongue. Laurel sighed with
relief and immediately began apologizing on her grandmother's
behalf. "I'm so sorry, Dr. Greenlea."

"David," he corrected her.

She barely heard him. "My grandmother was a very controlling
person and, I think, an unhappy one. She could be very unpleasant. I do apologize if she gave you a difficult time, and I'm glad
that at least she recognized the value of your program and supported your work financially."

His gaze was utterly open. "It doesn't bother you that I just
insulted her?"

Laurel searched for the right words. "Well, yes, frankly it does,
but mostly because she so often was everything you said."

"You don't mind that she left us all that money in her will?"

She could almost laugh at that. "I only wish she'd been as
wise with all her bequests."

He nodded. "Interesting." And it was as if he'd given her his
stamp of approval. The smile was equal parts charm and, unless
she missed her guess, flirtation. Leaning forward, he popped one
of Kendra's tiny, bedecked crackers into his mouth and murmured
between chews, "Very interesting, indeed."

Laurel was slightly disappointed when David Greenlea hurried
to pull out her chair at the dinner table, leaving Edward to do the
same for Kendra and Parker to pour the wine and begin carving
an absolutely luscious eye-of-the-round roast. Kendra passed

around the vegetables and hot bread, Darla already having been fed and sent off to the multipurpose room to watch a video with the volume appropriately low and the door open. Laurel tasted her carrots, a personal favorite of hers, and murmured approvingly. David grinned and waved a potato around on the end of his fork.

"It's a funny thing about these two," he said, indicating their hosts. "Alone, each is a capable if somewhat limited cook. Together, they're a gourmet chef." He forked the potato into his mouth and closed his eyes in ecstasy as he chewed.

"There's something you should know about David," Kendra said from her end of the table. "He can eat his weight three times a day and never gain a pound. It's disgusting, and he thinks he's a gourmet because of it. Oh, and he loves to observe." She waved a hand. "Doesn't make any difference what or whom, he just likes to watch and figure things out."

"Is that so?" Laurel murmured lightly, feeling his eyes on her right then.

"Comes with the territory," he said, cutting into his roast with relish.

"In other words," Parker said, picking up the banter, "he'll sit around your kitchen happily watching you labor over a hot oven and eat every bite of the meal without the least guilt."

"Hey, I'm nobody's fool," David quipped as everyone else laughed.

Laurel picked up another thread of the conversation. "What territory is that?"

"Hmm?"

"You said it comes with the territory, being observant, I mean. I just wondered, specifically, what territory that is."

Activity stopped all around the table, everywhere but over David Greenlea's plate. Smiling benignly, he continued cutting off bite-sized pieces of his roast and said casually, "Psychiatry." He laid down his knife and shifted his fork to his right hand. "I'm a psychiatrist."

Well, that explained a lot and seemed utterly irrelevant at the same time.

Kendra leaned forward and said, "Actually, David's being

modest. He's acting head of psychiatry at our hospital—the youngest ever.''

"The children's hospital?" Laurel said. "I think Edward said you were at the children's hospital."

"That's right," David told her, dispensing with a mouthful of beef and forking up another. "Our function there is primarily helping our patients and their families deal with the realities of serious illnesses."

"Ah. I'd think that would be very sad work."

He shook his head. "Not at all. We have our share of losses, of course, and those are always tough, but the vast majority of our patients go home happy and healthier. It's very rewarding, actually. It's much harder just to make my rounds at the county hospital across the street."

"Oh, that's right. I'd forgotten they were affiliated."

He nodded, busily swallowing another bite. "I'd rather deal with a diabetic child learning to deal with her illness any day than a coked-out prostitute convinced I'm her pimp come to kill her."

Laurel shivered. "How awful! How do you stand it?"

He tilted his head. "I want to help, and sometimes I actually do. It's definitely the successes that keep me going back."

"David volunteers in the chemical dependency unit," Kendra said. It was the last time she spoke until she rose to clear the table.

Laurel became aware, of course, that she and David were dominating the conversation, but he was an interesting conversationalist and her attempts to include the others, especially Edward, were greeted with little more than nods and smiles. She was not thrilled when Kendra rebuffed her offer to help clean up, saying that Parker and she worked best and quickest when it was just the two of them, then asking Edward to spend a few minutes with Darla. "I hate for her to spend the whole evening alone," she explained, "and she does love to have her uncle Eddie to herself now and again."

Laurel took that as a request to stay away and meekly followed David back into the living area, where he parked her in a corner of the couch, sat down next to her and casually asked her to tell him something about herself, since they'd talked primarily about

him all through dinner. Laurel glanced longingly in the direction in which Edward had disappeared and forced her attention on David. It wasn't his fault that Edward was ignoring her, and David did seem like a very nice man—very nice and very skilled. She didn't realize how well he'd coaxed her to open up to him until some time later when she found herself sniffing back tears and his arm coming around her in support.

"You know, don't you, that you were never the problem? The problem was always Virdel and those adults around you who failed to adequately stand up to her."

She nodded, feeling foolish and exposed. "What I never understood, though, is what made her that way."

He shrugged, holding her against his side. "It's hard to say without having had the opportunity to analyze her, but I'd say a very poor self-image was at the bottom of it."

She sat up straight, surprised. "You're kidding! My grandmother acted like she was God!"

"Perhaps she did that to hide her own fears of inadequacy and unacceptability," he suggested. "We'll never know now, but it's a reasonable assumption. I'd go so far as to say, in fact, that she was probably intimidated and threatened by you. She must have been dismayed at your ability to recover after every setback, and frightened by your determined quest for her love, a love she obviously didn't know how to give."

Laurel could only shake her head. "I wanted to quit, you know, but I couldn't help myself, not until very near the end, anyway."

He nodded. "It's perfectly normal to want the love and approval of the adults in our lives, Laurel. The only way to stop really is to realize that you've become more adult than they are capable of being."

That made perfect sense to her. "Yes, I see what you mean. That's pretty much what happened in my case. I gradually realized that I was the only reasonable, completely sane individual around, and it was more important for me to be that than to be loved."

He patted her shoulder. "You're a remarkable young woman to come to that conclusion on your own," he said gently, and she smiled her gratitude.

"Thank you."

"Personally," he went on in that comforting tone, "I think you're an extremely lovable person, too, but I suppose it's up to someone else to convince you of that. I wonder, could it be Edward White, perhaps?"

Laurel caught her breath. Why would he ask that? Had he seen something in Edward's manner toward her that she had not seen tonight? Her hopes for the evening suddenly lifted. As if summoned by the sound of his name, Edward walked into the room. His face seemed utterly impassive, but she thought she spied a flash of anger—or perhaps jealousy?—in the glance he directed at David Greenlea. David seemed to concur, for he smoothly but quickly withdrew his arm from around her shoulders and moved over on the sofa. Laurel followed, motioning for Edward to join them on her other side. He lowered his big frame into the corner she had just vacated and crossed his legs at the knee.

"You two have a nice chat?"

"A very nice chat," Laurel confirmed.

"Yes, indeed," David agreed.

"How is Darla?" she asked, just to make conversation with him.

"Just about ready for bed," he said, fingering the crease in one leg of his slacks as if it was the most interesting thing he'd come across in a very long time.

Laurel glanced at her watch, reminded that Barry would be sleepy-eyed by now, too, and bit her lip. A few moments later, the Sugarmans descended the steps into the living area, Parker laden with a tray of coffee and cups that Kendra dispensed as soon as he set it down.

"I'm sorry it took us so long," she said. "I didn't realize we'd made such a mess this afternoon. And you know how it is, the longer you let it go, the more difficult it is to clean."

Laurel nodded, accepting a cup of hazelnut coffee if the sublime aroma was anything to go by. The time had passed swiftly, but she was rather dismayed to realize how *much* of it had passed. Biding her time, she sipped her coffee and listened to the others chat. When Darla came into the room rubbing her eyes, Laurel

suggested that perhaps it was time for them to go. To her surprise, the Sugarmans protested adamantly.

"Oh, no! We haven't had much opportunity to visit yet," Parker said, to which Kendra added sheepishly, "I'm afraid we've been lousy hosts tonight, Please give us a chance to make it up to you." She looked pointedly at Laurel and then, oddly, to David, who seemed uncertain what response was expected of him. Edward, on the other hand, seemed to have no compunction about speaking for all three of them.

"We'll hang around for a while yet."

Well, Laurel told herself, it wasn't that she didn't want to get to know the Sugarmans better. She smiled and kept her mouth shut, wondering if Barry was missing her. Maybe she could slip away, find a telephone, and give Fancy a quick call. Meanwhile, she couldn't help noticing that Parker was looking at David rather oddly. David, for his part, pretended not to notice, removing his glasses and polishing them on his shirttail. Parker sent a desperate glance at Kendra, who scooped up Darla and announced that they would just put her down for the night and be right back. Laurel took advantage of the moment to ask where she might find a powder room, and was directed to a narrow hallway to one side of the kitchen near the front of the house. Perhaps she'd find a telephone somewhere along the way.

Edward watched as she climbed the steps to the kitchen area, then immediately turned his attention to David Greenlea. "Well," he demanded abruptly, "what do you think?"

David inclined his head, resettled his glasses and looked at Edward, realizing no doubt that Edward would have liked to use his fists to permanently plant those glasses in his face. "I think she's very lovely, very bright, and that I'd like to see a good deal more of her."

It was all Edward could do not to wring his neck. "Meaning what exactly?"

David tugged his ear, leaned forward and picked up his coffee cup, sipped and set it down again. Taking his time, he settled back, spreading his arm across the space on the sofa where Laurel had been sitting. "Do you really want to know what I think?"

Edward ground his teeth together, managing to get out "Not really, no, but I don't have much choice. Now do I?"

David smoothed the thigh of his chinos, then abruptly sat forward and pinned Edward with a direct look. "Let me ask you something. Just how far beyond business does your interest in Laurel go?"

Edward frowned. "It doesn't."

"Ah." David sat back again, apparently at his ease. "In that case, I don't mind telling you that she's saner than you are."

"That's your official diagnosis?" Edward asked sarcastically.

"That's my official diagnosis. Unofficially, I may as well tell you that I intend to ask her out."

Edward blanched. He'd sensed, of course, that David was attracted to her, and he suspected that it might be mutual, but confirmation was a little hard to take. He told himself that she deserved better than David Greenlea. He'd never liked David, no matter what Ken and Parker might say, but he was responsible for bringing him here tonight, so what could he say, really, if David wanted to go out with Laurel? It didn't have anything to do with the case. It wasn't any of his business. He wondered if Kendra and Parker would speak to him again if he punched out David Greenlea's lights in their living room. He swallowed down the impulse and several choice words that he couldn't say, but they didn't stay down. They climbed right back up his throat and got his tongue in a hammerlock. When he opened his mouth to breathe, they rushed right out.

"You've got some nerve, taking advantage of a woman in her position!"

"Taking advantage?" David exclaimed. "How did I take advantage? I did you a favor, if you'll recall. That's got nothing to do with Laurel herself."

"No?" Edward retorted. "Well, it smells to high heaven, if you ask me. Just how ethical is it for a psychiatrist to date a patient?"

"She's not my patient, nor will she ever be. And I'm not the one who set up this little farce. You are! How ethical is it to set up your own client for psychological evaluation with neither her knowledge nor her permission?"

"I didn't have any choice!" Edward shot back. "I had to know she was playing with a full deck. Otherwise, Kennison would eat us alive in court. And he still might. Damn!"

"If you ask me, Counselor, you should've thought of that before you arranged this secret psychoanalysis."

Edward didn't know what to think now. He didn't really even know what the problem was. He knew that he didn't like David Greenlea, and he knew that he didn't like David Greenlea draping himself all over Laurel. Most importantly, he knew that he'd never really seriously considered Laurel a nut case. But what the hell did it all mean? He pushed a hand through his hair in frustration, thought how Laurel would react to that and immediately set about putting it to rights again, only to draw up short, some sixth sense telling him that it was pointless.

She was there. He knew it as well as he knew his own name. She was there and she'd heard the whole damned thing, enough, at least, to hang him. Some part of him had always known that it would be so. It was utterly inevitable. And yet, the hardest thing he'd ever done was turn his head and confirm his worst suspicions.

It was the look in her eyes that he hadn't expected, that he couldn't take. She looked...shattered...broken. And he knew—too late—that he'd made the most colossal mistake of his life.

Chapter Nine

Laurel stared for a long moment. She felt frozen in place, as if this were eternity and she had been caught in a moment of hell, forever apart, forever suspended in the first unexpected stab of pain. She couldn't even think what this pain was. She only knew that it was inescapable—and deserved, though she couldn't say why just at that instant. Then she remembered. She had trusted. She had found the most responsible, fair, hardworking man available, and she had trusted him to care about her and her problems. And he thought that she was insane. Well, perhaps she was.

Without warning, her eyes closed, and she knew that the paralysis was past. She regretted that, for now she must do something. But what? She shook her head, surprised that it didn't hurt. Something hurt. What was it? Her hand rose automatically to her chest. Ah, God, not that. How long had it been since she'd lain awake at night, the pain in her chest so deep and wide and hollow that she had feared it would swallow her whole? She had protected herself so well after... She couldn't remember when she had learned to protect her heart from caring too much. How had she forgotten the way of it?

Her gaze moved automatically to Edward White, no longer dull Edward who looked as though he slept in those expensive but poorly fitted and unexceptional suits, the Edward who seemed to have forgotten that he had hair on his head until it hung over his eyes. This Edward was groomed to within an inch of his life, and a new knowledge struck Laurel. This wasn't the real him, either. He didn't know yet who the real Edward White was. How had she missed that? She had been there. Most of her life she had been the needy little girl without a soul to love her. Until Barry. Barry had made her grow up. He was the child, and he needed her to love him. The moment she had understood that, she had become her real self, not the little girl who needed love but the woman who needed *to* love. Why hadn't she seen the old her in the new Edward? Why had she let herself believe that he was as ready to love as she was?

Not insane, just foolish. Oh, so foolish.

She found no comfort in the thought, just as she found no comfort in Edward White's cool blue eyes. A hand fell upon the arm with which she had unknowingly hugged herself. She followed it to the person of David Greenlea, psychiatrist. She should be angry with him, perhaps, but somehow she couldn't muddle through the pain of discovery to any other emotion, and she could tell by the look in his eyes that he understood that. In silent acceptance of the comfort he offered, she nodded her head. His arm slid around her shoulders.

"I'm going to take Laurel home now," he said quietly.

The Sugarmans walked into the room just then, arm in arm, smiling at some whispered intimacy. Laurel welcomed the distraction with a dull sort of relief. Reacting by rote, she curved her mouth in a smile and said, "Thank you for a lovely evening." Her voice shook alarmingly. Her smile faded. Suddenly, tears filled her eyes.

Kendra was speaking. "Oh, surely you're not going now. We haven't had a chance—"

Laurel spun away and hurried blindly toward the door, stumbling when she came to the steps that led up into the foyer. Behind her she heard Edward say, "Let it go, Ken." He meant, let *her* go. Fresh pain blossomed in her chest and broke apart on a sob.

She clapped one hand over her mouth and reached for the door handle with the other. In another blessed moment, she was outside in the dark.

The evening was balmy, oddly serene, as if the night had hedged them in, protecting them from the city at large. Laurel felt as if, like Alice in Wonderland, she had fallen into a strange place and time. She did not belong, and she desperately needed to get away.

The door opened at her back, and David Greenlea walked through it. He flashed her a guilty look, then replaced it with a sympathetic smile. He laid a companionable arm across her shoulders and said, "Come with me."

She let him guide her to a bright red, German-made convertible parked directly behind Edward's big, boxy, sensible, luxury sedan. He put her inside and swung around the back, letting himself into the driver's seat. He started up the engine and reached for a switch on the dashboard. "I think we need to put the top down." An electronic hum preceded the retraction of the top by seconds, then gradually the heavy vinyl folded and slid away. David made a show of surveying the blank sky and sniffing the air. "Yes, definitely a night for putting the top down."

He was right. The cool wind calmed and engaged her as they drove through the city, and then she realized they were going in the wrong direction. She sat up abruptly, recognizing the upscale shopping area accessed by the Lyndon Baines Johnson Freeway. David immediately slowed the excessive speed of the red convertible and exited the freeway. Some blocks or more later, the neat, compact auto came to a smooth, uneventful stop at a red light. "Welcome back," David said succinctly. "Where to?"

She combed her hair with the fingers of one hand. "Home," she said, and then she fixed David Greenlea with a direct gaze and bluntly added, "but I have to pick up my son first."

Edward tossed back the second Scotch and hissed breath through his teeth to cool his tongue and throat. Liquid courage was a damnably unpleasant beverage, but he'd rather drink the whole bottle in a single slug than perform the task he'd set himself this day. Merciful God, the look in her eyes. The look haunted

him, no matter how hard he worked to hold it at bay. It came at him at odd moments—the hollow injury, the gaping disappointment, the self-deprecation and disillusionment. Why hadn't she slapped him or, better yet, doubled up her fist and knocked him off his pompous ass? But that would have been too easy. That would have engaged his fury and let him off the hook of sheer responsibility. Guilt. It roiled in his stomach with the Scotch, reminding him what a gutless wonder he was.

The bubbly waitress slid a plate of club sandwiches and potato chips across the bar top to him, but his appetite had gone again and with it the will to make himself eat. He'd prefer another Scotch, but he ordered a cup of coffee instead and forced it down in three long drinks, then paid the tab and walked out.

The sidewalk was hot. Summer was showing its face every now and again between the thunderstorms and tornado warnings that marked a Texas spring. Edward stripped off his tie and crammed it into his coat pocket before working loose the top two buttons of his shirt. He pushed back the unmoussed lock of hair that fell insistently over his forehead and got into the car, telling himself that it was time for another haircut.

He was embarrassed by the way his heart pounded and dread curled in his gut as he drove to the diner. The dusty lot was nearly empty now that the lunch hour waned. He parked as far from the door as possible and got out. A large part of him wanted to get right back in his car and drive away, but another part wanted—needed—to see her, and it proved the stronger. He gulped down the dread, pulled a deep breath of tepid, exhaust-flavored air and trudged, head down, to the diner.

He pushed inside in two long strides, giving himself no chance to back out, and immediately looked around. He found her before the brass bell attached to the door clanked back against the glass. She sat beside David Greenlea on a stool at the counter, half-turned as if expecting him. He clamped his jaw, wishing he could afford to throw David out on his face, but he couldn't. He told himself that maybe David's being here was a good sign. If she could forgive David his part in this conspiracy, surely she could forgive him.

Laurel slipped away before he got there, moving around behind

the counter to adopt the mein of waitress—and nothing more. He got no greeting, no expression to signal her feelings toward him, not even a flicker of recognition. He might have been a complete stranger. David Greenlea, on the other hand, swung around to hang his elbows on the edge of the counter and lift an inquiring brow at Edward. Edward lifted one right back. As far as he was concerned, Greenlea was his partner in crime, however reluctant the pairing. He tried not to think that his history with Laurel made him the more culpable party, but his training as an attorney wouldn't quite allow him to ignore that interpretation. Still, he told himself for the millionth time that she needed him to put forward her case and that in itself ought to get him a hearing. Hope existed.

He took the stool she had vacated and dared Greenlea to take exception. David merely shook his head and turned back to his lunch, his gaze settling on Laurel. Her hands trembled when she extracted the order pad from the pocket of her uniform skirt, but otherwise she gave no indication of anything amiss. If her smile was a touch practiced and her gaze not quite direct, well, only one who had been gifted with more could tell the difference.

"What can I get for you?"

Edward folded his hands and refused to answer. He wasn't here to play games.

After a moment, she dropped the pad back into her pocket and slid the pencil behind her ear. Turning away, she lifted a water pitcher and refilled David's glass. When she turned back to Edward, the pretense had been dropped. She sat down the pitcher and folded her arms. "Come to ask me to submit to psychiatric examination, perhaps?"

Her tone had a bite Edward had never heard before. He accepted it as his due, almost with gratitude. "No, but you can bet Kennison's going to hang a large part of his case on your mental stability."

"Don't you mean my lack of it?" she retorted.

He looked down to hide the smile that struggled for release, not realizing until that very moment how deeply he'd feared the damage he might have done that brazen spirit. When he'd con-

quered his expression, he looked up again. "You have given him some ammunition to support that argument."

"Him," she replied smartly, meaning that he, Edward, ought to have known better.

He nodded in agreement. "All right. I'm a slow learner, but you knocked me off balance. Give me that at least."

"Mmm." David Greenlea swallowed a french fry and nodded at Laurel. "The marriage proposal," he reminded her needlessly.

Her green eyes flashed. She frowned and bore down on him. "I explained that! It was a bid to secure his fee, a way to show him how serious I am about gaining control of my inheritance."

David shrugged and poked another fried potato slice into his mouth. Edward tamped down his irritation at the psychiatrist and concentrated on Laurel.

"So you told him about that, did you?"

"Why not?"

"You tell him about the kiss, too? How you knocked my socks off and—"

"What kiss?" she snapped. "It was more like punishment for my stupidity!"

"The first one," he admitted roughly. "Not the second."

"For which I slapped your face!"

"And then you went out with me again," he reminded her doggedly.

She murdered him with her glare, but he wouldn't be cowed, not with his former partner in crime sitting there basking in the fullness of her companionship and, worse, her obvious trust. He gave her back as level a look as he could manage, no easy feat when what he really wanted to do was fall on his knees and beg forgiveness. He was after more than forgiveness, however. He needed to regain her trust. How could he represent her in court if she did not trust him? But at bottom he knew it was more, even, than that. He didn't know why, but some sixth sense told him that he could not properly function without her trust. With a glance in Greenlea's direction, he made a deliberate bid for it. "Laurel, you found it in your heart to forgive me after I apologized before. More than ever now, I—"

The metal door behind the counter swung back and forth in

smaller and smaller arcs until it simply stopped, Laurel safely hidden behind it. Edward was left sitting there with his mouth open. She had walked out. She wasn't going to listen to his carefully prepared speech or his fervent pleas or anything else, apparently. And David Greenlea sat at his elbow shaking his head like some sort of all-knowing guru. It was all Edward could do not to wrap his hands around Greenlea's throat, but he managed. He'd be damned if he could resist taking at least one stripe off Greenlea's hide, though.

"Well, I see you've managed to paint me as the true villain in the piece."

To his surprise, Greenlea turned to face him almost with eagerness. "On the contrary," he said smoothly, "I've tried to explain to her all the valid reasons why you may have done what you've done."

"Valid reasons! What the hell would you know about my reasons for anything?"

Greenlea cocked his head. "Well, for one thing, I've made a study of human reasoning. It's part of what I do. For another, I've had insight from someone who may know you better than you know yourself."

Edward scoffed at the very idea. "Yeah, right. You've had a nice long coze with my mother, no doubt."

"No. With the woman you wanted to marry."

Edward went very still, torn between denial that Kendra could have discussed him in an intimate fashion with David Greenlea and the need to justify—and thereby accept—why she had done so. He shook off both, demanding, "What have you told Laurel about me?"

"Nothing she didn't already know."

"You son of a bitch!"

Greenlea shrugged unconcernedly. "Why don't you face facts, Ed? You screwed up. You couldn't face the idea that you might be falling for her, and you were looking for reasons to derail the relationship."

"That's just what I'd expect from you," Edward scoffed. "Typical psychobabble." It was, wasn't it? It had to be. The only woman who had ever meant anything significant to him was Ken-

dra, and Laurel was nothing, *nothing,* like Kendra. That didn't mean he didn't care about Laurel, though. On the contrary, he cared a great deal. Moreover, he owed her. Hell, the whole world owed her. He got up off his stool, ignoring Greenlea, and calmly walked around the counter and through the swinging metal doors. Laurel was sitting on the single bench in the long, narrow room, her head in her hands. She sniffed when the door fanned behind her and straightened. "Is he gone?"

"I'm right here, Laurel."

Dashing away the tears, she jumped up and rounded on him. "You're not allowed back here! Get out."

"Not until you listen to what I have to say."

She glared at him. "It doesn't make any difference."

"Then what can it hurt to listen?"

She frowned but was effectively caught. "All right, get it over with."

He walked around the end of the bench and moved toward her. She backed up until she was pressed against the metal door of one of a half-dozen lockers. "I came to ask your forgiveness," he began, "but if you can't give me that, then give me something else, for both our sakes."

"What is that?" she asked warily.

He took a deep breath. "Your trust."

She laughed, but it wasn't a pleasant sound.

"I know, I know," he said, "but I can help you, Laurel. I can win your case for you. I know I can. Let me, please."

She shook her head, wiping away fresh tears with the back of one hand. "I don't know, Ed. I just don't know."

"I do. I know I can win this one. I know as well that I don't deserve your trust, but if you'll give me the benefit of the doubt once more, I'll do my damnedest, I swear."

She sighed wearily and put the back of her hand to her forehead. "You don't understand," she said weakly. "There are things you don't even know."

"It doesn't matter."

She closed her eyes as if she found it too painful to look at him. "Maybe it doesn't," she said, "but I'm just not sure I can work with you." She opened her eyes but looked away from him.

"The thing is, David has a cousin who is an attorney, and I've asked David to speak to her on my behalf."

Edward's heart did a free-fall inside his chest. He tried not to appear as shaken as he felt, though, asking in a low voice, "Who would that be?"

Laurel named a fairly prominent local attorney with a busy and varied practice. Edward frowned, saying, "But does she have the steel to take on Kennison?"

Laurel sighed. "I suppose we'll find out."

Edward quickly realized that he couldn't say anything at that point to change her mind. He'd have to settle for wait-and-see. "Okay. If that's how it is, that's how it is. You can let me know later if you're going with her or not. If so, you can tell her I'll send over everything I have on the case."

She nodded almost desperately, her gaze carefully averted still. After a long silent moment, it became obvious that she wasn't going to say anything else and that she didn't want to hear anything he might have to say, either. He turned around and walked out of the room.

Greenlea was waiting for him. "Happy now?" he asked across the counter.

Ed put his head down and kept walking. When he rounded the end of the counter, Greenlea came off his stool. "Why can't you leave her alone, Edward? Ever thought of that?"

It seemed to Ed that Greenlea was purposely goading him. He ground his teeth together and walked on past.

"A kiss means nothing to you," David said, "but Laurel's different, you know. She takes these things to heart." That's when Ed decided to redesign the fit of David's jacket. He swung around and grabbed handfuls of tweedy white, black and gray, practically lifting David off the floor by it. He was heavier than he looked.

"What would you know about it?"

"More than you might like," David taunted.

The implications were clear, and Edward was suddenly seeing red. "If you've so much as laid a hand on her, I'll break you in half!"

"Now why would you do that?"

indeed? Some of his anger gave way to confusion.

"Relax," David said smugly, breaking Edward's hold with a swift, upward movement of his hands. He smoothed the front of his coat unconcernedly. Edward got in his face.

"Why should I?"

"Because," David replied smoothly, "all I'm offering Laurel now is just what she needs—friendship. Until she's ready for more."

"Yeah, right," Edward snipped. "A friend, with all the manipulative skills of a head shrink!"

For the first time, anger flared in David Greenlea's deep blue eyes. To his credit, he stood toe-to-toe with the several-inches-taller Edward. "I resent that."

"Then why don't you do something about it?"

For a moment longer, Greenlea stubbornly held his gaze level, but then something flickered behind his flashing blue eyes, something so near pity that Edward recoiled from it. "You don't need a beating, Edward. What you need is understanding. You see, Edward, we psychiatrists don't discard our humanity when we get the diploma. We're human like everyone else. We need human relationships...just like everyone else...*even lawyers*."

"Spare me," Edward said curtly, turning away. He strode as quickly as he could toward the door and still maintain his dignity. When he got outside and was certain that he couldn't be seen from the diner, he let go the rage and bitter disappointment. Then he drove to the body shop to get the dents taken out of the hood of his car before anyone could see them and remark about the stupidity of reshaping his automobile with his fists. The broken and bruised knuckles, like his pride—and his heart—he nursed himself.

"You're too good to us," Laurel said softly, tugging the blanket into place and tucking it around Barry's limp body.

David leaned close and remarked quietly, "He did enjoy the park, didn't he?"

Laurel smiled, tears gathering in her eyes. "He must have run five miles today. And two weeks ago, he wasn't even walking yet!"

"I thought sooner or later he'd get tired of picking himself up

off the ground," David whispered, laughter putting hitches and whistles in his voice.

Laurel sighed. "That part wasn't fun for me."

"I know," David said, sobering and laying a hand upon her shoulder, "but you managed very well. You did just what a good mother should do—you kept your winces hidden and you let him pick himself up and go again."

"He has to learn," she commented dismissively, moving across the dimly lit room to put space between them and the crib.

"Yes," David agreed, "but another mother in your position and with your background might have great difficulty letting him."

Laurel gave him a dismissive look. "That would be selfish."

"Yes, but another person might not realize that, and if you attempt to turn aside this compliment again, I'll have to lower my assessment of you to 'near perfect.'"

Laurel laughed behind her hand. It felt so good to laugh every time he made her do it. If only she didn't feel so numb the rest of the time, numb and yet hovering on the brink of collapse, tears ever threatening. The laughter died, leaving her feeling rather forlorn again. She turned away before he could see it in her eyes. He was too good at reading her. He was too good at a great deal, and any woman in her right mind would be passionately in love with him by now. Oh, why couldn't she do the sensible thing for once? Why must she dream of the unattainable? Hadn't she learned anything from all those years of trying to win her grandmother's love?

As usual, David seemed to read her thoughts. He reached out his hands and sent them gliding down her arms, then brought them back to pat her shoulders comfortingly. "How about dinner?" he suggested. "We'll order in and eat sitting on the floor, Oriental-style."

Laurel smiled, about to turn him down, but a knock upon her door sent her hurrying in that direction instead. Intent upon keeping whoever was there from waking the baby, she yanked open the door without first checking through the spy hole. A deliveryman stood on the landing, a baseball cap askew on his balding

head, a pencil behind each ear, clipboard braced against one hip. "Laurel Miller?"

"Yes?"

He turned his back, walked to the railing, leaned over it and bawled down into the stairwell. "Bring 'er on up, boys!"

His booming voice echoed off concrete and steel, swelling until it rattled the windows in their frames. Behind Laurel, Barry's thin wail erupted, growing quickly into a scream of sheer misery. Laurel spun away, resisting the urge to tip the ignorant deliveryman over the rail, and met David halfway across the room, a bawling Barry in his arms.

"Mama!" Catching David unaware, Barry launched himself at her—and very nearly wound up hitting the floor headfirst.

"Barry!" She caught him at the last instant, hauling him up into her arms, her knees threatening to buckle in relief. Frightened, Barry's screams reached new decibel levels. Laurel backed up and leaned against the wall, jiggling him up and down and muttering sounds of comfort.

She had calmed him to sniffles and was trying to find an opening amid an ever-changing tumble of little arms and fingers in order to wipe his nose with the tissue David had brought her, when three men entered her apartment carrying a sofa covered in heavy plastic.

"What on earth?" Even as she spoke, the men placed the sofa in the center of the floor. "What do you think you're doing? I didn't order that!"

"Yes, ma'am," said the man with the clipboard as a second man disappeared outside once more and the third began ripping off the plastic, "but the boss said we was to leave 'em anyway, seein' as how they're paid for." The third man rolled the plastic sheeting into a huge ball and took it away. "We're not to leave behind any refuse neither." With that he flipped the clipboard beneath his arm and turned to follow the other two out the door.

David stepped forward. "One moment please." He reached for the clipboard, scanned the top page, lifted it and scanned another.

"Did you do this?" Laurel demanded, but he shook his head.

"Not me. I wouldn't have the guts." He handed the clipboard back to the deliveryman, who turned and walked out just as the

first man reentered carrying a tall lamp and what appeared to be a set of bedsheets. "You'll have to thank your attorney for this little surprise," David went on. "It's a sofa bed you know. Just the thing for a studio apartment." He wandered over and ran a hand along the low, softly padded back. "I wouldn't have thought Edward knew flowered upholstery existed."

Laurel couldn't get her mouth closed. Edward? Edward had bought her this furniture? This Hide-A-Bed sofa? A real bed? She shook her head, managing to croak out, "No."

David lifted his head. "Yes, indeed."

The clipboard carrier and the second man returned, hauling a chair that matched the sofa. They ripped the plastic off and disappeared with it. David walked over and touched the back. The chair swayed gently back and forth. "Rocker," he announced succinctly. "Appropriate, wouldn't you say?"

The final piece was a tabletop television, complete with its own table.

Laurel looked around the now-crowded room with mingled wonder and dismay. What did it mean, all this largesse? Was it a plea for forgiveness? A declaration of feeling? She closed her eyes, then opened them again to find the clipboard and an ink pen thrust at her.

"Sign here."

She looked at the line with the big X scrawled at one end of it and thought of Edward picking out these pieces for her. Then Barry made a grab for the pen, and she was suddenly fending him off, the pen in her own hand now. Should she sign? Could she accept these things from him? She cast a longing glance at the sofa bed, steeled herself and laid the pen on the clipboard. "No, I—I can't. You'll...have to take them all back."

The man shook his head. "Uh-uh. Like I told you, we can't take 'em back. You sign or you don't sign, but the stuff stays. Only difference is, you don't sign, the boss's gonna chew my..." He cleared his throat. "Anyhow, I wish you'd sign."

Laurel looked to David for guidance, but he merely lifted his shoulders in a shrug. Frowning, Laurel snatched up the pen and signed her name after the X. The man straightened his ball cap and said, "That's it, then, boys. We're outta here."

David whipped out his wallet and began extracting dollar bills, but the man lifted his clipboard in refusal. "Naw, see, we done been tipped. The big guy, he said we wasn't to take nothing else."

David stashed the bills, folded his wallet and slipped it back into his hip pocket. "Have a good one, then, guys."

"No problem." They went out and closed the door behind them.

Laurel walked around the rocker, wary lest it spring to life and bite her. David chuckled and shook his head. "Sit down and rock the baby back to sleep. Then I'll help you move it all into place." He looked around. "I guess I could deflate the air mattress while you're at it." He maneuvered around the sofa and sat down on the floor near the corner where she kept her "bed." She sat down in the rocker, frowning to find it exceptionally comfortable, and helped Barry find a relaxing position.

He stared up at her for several minutes, occasionally patting her chin, then poked his middle finger into his mouth and closed his eyes. He'd recently replaced his pacifier with that middle finger, and she couldn't for the life of her figure out what had prompted it. One thing about a finger, it didn't get lost. She couldn't very well take it away from him, however. She continued rocking gently until his little face went so lax that he began to drool. Then she tugged the finger from his mouth and rocked a minute or two longer before carefully rising, winding her way to the crib, and lowering him into it. He turned onto his side and stuck his finger into his mouth again. Sighing, Laurel tucked the blanket around him and turned to face a more immediate problem.

David was watching her, the deflated and folded air mattress in his arms. "Where do you want this?"

Laurel put a hand to her hair. "I don't know." She looked around her. "I don't know where I want anything. Or if I want it at all."

"Don't be silly," he said. "Why wouldn't you want it? You obviously need it...and Edward obviously needs to give it to you."

That, of course, was the problem. "He doesn't need anything from me. He's just trying to salve a guilty conscience."

David bowed his head, considering, then he lifted it again to

give her one of his let's-be-honest looks. "Can you really not forgive him, Laurel, or is it something else?"

She frowned. "I don't know what you mean."

"Don't you?"

She hated it when he did that. She never knew what he wanted her to say, and she never enjoyed searching for it. Wandering over to the rocker, she dropped back down into it and threw one long bare leg over the padded arm, flipping her sandal against the bottom of her foot. "Stop playing psychiatrist," she grumbled.

David moved to the end of the sofa nearest to her and sat down, leaning forward in that earnest way of his. "Can't. A psychiatrist is what I am. Besides, I hate dishonesty, even if it's yourself you're lying to."

Laurel wrinkled up her nose. "I'm not lying to myself."

"No?"

She tugged at the hem of her shorts, refusing to look at him. After a while, she grudgingly gave in. "How am I lying to myself?"

As usual, he turned his answer into a question. "Haven't you already forgiven him, Laurel?"

She averted her eyes again. "What makes you say that?"

"Oh, the way you've been defending him to Fancy lately, the detailed explanations about how he might have come to his erroneous conclusion, the self-deprecating disclosures about your past, the careful way you've omitted any reference to kissing him."

Laurel felt the color drain from her face and then surge back again, stronger than before. She swallowed a lump in her throat, kept her eyes on the hem of her shorts and shrugged. David leaned back and crossed his legs.

"Well, you did slap him. Maybe you hated his kisses."

She glowered, but she couldn't hold it and wound up screwing up her face in a grimace. David folded his arms, sighing.

"Hmm, I didn't think so."

Exasperated, Laurel lashed out. "It doesn't mean anything!"

David leaned forward, elbows on knees, tone and expression earnest. "I think you're in love with him."

Laurel sucked in her breath suddenly, whispering, "No." Desperately she shook her head. "No. Don't say that, please!"

David let his head drop. For a long moment, he seemed to be thinking, but then he looked up again, and that comforting smile was in place. "What about dinner? We've got this lovely furniture to sit on now, and even a television."

Laurel made herself relax. If there was something a little desperate about it, if her heart was beating painfully, she didn't want to think about that. She didn't want to think at all. Later she would decide what to do about the furniture, about Edward, about everything. Later.

She put on a watery smile. "Chinese or Italian?"

Chapter Ten

Edward stripped off his tie, tossed it into the middle of the glass-topped table and unbuttoned the top three buttons of his shirt. It was too damned hot for May. It was too damned hot for anytime, especially nighttime. He didn't know what he was doing here anyway. He had work to do, and he was in no mood to sit here alone on the Sugarmans' back deck listening to the bug zapper electrocute innocent winged insects. He grabbed the tie, stuffed it into his pants pocket and got up to go, snagging his coat from the back of the chair. He met Parker and Kendra in the doorway. Kendra carried a plate of sandwiches, and Parker a tray of tumblers filled with ice tea. Kendra put up a hand to block his way.

"Oh, no you don't. You sit right back down there and relax. I've made you some sandwiches."

"Better do as she says," Parker told him, slipping around them both to place the tray on the table. "She's using her nurse's voice." He winked. "She'll be ordering restraints next, and you know I can't resist her in that mode."

Kendra scolded him with narrowed eyes and plucked Edward's coat out of his hands. "Sit."

Grumbling, he turned around and took his place at the table. Kendra set the plate of sandwiches before him. "Eat."

"I'm not hungry."

"That's obvious." She draped his suit coat over the back of his chair, then pulled out the chair on his left and sat down. "You've lost weight. You're not taking care of yourself."

"Something wrong?" Parker asked, every syllable rife with special meaning.

He knew what they thought, that he was wasting away with guilt over Laurel. Well, they could think what they liked. He'd been over and over it in his mind, and he figured that he'd done the best he could where Laurel was concerned. It wasn't his fault she'd done all those stupid things. No one could hold *him* responsible for how things had seemed. He wished that she hadn't found out about the scheme to have Greenlea secretly evaluate her, but he couldn't do anything about that now, and if anyone was to blame, it was Greenlea.

As for himself, if he could change anything, he'd change those kisses. He'd make those kisses never happen. He'd go back to that moment in his office when he'd thought to teach her an obvious lesson and he'd simply sit there looking at her like she'd lost her mind until she realized her stupidity. He'd go back to that electric moment in his car when he'd never wanted anything so much as he'd wanted to lock lips with her, and instead he'd smile politely and say, "Let me walk you to your door." And then he'd go home without getting his face slapped, which, by the way, was suitable recompense for his own stupidity. Add to that the fact that he'd spent a small fortune for furniture to make her current circumstances more comfortable, and he'd done everything he could do to make amends. If she was too ill-natured to respond with more than a hurried telephone call to tell him that she wasn't sure she could keep it, he'd be damned if he'd go around on bended knee to beg forgiveness. Been there. Done that. No, he wasn't eaten up with guilt. He was just too busy, always too busy—and too much alone.

He picked up the neatly sliced triangle of sandwich on the top of the stack and bit off at least half of it. Laurel sat back in satisfaction. Grinning, Parker passed him a glass of cold tea. He

gulped from it, felt the hard cold slide down his throat and sighed, rolling his head side to side to get the kinks out of his neck.

"You're working too much," Kendra said.

Ed shrugged. "Story of my life."

"Not yet," Parker said, "but if you're not careful, it's going to be."

He shrugged again and bit off another huge bite of sandwich. They sat in companionable silence for some time, listening to the *zzzt-zzzt-zzzt* emanating from the corner of the house and the distant hum of traffic, basking in the soft light of the gas lamps. Before he knew it, Edward found an empty plate beneath his fingertips. Kendra started to rise.

"I'll make you another."

He waved her back down into her chair. "No, no. I'm full." He patted his flat middle and slid down farther against the padding of the green metal chair, bracing his bent knee on the edge of the table and leaning his head back against cool metal that quickly heated to body temperature. "Hell's bells, it's hot."

"Yes, it is." Kendra sighed and lifted the weight of her hair up off her shoulders.

"Well, I like it," Parker said. "Tomorrow I'm going to lie out in the sun for a while."

Edward snorted, and Kendra delivered a minilecture on the evils of overexposure. Parker just grinned at them. "He's not going to lie out and bake," Edward said. "He's just yanking our chains, wanting you to fuss over him and me to think I'm the only one working day and night."

Parker didn't deny or confirm, but no one expected him to. He kicked back in his chair and propped his feet on the rim of the table. "Speaking of work," he said, "how's the case coming?"

To his irritation, Edward felt himself go very still. "What case?"

Parker slid him an innocent look. "You know, the Kennison thing."

Kennison. Edward barely restrained himself from gnashing his teeth. "Aw, you know how it is—things creep along, then suddenly they bust loose."

"So you're saying it's creeping along?" Parker asked, deliberately pressing.

Edward bit back a caustic reply and forced himself to remain calm. "Actually, it's sort of on hold," he managed to say, "and a good thing, too. I've got more than I can do these days."

With a single look, Parker passed the torch to Kendra. Holding that gaze, she asked of Edward, "Have you spoken to Laurel lately?"

Edward set his back teeth. "No."

"I thought of sending around a note," she said contritely, "but David offered to convey our apologies verbally instead."

David. Edward put a firm cap on the swelling of his rage. Once he was fairly sure that it wouldn't choke him, he reached for his tea glass and drained it, then sat up, stretched and said, "Well, I'd better get back to it. Those briefs don't write themselves."

Kendra mouthed a silent message to Parker, who appeared not to heed her. But then, just as Edward reached the door, Parker spoke up. "They're dating, you know." He turned to skewer Edward with a glance aimed over his shoulder. "David and Laurel, that is."

Edward forced his hand around the doorknob, but turning it seemed beyond him. Parker went on.

"I think it's getting serious. What do you say, Ken? Does David seem serious to you?"

"Very much so," she replied softly.

Edward snatched his hand off the doorknob and turned around. He meant to say something innocuous. He meant to wish them well or some such nonsense. Instead, the words that fell out of his mouth were "I knew that snake couldn't be trusted!"

"What snake would that be?" Parker quickly rejoined.

Edward took a menacing step forward and shook a finger in Parker's too-composed face. "I never should've let you talk me into bringing him in on this! Damn! Why didn't I follow my better judgment?"

"Me?" Parker retorted. "You and Kendra masterminded that, old buddy. If I remember correctly, I never thought there was anything wrong with her to begin with—other than that odd notion about marrying you!"

"*Odd* is the key word here, *old buddy!* And it's got nothing to do with marrying anyone! That woman is trouble walking, and he's welcome to her, by golly! He *deserves* her. Hell, they deserve each other! She can drive him crazy, and he can heal himself!" He waved a hand dismissively. "Why would I care? Why am I even wasting breath on this?" Throwing up his hands, he turned to go. Kendra stopped him with one softly spoken sentence.

"Because you're in love with her."

He froze in his tracks. For just an instant he felt a rush of emotion so strong that it terrified him. He slammed the door on it, and with eerie calm, rounded on her. "You, of all people, ought to know better."

She stared at him, and for a long moment the old connection held—comfortable, companionable, predictable, safe. Then Kendra broke it, and with nothing more than her eyes, telegraphed a message to her husband. Immediately Parker hopped up and headed for the door, announcing that he really ought to check on Darla. Edward had the feeling that he should follow right on his heels, but for some reason he stayed. Kendra got up and wandered to the deck railing, where she turned and leaned back, her arms folded across her middle.

"Have you looked at yourself lately?"

He sniffed and stuck his hands in his pants pockets. "Don't be silly. I still shave every morning."

She ignored that. "You've given up the trendy cut for a more manageable style that's a little shorter in the front. It becomes you."

He shrugged and muttered, "Too much trouble the other way."

She nodded. "And it wasn't really you, no more than that overgrown mop you used to wear. But this...this is you."

He didn't bother saying thanks because he knew she was making a point, however obscure at the moment. "Yeah, so, I finally figured out the hair thing."

"It's more than that," she told him. "You're wearing those clothes like they were made for you."

He looked down at himself. "They might as well have been. That crazy tailor can find more adjustments to make than these things have seams."

"The point is, you finally know what looks best on you."

"Somebody finally *told* me what looked best on me."

"I figured that, but it wasn't Walden, the tailor. He's more concerned with meeting his sales quotas than helping his individual customers find their own personal styles."

Edward frowned at that, but he was big enough to confess. "It was Laurel. She's got an education in fashion design. I figured she knew what she was talking about, considering she always looks like she just walked off the cover of a magazine."

"Good move," Kendra told him, one eyebrow held aloft. "Doesn't that tell you anything?"

"It tells me she can dress. She might have been sleeping on the floor in a rented cave when I met her, but by golly, she looked good doing it."

"You're being mean," Kendra said. "None of this is her fault. My word, after everything that's happened to her, it's a wonder she can function at all. David says—"

"Oh, spare me what David Greenlea might have to say! Of all the people on this earth, Ken, you're the last one I expected to talk to him about me, about *us.*"

"Oh, Ed, don't you see that I'm very concerned for you? We all are."

"Nothing to be concerned about," he muttered.

"Isn't there?" she asked softly.

He stood for a moment, confused and conflicted. What was happening to him? Dear God, why couldn't he get a handle on this?

"Ed, you're going to regret it if you don't face up to your feelings for Laurel and do something about them."

"There's nothing to do."

"Isn't there?"

Her prodding infuriated him. "You talk like I ought to run out and grab a license and a ring, and you of all people know that's impossible for me!"

"Oh, Ed, get over it!" she shouted back. "You're not in love with me and you never have been!"

"How can you say—"

"Because it's true!" She doubled up her fists and brought them up to her forehead in frustration. "Ahh!"

He'd never seen her like this. He didn't know what to make of it. And it hurt him that she could say these things to him. "I've always loved you," he said defensively, and she dropped her hands.

"Not like Parker loves me. Not like I love him. Not like you love a wife, a mate, a partner, Ed. Don't you see? Parker makes me more than I ever could've been without him, and vice versa. We balance each other. We make each other shine, sometimes by rubbing each other the wrong way—but in the right way, somehow. That's what Laurel does for you. Take a long hard look, Ed, inside and out, because it's more than appearance. It's... passion, intensity. It's...scary as hell," she admitted. "I know what you're feeling, because I've been there myself. I was terrified of Parker. Yet, deep down where it counts most, I always knew that he and I were an explosive combination—just as I knew that, as much as I do love you, the two of us together are dull as dishwater. We're too much alike, you and I. We need Parker and Laurel to shake us up, to pull us out of our comfortable ruts, to make us live life to its fullest. And they need us to lend a calming influence. They need our dependability and our willingness to shoulder the responsibility, to make them believe in their own worth and maturity. It's a perfect combination of strengths and weaknesses, Ed. Don't let it pass you by. Please."

He didn't know what to say to all that. She was right about her and Parker. He could see it every time they were together. It was why he couldn't stay away, why he couldn't give them up— either of them. Together they had built a real family and a real home. This was the only place he felt really comfortable, the only place where he found the hope to keep on keeping on, day after day, case after case, fight after fight. But how could he believe that he could have all this with Laurel? How could he pin his hopes on a quirky, battered little debutante so desperate that she would waltz in off the street and ask a complete stranger to marry her? How could he even make a judgment call on the possibility when there wasn't a snowball's chance in hell that she'd ever

forgive him for that stupid setup almost a month ago? Aw, God, what had he done?

"I'm screwed," he said bleakly. Kendra strolled over and put an arm around him. He pulled her close against his side.

"You never know until you try," she said hopefully.

The love he felt for Kendra Sugarman in that moment was real enough, but hugging her was like hugging his mother—and it always had been. The correlation made him chuckle, and he said against the top of her head, "Think you're ever going to get me raised?"

She laughed and shook her head. "I've done all I can. It'll take a better woman than me to top you off." She looked up then. "A better woman *for you,* that is."

He knew, finally, who that was, thanks to Kendra, thanks to his friend, Kendra Ballard Sugarman. His friend. His very dear friend.

He closed his eyes. *Please, God, don't let it be too late for more. I need so much more.* He needed Laurel.

He didn't know how long he'd driven aimlessly around the city until he glanced at his watch. Almost eleven, but when he realized that he was within a block of Laurel's apartment building, he knew he was going to stop. He had to try again, and this time he could be completely honest with her.

Ken was right. Maybe it was the old adage about opposites attracting. He didn't suppose it mattered; all he knew was that he'd been powerfully attracted to Laurel Miller from the first moment he'd laid eyes on her—and that had scared the hell out of him.

It had been easy to be in love with Kendra. She was safe, comfortable, easily admired. He almost always knew what she was thinking, how she would view a thing. In some ways, having Kendra married to his best friend was like having his cake and eating it, too. She was there for him more than she had been after their initial breakup, and if she was untouchable... He wondered when that had stopped bothering him, or if it ever had, really. Even when he had realized that she was falling in love with Parker and making their marriage real, his concern had not been that

she would be forever unavailable to him, but rather that Parker's lovemaking would change her somehow, make her less than she was. He'd been wrong about that, of course, and he'd known it for some time. He'd been content with the situation, even happy for her and Parker. His love for Kendra had changed, or else it hadn't been what he'd assumed it to be all along. And hadn't Ken tried to tell him that when she'd broken their engagement? Hadn't she told him repeatedly since? But he had hung on to his illusions. They made him safe. How could he fall in love elsewhere if his heart already belonged to an unattainable woman? Safe.

Until Laurel. And Laurel was another proposition altogether. Could he find a riskier female, a woman with more problems? In many ways, Laurel was still an unknown quantity. Was she capable of loving with the same ferocity and commitment that he witnessed between Kendra and Parker? Would her passion match his? Was she brave enough to love after all she'd been through? He knew that she was loyal and unapologetic where her friends were concerned, but he knew, too, that her marriage had foundered. She was impulsive. She was fiery. She was an enigma. But she was definitely *not* crazy. And he couldn't get her out of his head no matter how hard he tried.

He parked and got out of the car. What if she closed the door in his face? What if she told him to go away and never come back? What if David Greenlea was there? What if she and David... No, he wasn't going to think about that. He didn't dare.

He kept his footfalls quiet, coming down gently on his heels and slowly rolling forward onto his toes, step after step after step after step. He didn't want to alert the neighbors, and all the windows were open because of the heat. He could see from the top of the landing that even her window was open. The clothing that had been hung there had obviously been moved. The lights were off, but he felt certain that she was there. She wouldn't have left the place open. Maybe he could wake her without alerting the rest of the occupants of the building.

He moved quietly along the landing, listening to the muted sounds of voices raised behind closed doors and televisions being played too loud. From somewhere just ahead, a baby cried for its mama. Ed slowed and eased up to Laurel's door, pausing to con-

sider his next move. Did he knock lightly or call to her through the open window? The baby wailed, sounding as though it were right inside Laurel's apartment this time. Then suddenly the light came on inside.

"Mommy's here," said a soft, sleepy voice. A familiar voice. Laurel's voice. "Mommy's here, honey."

It hadn't really registered yet, not as a coherent thought. It was just a niggling possibility floating on the edge of his consciousness, and he automatically stepped to the window to see what his eyes could tell him about the idea now beginning to form in the back of his mind. He watched her rise from the bed, the bed that unfolded from the sofa he had sent her, the one she wasn't even certain she would keep. She wore a skimpy little cotton gown that looked yellow in the yellow light of the lamp he had purchased. He watched her long bare legs as they moved the few steps across the room to the crib against the opposite wall. He held his breath as she bent and lifted the crying child onto her shoulder. His bright red head snuggled against her in a gesture performed hundreds of times before, golden eyes gleaming with tears. She patted his back.

"Those new teeth coming in are hurting again, aren't they, angel?" She picked up a small bottle from the counter and moved to the side. "Well, Mommy can fix that, for a little while, anyway."

She sat down in the rocker, the one that matched the sofa, the one he had bought for her, the one that was part of his peace offering, his way of making amends and salving his conscience. He had wanted to make her life better somehow. The rocker had seemed appropriate, and he knew now why. He listened as she coaxed the little one into opening his mouth, presumably so she could rub something foul-tasting but helpful onto his gums.

Stunned, he stood there and listened to it all. He heard her comfort the boy, rocking him gently in the chair until his whimpering and snufflings had ceased, until he slept again, safe in his mother's arms.

After a long while, she stood and carried the boy back to his crib. She smoothed his hair and smiled down at him. A mother's smile. Then she tiptoed back to the bed and lay down. She turned

off the light and rolled onto her side, sighing with the weight of responsibility on this too-warm night, the responsibility for her child. Her child.

Ed shifted slightly to one side and lifted a forearm to lean against the rough wall. His head was spinning. How could he not have known? It had been obvious all along. Why hadn't he seen? Maybe he hadn't wanted to see the truth. Suddenly he knew why. He didn't want to think that Barry was Laurel's because he didn't want to think who his father might be.

His mind was already whirling with possibilities, each one more awful than the last, each one damning her more surely, ripping his heart a little deeper. If he could have trusted himself not to throttle her, he'd have awakened her then and demanded the truth, but he knew better than to attempt that, and yet he had to know. God help him, he had to know.

He didn't bother to soften his footsteps as he left that place. He ran all the way to the car, and his tires squealed when he swung the car out onto the street. He didn't care who heard, didn't care who saw, and the level of his distress told him what he'd been slow to realize: the depth of his feelings for her. His mind was busy with visions of Laurel and a parade of men, from that damned gardener at the asylum to Bryce and David Greenlea and a faceless army of others, one of them the father of her child. He had to know that man's name—and he knew one person more likely to tell him than any other.

He drove up in front of the Heffington mansion, lighting up the motion detectors that rimmed the drive. He slammed the door when he got out of the car. He wanted Miller to have plenty of notice that he was coming. To that end, he not only leaned on the doorbell but beat on the door with his fist until someone switched on the chandelier in the foyer.

"Who is it?"

Good, Bryce himself had come to check out the new arrival. Ed laid his fist against the door again and shouted, "Ed White!" Then he backed up to make himself visible through the peephole, allowing every bit of his agitation to show. He counted on Miller's curiosity, and Miller didn't disappoint him. The door cracked open several inches. Ed saw no sign of a chain. Dumb cluck

probably thought he didn't need one. Edward denied the impulse to shove his way inside and instead forced himself to speak. "I've got to talk to you. Open up."

Miller eyed him suspiciously. "You drunk?"

"Not yet."

The door opened a little wider. "This about Laurel?"

"Who else?"

Miller opened the door all the way and stood leaning against the frame, a grin on his face. "Got you tied in knots, does she? I warned you about her."

Edward forced himself to remain calm. "Can we go inside?"

Miller shrugged and turned away. Edward followed him down the hall to a sort of den furnished with heavy leather pieces and a home theater setup, complete with big-screen TV. The "maid" was curled up in one corner of the sofa watching a video. Bryce flipped on the overhead light and used the remote to turn off the TV.

"Hey, I was watching that!"

"Now you're not, so get out."

She uncurled from her corner and stood, displaying long bare legs so thin, Ed wondered that they could support her. Wearing nothing but a T-shirt and panties, she flounced from the room, pouting. Both men ignored her. When she had gone, Bryce folded his arms, tucking his hands into his armpits and leaned against the arm of the sofa. He didn't offer Edward a seat.

"What's Laurel done now?"

Edward didn't even attempt to answer that. He had questions of his own and only one way to get answers for them. "Are you the father of Laurel's baby?"

Bryce Miller looked as if an invisible fist had bopped him on the nose.

"Laurel's *pregnant?*"

"No!"

"But you just said—"

"Never mind. I—I've obviously come to the wrong place." Bryce wasn't a good enough actor to feign that much surprise. He'd made a mistake coming here, but he couldn't, for the moment, figure out how. He turned and headed for the door, hoping

for a quick escape, but his luck, such as it was, was holding. Miller beat him there and flung himself into the void.

"You're telling me that Laurel's already *got* a baby? When? How old is it? What's its name?"

Edward shook his head, more miserably confused than ever before in his life. "Get out of my way!"

"Hell, no! If Laurel's got a kid, I ought to know about it. I was married to her, for pity's sake!"

He had a point, but Edward knew he wasn't thinking clearly enough to consider all the ramifications. He tried to fob off Miller with a single answer. "His name's Barry."

"Barry!" Miller's eyes widened. "Barry was my uncle's name."

Ed tried to shoulder his way past Bryce. "I have to go."

Bryce seized him by the shirtfront. "What color is his hair?"

Ed took a look at the other man's golden-brown mop and answered him, more concerned about holding on to his temper and getting out of there than giving away possible secrets. "Red. Now let go of me!"

Bryce Miller looked at him as if only then realizing what he was doing. He backed up a step and loosened his grip on Ed's shirt. "How old did you say the kid was?"

Ed slid out into the hallway, muttering, "I didn't."

"Year maybe? Somewhere around there?"

"Maybe."

Ed hurried down the hall, through the door and out onto the drive. His last view of Bryce Miller showed him that the other guy was grinning like he'd won the lottery, and Ed had the sinking feeling that he'd given the louse the winning number. Once in the car, Ed sat with his head in his hands, trying to think. Had he been wrong? Was the child really Laurel's, or had he misunderstood? One thing was certain—Bryce Miller hadn't known about the boy. Then what the hell was going on? Could Laurel have managed to keep a pregnancy secret from her estranged husband? Maybe. But what about her divorce lawyer?

He turned that idea over in his mind. Hardacre had to know. He *had* to. Bryce had guessed correctly when he'd asked if the kid was a year old or so. That meant that Laurel had to have been

pregnant during the divorce proceedings. Who else but Hardacre would have seen her during that period on a regular basis?

He knew one place where he might find Hardacre this time of night. He used to hang out at a bar down on Greenville Avenue. It was a long time since Ed had been in there himself. It was one of those places that seemed to have slid downhill, its clientele changing over time, but it was still worth checking out. Even if Danny Hardacre wasn't there, Ed himself could use a drink. And if Hardacre was there, well, this time he wouldn't go in shooting his mouth off. This time he'd use his supposed skills to get the answers he needed. He was a lawyer, after all, and he used to be a good one.

He drove to the bar on lower Greenville Avenue. The facade was shabby and run-down. The sidewalk in front was littered with broken bottles and other even less savory trash. He nodded to the ponytailed bouncer keeping a watch on the front door and pushed through a black curtain into the bar. It was an arrangement meant to facilitate collection of a cover charge; it also gave the bouncer a chance to warn management if the cops came in to check out the validity of their liquor license or the IDs of their clientele.

A look around the room showed him Danny Hardacre sitting at a table with a woman and two other men. The woman looked like she could eat nails for breakfast and come back for more. The two men flanking her could have knocked her away from the table with the same concentration and caring they'd put into swatting a fly. Rough company. The rest of the patrons were of the same ilk. He swallowed down his concerns and moved to the bar, where he ordered a beer before sauntering over to the table, a smile pasted on his face.

"Hey, Danny. Long time no see."

Danny looked up at him. The way his eyes rolled around in his head, Edward assumed that he was more than halfway to being unconscious. Clearly, he wasn't sober enough to recognize a colleague. Edward looked at the woman at the table and stuck out his hand. Her long, straight hair was so black, it looked like she'd dyed it with ink. If so, she'd used the same substance to shadow and outline her eyes. The dark makeup, along with burgundy lipstick and the gold ring in her left nostril made her look hard

and cold, an impression that her low-cut, black leather vest and frayed jeans did nothing to dispel, despite the amount of skin they displayed. Ed noted that the upper swell of her left breast had been tatooed with the image of a broken heart, denoting either an unsuspected emotional vulnerability or a beloved pasttime. His money was on a very literal interpretation of the latter. Nevertheless, the corners of her garish mouth lifted in what might have been a smile. He identified himself. "Edward White."

Her hand rose and curled around his. Two-inch nails painted shiny black lifted the hair on the back of his neck. She identified herself, improbably, as the Virgin Mary, then got up and left the table without another word. The two men did the same, one of them baring his teeth at Edward as he walked away. They took up places at the bar and cast him sullen glances. It occurred to Ed that, if he should leave Danny Hardacre here in the company of that bizarre trio, he might well see Danny's name listed in tomorrow's crime report. On the other hand, Hardacre was obviously well-known in these parts. He had to know what kind of company he was keeping. Either way, it wasn't Ed's problem.

Ed sat down and sipped his drink. Danny Hardacre's head came up. Heavily graying, lank brown hair fell into one bloodshot eye. Danny pushed it away with the back of his hand and smiled.

"I know you. You're, uh, Eddie White."

Edward ground his teeth together. No one but his mother and little Darla could get away with calling him Eddie. He forced a jovial smile. "How you doing, Danny?"

Danny waved a wobbly hand. "Sho-sho. How're you?"

"Fine. Just fine. I, um, met a friend of yours the other day."

"Frien'?" Danny wrinkled an already furrowed and rather pasty brow as if the idea of his having a friend was foreign. "Wha' frien'?"

Ed sipped his drink and said casually, "Laurel Miller."

Danny's spine snapped straight. He looked Edward right in the eye. "You know Laurel?"

"I know her."

"How come?"

"I'm considering her case."

"Agains' Kennison?"

"Yeah, her case against Kennison."

Danny sighed. "Save yourse'f the time and hassle. You can't win agains' Kennison."

"No? Why's that?"

Danny leaned over the table and gagged Edward with his ninety-proof breath. "He'll get somethin' on you—an'thin'. He'll make it up, an' he'll hold it o'er your head like the swor' o' Demelin, er, the swor' o' Dameldin, the swor'..." He waved a hand dismissively and said, "An ax."

Which would account for that absurd property settlement and inheritance oversight, Ed remarked silently. At the moment, however, the case was secondary in Edward's mind. He turned the conversation back to Laurel. "I've heard that you and the ex-Mrs. Miller were engaged to be married."

Danny snorted. "You hear' that?"

"Well, something like that."

Danny shook his head, nearly lost it and parked it on his fist, cheekbone to knuckles. "Where'd you hear that?"

"Does it matter? I mean, you didn't marry her, obviously."

Danny snorted again, then hiccupped. His head fell off his fist, and he slid down to support it on the back of his chair. "In your dream. No, I mean, in my dream, or..." He sighed.

Edward fortified himself with a draught of beer and asked the definitive question. "What happened? Did you break it off because of the kid?"

Danny lifted his head and stared at Edward, eyes narrowed in an apparent attempt to bring him into sharp focus. "What kid?"

"Laurel's little boy."

Danny stared, mouth open, for some time. Then suddenly he began to snigger. "She ain't got no kid!" He pushed up straight in his chair and laughed at Edward. "Kennison tell you that?"

Edward looked down. "No. I've seen him, Laurel's little boy. His name's Barry, and he's about a year old."

Danny put a hand to his head. It was painful watching him trying to do the math, but he finally figured it to his own satisfaction. "No," he announced, straightening again and pulling in a deep, fortifying breath. "No way."

Ed's heart leapt into his throat. "Are you sure?"

Danny swallowed a belch. "On'y kid Laurel ever had aroun' her was that skinny li'l redhead sis'er of Miller's, an' she was eighteen, nineteen...ol' enough to have a kid herse'f."

"Redhead?" Edward latched on to that one word. "Did you say she was redheaded?"

Danny shrugged. "Yeah, but she wa'n't nothin' nex' to Laurel, you know? Laurel...now there's a woman t' make your head spin. Oh-oh." He dropped his head into his hands, as if afraid it would spin right off his skinny neck. Ed knew exactly how he felt. His own head was spinning.

Was it possible that Barry was Bryce's sister's kid? He remembered Laurel mentioning Bryce's younger sister as a factor in delaying her divorce. She had said, in fact, that once her sister-in-law had left, there had been no reason to sustain the marriage. What was her name? Ed was sure Laurel had mentioned it. Dionne? Yvonne? Avon! And Barry was named after Bryce and Avon's uncle! Avon had to be the mother. She could have returned to Laurel later, after the divorce had been filed. Where else could she have gone if she'd been pregnant? After the baby was born, she might well have entrusted her child to Laurel. Yes, of course. That's exactly what she'd have done. But why keep knowledge of the child from Bryce? Why—

Suddenly his blood ran cold. He shot up from his chair. "I have to go!"

Danny's chair hit the bare cement floor as he got to his feet. "Yeah, gotta go. Gotta go." He wobbled, straightened, then staggered into a neighboring table, chairs screeching and tumbling over. Ed grabbed his arm to keep him from falling.

"Whoa! You'd better sober up some first."

"Yeah, sober up." Danny yawned, swaying. "You take me home, I'll swober up, I s'ear." He attempted to cross his heart and poked himself in the eye. "Ow!"

Edward shook him. "Danny, I can't take you home."

Danny nodded. "Yeah. Okay. I got some frien's." He lifted a hand and yelled across the room. "Hey, Mary!"

Ed glanced at the unsavory trio at the bar. Some friends. They'd slit Danny's throat for a nickel. The two men were sitting there laughing at him now even as "Mary" wove her way toward them.

Ed made a quick decision. Okay, he'd stupidly given Bryce another weapon against Laurel. No doubt Kennison was preparing custody papers now, and he had to tell Laurel what he'd done, but the threat wasn't immediate. He'd have time to get Hardacre home first. He tugged Danny's arm.

"Come on, pal. Say good night to the black leather virgin, and let's get out of here."

"Mary" spat a stream of foul words at Ed as he dragged Danny from the bar, but the bouncer stopped her from following them. Ed was sure that he heard the click of a clip sliding home as he shoved Danny out onto the sidewalk, but he wasn't about to stop to see which party had pulled the gun. He didn't look back until the car had safely merged into the flow of traffic moving sluggishly along the street. Only then did he breathe easy, and somehow even that did not loosen the knot in his stomach. Nothing would until he saw Laurel again, told her what he'd done now and pledged her not only his help but also his heart. What she did after that would determine whether he spent the rest of his life regretting what he'd done or making it up to her. He knew he didn't deserve a chance at the latter, but he was selfish enough to hope for it. Love, he was discovering, could be a little selfish.

Chapter Eleven

Danny Hardacre lived in an old frame house in Oak Cliff, apparently alone. Ed had to raid his pockets for the keys, unlock the door and carry a loudly snoring Danny inside. Ed dumped Danny on a ragged couch in the small, cluttered living room, which reeked of cigarettes. He tossed his business card on the coffee table and locked the door as he left.

He drove straight to Laurel's apartment building, climbed the stairs in a hurry and rushed to her door. But there, once again, he paused. If she was sleeping, should he wake her and the baby for so selfish a cause as unburdening himself? Was a warning in the middle of the night really necessary? He moved to the window, leaned a shoulder against the frame and carefully craned his neck to take a look inside.

She had been up again since he'd been here earlier, for the light over the tiny kitchen sink had been switched on and left to burn. He remembered from the Sugarmans' experience that cutting teeth could be a torturous experience for baby and parent alike. Laurel and Barry both probably needed every moment of

sleep they could get right now. He rubbed a hand over his mustache and forced his mind into logical thought.

All right, if Bryce was Barry's uncle, he could raise a real stink about Laurel having custody, as she was no real relation. On the other hand, this Avon character must have meant Laurel to have care of the child or she would have at least informed her brother of the baby's existence, so Laurel had that in her favor. Financially, Bryce could claim superiority, but Ed could argue that as trustee of the Heffington legacy, Miller was obligated to provide for Laurel—if not relinquish control of the actual trust—and thereby, Barry as well, so long as the child remained in Laurel's custody. That ought to nullify the question of finances. Meanwhile, Edward would see that she was set up in better residential circumstances. The real problem would be Laurel's background. He'd have to defuse that, but he'd known it for some time now, and he knew just where to start. He'd call his investigator again first thing in the morning.

Bryce would still have a powerful weapon in Barry. By simply threatening to remove Barry from her care, he could force Laurel to give up her fight to gain control of her inheritance. It was up to Ed to convince Laurel that they could win. He didn't see how waking her and Barry in the middle of the night with bad news would accomplish that goal. As badly as he wanted to see her, speak to her, touch her, it could and should wait. And so could his confession, thankfully, for he was beginning to dread what he had to say. Maybe it would come easier if he could tell her that he was already at work resolving the crisis. He'd call the investigator tonight, no matter the hour, and start drawing up the papers for a permanent custody order. He'd do anything necessary to keep her from being hurt again, whether she was willing to forgive him or not. He owed her that much. The truth was, though, he couldn't any longer do anything else, thanks to his own impulsiveness. Never mind that he'd never been impulsive before Laurel!

He stood there awhile longer, listening to Laurel's slow, even breaths as she slept on the sofa bed beneath the window. He couldn't see her, and that was just as well, for if he could stand here and do this, so could another man, and he could hardly bear

the thought of someone else standing this close, listening as she slept, let alone watching her. Tomorrow he'd warn her to get curtains up and keep them closed. Better yet, tomorrow they'd start looking for a safer, quieter place for her and the baby. He couldn't think of any better place than his own, but he couldn't count on that suggestion being accepted. Hell, he'd be lucky if she even talked to him after this. That in mind, he tore a page from his pocket notebook and wrote a note requesting that she call him at first opportunity either at home or the office. He stressed that it was very important, and pondered a long while over the closing. He wanted to write that he missed her. For one insane moment, he even considered writing that he loved her, but in the end he merely signed it, wedged it into the crack between the door and the frame and took himself off again, quietly this time, to plan and plot—and hope.

When the baby woke again, Laurel groaned even as she sat straight up and pushed back her hair. She jumped out of bed and ran to the crib. He was standing by the time she got there and holding up his little arms. She could see that he was soaked and, worse, flushed with the bright-eyed look of a fever. One touch of her wrist against his little forehead proved his temperature had risen alarmingly. Quickly she changed him, which made him not at all happy. He screamed so loudly in fact, that the people next door pounded on the wall. Laurel quieted him as best she could, but the lotion for his gums did not relieve his pain. From the way he pulled at his little ears, she suspected that they were dealing with an infection, a not uncommon occurrence with teething babies, especially those slow to get in their teeth. She gave him drops of an over-the-counter medication she kept for such emergencies, and that aggravated him even more. Poor darling was desperately unhappy. He couldn't understand why he was suffering or tell her what he wanted her to do to make it better, and that would make anyone cranky.

After much soothing and crooning and rocking—thank God for that chair!—she got him calmed down enough to sleep lightly. She put him into his cumbersome combination safety seat and carrier. He was much too heavy to easily carry that way, but she

didn't want to wake him. Quickly she changed into a pair of jeans and a soft, short-sleeved, lilac-colored sweater cropped just at the waist. After brushing her teeth and hair and washing her face, she put together a bag of necessities, slipped a dollar's worth of quarters into her pocket for easy access and hurriedly left the apartment. In her haste, juggling baby and carrier and bag, she failed to see the small, folded note that fluttered silently to the landing behind her. A moment later, a gust of wind swept it into the open stairwell, ruffling Laurel's hair and the baby's blanket, and sweeping the note beneath the banister and down, down, down to a resting place beneath the stairs. Unknowingly, Laurel stepped over it on her way, precious cargo in tow, to the nearest telephone.

Her first call was to Fancy, who didn't answer. Presumably she was already on her way to the diner. So Laurel called there next, but no one answered there, either. Finally she called David, who promised to come immediately. While she waited, she phoned the pediatrician and left David's number with his service.

That last effort proved needless, however, for David himself took care of Barry. Laurel had forgotten that psychiatrists were also medical doctors until David reminded her as he drove her and Barry to the hospital emergency room, where he appropriated an examination table, instruments and even samples of an antibiotic and decongestant to fight Barry's ear infection. In little more than hour, they were home again, Barry sleeping peacefully for the first time in days.

Laurel looked at David, so handsome in his sleek golden blondness, and felt a very real affection deepened by immense gratitude. She put out her hand. "Thank you. I don't know what we'd have done without you. You've been so good to us."

"You're easy to be good to," he told her, smiling. "Is there anything else I can do before I go?"

Laurel shook her head, then stopped. "Oh, yes, if you wouldn't mind calling the diner for me. I can't go in with the baby so sick, and I can't leave him to get to a phone."

"No problem," he told her. Then his voice took on a deeper, huskier tone as he said, "I'd do more, you know, if you'd let me. I could always take you home with me, and you could call from there. I have everything else you need there, and I could check

on you throughout the day. And you'd be so nice to come home to.'' This last he said with a plaintive smile, but Laurel shook her head and lifted a hand to cup his smooth cheek.

Unbidden, memories swamped her. She could almost feel Edward's rough, heavily shadowed skin rasping against her cheek as his mouth plied hers, his mustache tickling her nose. Shuddering, she threw off the memories. Concern written all over his face, David pulled her into his arms and held her tenderly against him.

''Hey, it's all right. You can't blame a guy for trying, though, especially when the lady in question is as desirable as you.''

''Oh, David,'' she said, wishing that she could feel more for him—and less for Edward White. That wish alone, never mind the deep affection she bore him, was reason enough not to pull away when he put his mouth to hers. She felt a sad regret when he moaned and tightened his arms about her, holding her fast while his mouth manipulated hers.

She could find nothing not to like about his kiss. He was, in fact, quite a skillful kisser, and she felt flattered that he had chosen her to kiss, for she knew that this was no idle flirtation. And yet she felt oddly untouched, even removed from the experience. She felt in no danger of doing something foolish, such as finding herself naked and flat on her back, making love with a man she barely knew. In other words, he simply did not affect her as Edward had, and that was a pitiable shame, for unlike Edward, David Greenlea was a man ready to love and to give himself fully to it. If only she could return the feeling as completely as he deserved and needed.... But she could not, and nothing told her so as plainly as this.

He must have sensed it, too, for he slowly broke apart their mouths, sighing with resignation. He brushed her cheek with the backs of his fingers. ''Well,'' he said, ''I knew it was a chancy thing.'' She looked away, sorry for him.

''I'm the worst kind of idiot, I know.''

He shook his head and set her back from him. ''No, you're just in love with the wrong man—or the right one. I don't honestly know.''

Neither did she, not that it mattered. ''I don't suppose he can

be the right one if he's not in love with me," she pointed out softly.

David bowed his head, obviously choosing his words with care. "I'm not so sure about that. I don't think Edward himself knows what his feelings for you are. Give him some time. Clearly, he's made overtures. Perhaps if you followed up on that..."

She glanced around her at the furniture that had made her life so much easier, and considered. Had something more than guilt prompted his generosity? She was afraid to find out. Besides, now wasn't the time. She had a sick baby to tend to. David laid his hand on her shoulder.

"I have to go," he said, "and you look like you could use some sleep."

She nodded, too eagerly, probably. "Thank you again. Don't worry about us."

He simply smiled and left her. She locked the door behind him, sad all over again, and wandered over to look down at the sleeping baby. As usual, her heart lightened. Whatever or *whomever* else she might not have, she had him, this delightful, sometimes wearying, extremely precious little boy. In a very real way, he had saved her—from herself, from her demons, from her past— and she had never dreamed that she could love as selflessly as she loved him. Her son. In every way that counted, he was hers, and nothing could ever change that. Not for her. Nothing.

She didn't call. He went so far as to phone the diner in search of her, but only to be informed that she was not working. He tried to ask a few questions, to find out if it was a scheduled day off or if there was a problem, but Fancy hung up on him. He could only assume that all was well. Surely Fancy wouldn't let her understandable prejudices against him keep her from informing him if Laurel should have a problem with which he could help. The message seemed pretty clear: She wasn't going to forgive him; she wasn't even going to talk to him, no matter how important it was, no matter what he did.

After mulling it over fruitlessly for hours, he decided to swallow his pride and put in a call to David Greenlea. It was some

time before David got back to him, and then the conversation didn't last long.

"David, I've got to talk to Laurel."

"Not a good idea, not today."

"This is important, David. It has to do with Barry."

"It'll have to wait anyway, Edward. Barry has a serious ear infection. They hardly slept last night. I'll be taking them dinner later, and I'll tell Laurel then that you need to speak to her. But, Ed, don't be surprised if you don't hear from her. Now I've got rounds to make." With that he hung up.

Ed figured David would be with her tonight. Tomorrow he'd press her for a meeting. He figured he'd better be prepared to find her other legal representation after that. No doubt that would be best for both of them, but he couldn't deny the pain the thought caused him.

When the phone rang just past midnight, he was so sleep muddled, he first wondered why the receptionist didn't get it. Then he sat up in bed, glanced at the luminous dial of his bedside clock, switched on the light and caught the phone just before the answering machine kicked in. His mind was in such a state that he hadn't yet connected this midnight call with any reason for alarm when he heard David Greenlea identifying himself. His next words threw Edward into a panic.

"Laurel's in the emergency room."

Ed was halfway to his pants before he thought to snatch up the abandoned receiver and ask which emergency room. The county hospital, of course. Where else, with David on the staff there? He didn't bother to ask why David was calling *him*, or anything else. He just jumped into a pair of jeans, pulled on the first shirt that fell to hand, grabbed his athletic shoes and was out the door in a heartbeat.

David was waiting for him just inside the hospital's sliding doors—David and what looked like half of Dallas. Edward took in the chaotic scene and exclaimed, "Some kind of catastrophe?"

David glanced around in surprise. "No. No, no, just your normal, run-of-the-mill Wednesday night/Thursday morning variety."

Edward's eyes rounded. David smiled sympathetically. "You should see it around here on the weekend."

"No thanks. Where is Laurel? Is she hurt, sick, what?"

David's face grew taut and grim. "He hit her, Ed. The son of a bitch hit her—and he took Barry."

Edward felt as if he'd been hit in the solar plexus. He bent forward as if absorbing the blow. "I'll kill him" were the first words out of his mouth. "Oh, God, this is all my fault" were the next. Neither of them had mentioned a name, but they both knew the culprit could be none other than Bryce Miller.

David grabbed Edward by the arm, his demeanor and tone that of the stern professional. "There isn't time for that. She needs you now. She was absolutely hysterical when I got here."

That in itself was alarming. "She was that bad, bad enough they wanted a psychiatrist?"

"No, no." David shook his head impatiently and started off across the room, motioning Edward to follow. "I was in here with her just this morning to treat Barry's ear infection. He's cutting teeth. It's a standard complication. Anyway, I guess it got around the hospital, so when Laurel named me as her doctor, they put two and two together. Normally they'd have discounted that, knowing I'm psychiatrics."

"How'd she get here?"

"Someone in the apartment complex heard the commotion and called 911. The police insisted on bringing her in, but so far, Laurel's refused to talk to them. She says she won't talk to anyone but you."

That gave Edward a surge of determination. He calmed himself, and the years of training and experience kicked in. He had himself well in hand by the time David whisked back a curtain, revealing Laurel sitting dejectedly on the side of a gurney. Then she looked up, and rage unlike anything he'd ever known utterly defeated his professionalism for several minutes. Rage and heartsick concern. Automatically he stepped forward and opened his arms. She flew into them, sobbing against his shoulder. He held her tight.

"It's all right, honey. He won't get away with this, I promise you. Whatever it takes, whatever I have to do, he'll pay. I swear it."

"I don't care about that," she sobbed, looking up at him.

He cradled her delicate face in his hands and tilted it gently. She had a lump below her right eye and a scrape above it. Her lip had been busted, and her nose and chin scratched. He could see the beginnings of bruises. "I care," he said, feeling his own eyes begin to burn.

She caught hold of his wrist. "I have to tell you something."

"Anything."

"B-Barry, he-he's mine!"

"I know, honey." He didn't say how, and she didn't ask.

"Bryce t-took him. He was c-crying. He's sick, and he needs me!"

"We'll get him back."

She seized on that assurance just as she seized handsful of his shirt. "Yes. Get him back. We have to get him back!" She swayed on her feet. Edward dropped his hands away from her face and scooped her up into his arms, carrying her back to the gurney.

"Listen to me," he said, laying her down and leaning close. "This is important, honey. Is Bryce's sister Barry's real mother?"

"I'm his real mother!" she exclaimed hotly. "Avon gave birth to him, but that's all! I've had him since the day he was born, even before. She stayed with me while she was pregnant, because she didn't want Bryce to know. I brought them home from the hospital and took care of them. Then one morning I woke up and she was gone. She left a note saying that she knew I'd take good care of him, that I'd be a better mother than her and that she wouldn't worry knowing that he was with me."

"Do you still have that note?"

"Yes. I keep it in Barry's baby book."

"Good. What else did it say?"

"Only that she was sorry and that she had a little insurance policy that she was going to make over to me so that he could have it if anything happened to her."

"Wonderful! Better and better. Now then, I want you to give a statement to the police."

She lurched up onto her elbows. "But Bryce said if I did that I'd never get Barry back!"

"I don't care what Bryce said. I'm the attorney here, and I'm telling you that we have to give a statement to the police—and then we're going to file a complaint and swear out a warrant and petition for a restraining order."

"He said he'd take Barry and go away where I couldn't find him."

"He's not taking Barry anywhere," Edward promised her. "As God is my witness, Laurel, you'll have that baby back in your arms before breakfast."

Her wide green eyes searched his and obviously found what they needed to see. She nodded wearily. Edward turned to David, who stood silently by the curtain. "Can you get someone in here?"

"The police officer who brought her in is waiting in the lounge. I'll send someone for him."

"Thanks."

Ed watched him walk away, then pulled a chair close and sat down next to the small bed, taking Laurel's hand in his. There was so much he wanted to say, but he didn't know where to begin. She surprised him by speaking first.

"I'm sorry, Edward."

"What have you got to be sorry for? I'm the one who betrayed your trust. Laurel, I can't tell you how very sorry I am that I ever even questioned your mental stability. I should have known better."

"It wasn't your fault. I know I've done some stupid things."

"In the past," he told her, "and not so stupid when you take everything into consideration. Even David agrees with me."

She laughed at that, accompanied by winces. "He's been a good friend to me, Edward."

"I know. And to tell you the truth, I'm a little jealous."

Those gemlike eyes sparkled. "Really?"

He nodded and confessed, "I guess, despite everything I've done and said, I've wanted all along to play the part of your white knight—no pun intended."

"No pun," she said, squeezing his hand, "just an apt description."

He leaned close and brushed back a wisp of her pale hair. His

heart was beating with slow, sure strokes. He'd never been so certain of anything as what he was about to say. "Laurel, sweetheart, I—"

"Ms. Miller?"

Edward swallowed the words with a growl and looked over at the policeman. He got up and offered his hand. "I'm Mrs. Miller's attorney, Edward White."

They shook hands. "Officer Howard."

"She'd be glad to make a statement now. Thank you for your patience."

The policeman nodded and brought up a clipboard. For the next several minutes, Edward stood at Laurel's side while she answered questions in a soft, weary voice. When that was done and the policeman left to file his report, a nurse came in with papers to be explained and signed, releasing Laurel into Edward's care.

"Do you have insurance, ma'am?"

Laurel shook her head. "No, but—"

The nurse waved away further concern. "That's all right. Dr. Greenlea has taken care of everything. I just thought I'd ask."

Laurel looked at Edward in surprise. Edward turned to the nurse. "Where is Dr. Greenlea?"

"I couldn't say. Home, I suppose, but he left this for you."

She slipped a folded piece of paper from her pocket and passed it to Edward. He unfolded it and read, "She belongs with you. I know now that you'll treat her right. Call me if I can help in any way. David."

Edward pinched the bridge of his nose. Mark down one more error in judgment that he'd made. David Greenlea was a decidedly more decent fellow than he'd ever given him credit for being, and it was obvious that he truly cared for Laurel. Maybe she didn't know that. If he was half the man Greenlea was, he'd tell her himself.

"What does he say?" Laurel asked.

Ed folded the note and put it in his pocket. "Just that we should call if we need him." So much for measuring up to David Greenlea's standard. But he wouldn't worry about that now. First things first. And the first thing was to get her settled someplace safe.

One place came immediately to mind. "I have to make a phone call, honey. Will you be all right here for a minute or two?"

She assured him that she would be, and he walked out into a hallway where he'd seen a pay phone. In his earlier haste, he'd forgotten his cell phone. He dialed up the Sugarmans. The phone rang only once before Parker's gruff voice greeted him. Ed apologized for the hour, then quickly brought Parker up to speed, finishing with "I wouldn't ask, good buddy, but I've got an important matter to take care of, and I don't want Laurel left alone while I'm gone."

"You're going after the baby," Parker surmised correctly.

"I have to."

"I understand," Parker said. "Need some help? I seem to remember you kept the car running for me once."

"Would Ken shoot me if I said yes?"

"You forget that she's been in Laurel's shoes."

"No, I don't, and Laurel won't ever forget it, either, after tonight."

"I'll put clean sheets on the bed in the guest room," Parker said and hung up.

When Edward told Laurel where they were headed, once they were in the car, she protested. It was too late, an imposition, and finally, "Have they changed their minds about me?"

He was surprised. "No. There was nothing to change. Parker thought I was the crazy one from the beginning, and Kendra simply didn't know you. They both feel bad about what happened, but please don't hold it against them. I'm the one to blame."

"I thought we'd dealt with that," she said quietly.

He reached across the car and took her hand in his. "I'll make it up to you, I swear."

"Just bring my baby home," she said. "I don't care about the rest anymore. He can have it all. I just want Barry home."

"That's exactly what he wants you to feel and say, Laurel," Edward pointed out. "You leave everything to me, all right?"

She nodded, and he marveled at the trust in her expression. God, could he get lucky enough to work this out? He still hadn't told her that he was the one who had spilled her secret to Bryce. Pretty soon now she was going to start wondering how Bryce had

learned about his nephew, and when he had to tell her... He didn't even want to think about what might happen then. *First things first*, he reminded himself. Kendra was practically waiting for them in the doorway. She took one look at Laurel and threw her arms around her. "You poor thing! Don't you worry. Come in and let me make you something to drink. What drugs did they give you at the hospital? We don't want any negative reactions. Let's get an ice pack on that cheek."

Laurel pulled out the papers they'd given her at the hospital and put her head together with Kendra, deciphering them. Edward pulled Parker aside. "You sure you want in on this? Bryce is no grandmotherly baby-sitter."

"All the more reason not to go alone."

"Thanks. I appreciate that, and frankly, I need someone around to make sure I don't kill the guy."

Parker sucked in a deep breath and looked over in Laurel's direction. "I hope I'm up to that."

"So do I."

Kendra offered Laurel a fresh nightgown. Edward realized then that she was wearing that little cotton job over a pair of gray knit pants and under a denim jacket. His mouth went dry, remembering how she'd looked sans pants and jacket, and then he realized that must have been exactly how she'd looked to Bryce Miller when he'd forced his way into the apartment and started hitting her. God help him, he *would* kill the worm. To distract himself from his anger, he offered to go by Laurel's apartment to pick up some necessities. She gave him her keys and tried to suggest a list of things to get, but the drugs they'd given her at the hospital and Kendra's herbal tea, compounded by the drain on her emotions, combined to rob her of her last shreds of energy. She was almost asleep sitting up. Kendra took her off to bed, promising her that Parker would know quite well what to bring for her and the baby. She cast a last, lingering look in Edward's direction, a look so full of trust and hope that it nearly brought him to his knees.

He didn't realize how strongly he'd reacted until he felt himself gasping for breath and Parker's hand on his shoulder.

"Welcome to the wild world of love, buddy mine," Parker

told him. "Don't worry. Kendra will take care of her tonight, and you'll take care of everything else in time."

"I hope so," Edward said, his voice thick with emotion, and then he told Parker what he'd done.

Parker thought a moment and shook his head. "Well, it won't help to stand around here worrying about it. We have work to do."

"Right," Edward agreed. "First things first." It was becoming his mantra.

They went to the apartment first. Parker advised Ed that he'd need diapers and a few changes of clothes for the boy, a bottle or two, a small bag of toys. They found his medicine in the cabinet and the car seat at the foot of the crib. Parker decided that they should take those things, too. Ed himself went through Laurel's things and chose some jeans and shorts, a casual dress or two, a variety of blouses and tops. He dug through her underthings, doggedly choosing the least provocative things and tossing them into the bag he'd found in the closet. He added a pair of silk pajamas, a nightshirt and a thin cotton bathrobe—all summerweight things. When he came to the bathroom, he again let Parker advise him and wound up with a hair dryer, brush and comb, a small bag of cosmetics that sat on the counter next to the sink, a stick of deodorant, shampoo and conditioner, a spray bottle of some kind of hair stiffener and a toothbrush and tube of paste.

"That ought to hold her for a day or two."

Parker looked at the shoe boxes stacked nearly ceiling to floor and said, "I think you may have forgotten something."

It took Ed ten minutes to find a simple pair of sneakers and a pair of frilly house slippers, pink satin with some sort of feather stuck to the toes. They wagged it all down to the car and stowed everything in the trunk except the safety seat, which Parker expertly belted into place in the back seat.

From there, they drove to the Heffington manse. Motion detector lights flashed on as they drove up to the house. Both men got out, leaving the car doors open and the engine running and walked up to the front door. They could hear a baby in deep distress screaming at the top of his lungs and a man and woman shouting at each other. Parker pounded on the door, but Edward

wasn't waiting to be let in. He tried the door, found it was locked and calmly kicked it down.

"Ed!"

But he wasn't waiting around to be told to calm down—or for the police to show. He had little doubt that he'd set off an silent alarm. He strode into the entry, got his bearings and turned toward the foot of the stairs. He met Bryce Miller and the skinny maid coming down. Bryce broke off yelling at her to "do something about that damned kid!" and started yelling at Edward to "get the hell out of my house!"

Edward helped himself to a handful of Miller's T-shirt and nearly yanked him out of his jockey shorts. Parker came up on Edward's right and said, "I'll find the kid. Don't kill him too bad until I get back."

The "maid" jerked her head toward the right. "I'll take you to him. He ain't done nothing but cry since he got here."

"You're supposed to be helping me!" Bryce bawled at her.

She bawled right back. "I told you I don't know nothing about kids!" She shook her head, apparently uncaring that Bryce was likely to get his face broken in several places during the next few minutes, and started back up the stairs, Parker hurrying her ahead of him.

Edward was free to concentrate fully on Bryce Miller, and Bryce wisely did not appreciate the look in Edward's pale blue eyes. "I didn't mean to hurt her!" he exclaimed. "I lost my temper. You can understand. She kept my nephew from me all these months and—"

He never finished the sentence. Having Edward's fist in his mouth made speech difficult. He was crawling up the stairs backward when Parker reappeared with Barry. The poor little tyke's face was swollen from his tears. His nose was running and he had crammed his fist into his mouth to hold back the howls while he tried to make sense of this latest business. He cocked his little head at Edward, red hair standing up straight as if from an electric charge, and seemed to recognize him. At least he seemed to know with whom he'd last seen this big guy. "Mama?" he said, between gasps.

"That's right, pal. We're taking you to Mama," Edward told him while Parker attempted to smooth down his hair.

"She's not his mother," Bryce spat.

Edward motioned for Parker to take the child downstairs, waited patiently until they were on their way, then reached down and yanked Bryce Miller onto his feet. "Listen up, scum," he said, getting right in Miller's face. "I know you weren't bright enough to act on your own. Left to your own devices you certainly wouldn't saddle yourself with anybody's kid, nephew or no. So this message is for Kennison. He went over the line on this one, and he's going to pay for it. That's a promise."

The maid folded her arms and harrumphed. "I told him it was stupid. Let Abe take care of the kid then, I said, but did he listen? Does he ever?"

"Shut your face, Pamela!" Bryce snarled.

"You just try to make me, you worm. I'll tell everything I know, and where'll you be then? I'll tell you where. In the pen, that's where!"

Edward grinned. "I think it's unanimous, Miller. You're a new life-form, something lower than pond scum. Pond scum will look good next to you if you ever lay hands on another woman again. You hear me?"

"I'm not afraid of you," Bryce said in a wavering voice. "I'll call the police."

"You do that," Edward advised. "It'll save them having to come find you. The warrant should be just about ready."

"You won't get away with this!" Bryce said.

"Oh, I think I will," Ed said and calmly bloodied his nose. He bent over and wiped his knuckles on Miller's T-shirt, flexed his fingers and took a business card from his wallet, flipping it at Pamela. "Just in case you need someone to talk to."

She shrugged. "We'll see."

Ed looked down at Bryce, who was writhing on the stairs, holding his nose and howling like he was dying. "I wouldn't stay around here. Sooner or later, he'll be wanting a punching bag to take out his frustrations on."

She sneered at the pathetic excuse for a man on the floor. "He ever hits me, I'll cut off his—"

Edward put back his head and laughed. "You do that."

She grinned and slipped the card into the pocket on the front of the man's shirt she was wearing, presumably Bryce's. "I can forget what happened to that door if you want."

Edward chuckled and started down the stairs, calling back over his shoulder, "Don't bother. I won't mind paying the damages, not one bit."

The last thing he heard was her foot connecting with some part of Miller's anatomy and her strident voice saying, "Now there's a man. Not like you, always skittering around after that cold ghoul Kennison."

She went on, but Edward had heard plenty, more than enough, in fact. And he could still use both hands. All in all, a very satisfying experience.

Chapter Twelve

Laurel awoke with a jerk, disoriented, aching, alarmed. Where was she? What had happened? It all came back in a rush. Bryce ripping the screen out of her window when she wouldn't open the door, stepping in, walking across her folded-out bed and to the crib, where she'd taken up a protective stance, his shouts, her begging, the baby's screams, the slap first and then his fist, and finally the struggle at the door, being shoved down repeatedly, Barry screaming for his mama as Bryce carried him away from her. She had found herself on her knees on the landing, hugging her middle to keep herself from flying apart. She remembered the neighbors gathering around her, the sirens in the distance, and realizing that the high, keening sound was coming from her own throat. Her worst nightmare had come to pass. Bryce had taken her son.

But then Edward had come, promising that all would be well, and somehow she had believed him. She remembered his arms about her and the warmth of his voice, exactly as she had imagined they would be. The rest was pretty blurry. She knew that she was at the Sugarmans' and remembered Kendra's herbal tea

and being put to bed as if she were the child, and she remembered that Edward had promised her she'd be back with Barry before breakfast. She squeezed her eyes shut and prayed, then tried to lull herself back to sleep, but it was no use. She could feel herself trembling from the inside out, and her mind would not block images of Barry reaching for her, his face contorted in fear. After long, restless minutes, she got up and looked around the small, elegant room.

Her bathrobe had been laid across the foot of the bed, and a pair of her slippers sat side by side at the foot. Edward. She felt warmed, despite the cold knot of fear in her stomach. Donning the robe over her borrowed gown, she visited the tiny bathroom, then put her feet into the slippers and stepped out into the hallway. Taking a moment to orient herself, she tiptoed toward the door to the living area, making her way by the half-light of early morning. The house was still and silent. She moved out onto the columned room and wandered toward the kitchen. To her left, she spied a soft, flickering, bluish light.

Remembering that the Sugarmans had referred to a multipurpose room, she moved to the partially open door and peeked inside. The flickering light came from the television across the room near the fireplace. Someone had gone off to bed and left the TV playing. With the sound turned down, they had probably forgotten about it. She knew how that was. Several times lately, she'd lain in bed alone at night and watched the silent screen while Barry lay sleeping nearby, only to wake and find that it was morning and the television played on. She walked around the end of the big overstuffed sofa and switched off the power. When she turned, it was to discover the most precious sight she'd ever seen.

Edward lay on his back on the sofa, knees drawn up to accommodate his height, one arm dangling over the side, knuckles on the carpeted floor. His short hair was mashed flat, and his jaws and chin were covered with a dark, rough shadow. His mouth was slightly ajar beneath the heavy brush of his mustache. He looked utterly charming, but what took her breath away and brought instant tears to her eyes was the sight of her small son cuddled against Edward's chest, his bottom tucked into the curve

of Edward's arm. He was on his stomach, and the drool from his mouth had wet a spot the size of Laurel's fist on Edward's shirt.

Laurel covered her mouth with her hand to stifle the sob of pure joy that immediately rose from her throat. He was here, sleeping peacefully, safe, well, and she knew exactly whom she had to thank for it. She went down on her knees next to the couch and lifted Edward's hand in both of hers. He jerked slightly and moaned. His knuckles were scraped and swollen, and she had no doubt how that had happened. Tears of gratitude rolled down her cheeks. She kissed those bruised knuckles, feeling the slight pull and sting of her busted lip.

When she lifted her gaze, it was to find him staring at her, his sleepy face unusually solemn. "You brought him home," she said softly.

His hand turned in hers and lifted free to cup the back of her head. As naturally as breathing, he pulled her to him, and just as naturally, she went up on her knees and bent her head. Their lips met, gently at first, all softness and comfort. Then she sifted one hand into the thick, springy pelt of hair on the top of his head, while the other slipped up his prickly throat to the underside of his chin. The pressure of their mouths increased proportionally, as did the rasp of his beard and the prickle of his mustache, and she shifted the slant of hers to accommodate the tiny split near one corner of her upper lip. Edward moaned softly, and the hand at the back of her head became an arm curled around her neck. His tongue slid into her mouth, and her own welcomed it with languid undulations and curling strokes. It was like swallowing fire and being licked by it in every sensitive spot in her body. It was lightning followed by bright, leaping flames that roared quickly out of control. Overwhelmed, she sat back on her heels with a gasp, breaking the kiss, the fingers of one hand going to the split in her lip.

Edward glanced down at the little one snuggled against his chest, then back at Laurel. "Did I hurt you?" he whispered worriedly.

She shook her head, smiling behind her hand.

"You sure?"

She dropped her hand and leaned close again, bringing her mouth to his ear, where she whispered, "I'm sure."

He turned his head far to the left, until they were nose to nose. "Then why did you stop kissing me?"

She sat back again, searching for the right words. "I suppose you scare me a little," she finally admitted. "It's like turning on the faucet for a drink of water and finding yourself in a flash flood. I don't know if I swim well enough to survive it!"

He lifted his hand to stroke her cheek. "I won't let you drown, sweetheart. I promise."

Tears came to her eyes. Oh, how she wanted to believe him, but it was so hard to trust again. She grasped his wrist, amazed at its thick strength, and whispered, "What does that mean, Edward?"

He cleared his throat. "It means that I—"

Suddenly Barry squealed, curled his body in a stretch and screwed his face up in preparation for a full-blown howl. Then Laurel spoke to him, and his little eyes popped open. Howls turned to smiles. He pushed up onto his knees and elbows and literally crawled over Edward's face toward her, babbling merrily. Edward and Laurel both laughed. Then Edward bolted up, holding Barry at arm's length.

"Whew! Bad diaper!"

Laurel swept him into her arms and hugged him tight. "Oh, I'm so glad to see my sunshine boy!" She pushed him out to arm's length again. "Golly, you reek. Let's get that diaper changed." She looked at Edward, eyes shining. "Where are his things?"

"Here." Ed leaned over the end of the couch and pulled up a bag crammed full of baby paraphernalia. Laurel sat down and laid Barry on the cushions. Talking and tickling, she got him undressed and changed. He alternated between laughing and crying, between jabbering incoherently and cramming his fist into his mouth.

"He did that last night," Edward commented.

"Stick his fist in his mouth? Means he's hungry, poor munchkin."

"No, I mean babbling."

"Oh. He's been doing that for a while now. I think he knows exactly what's he's saying and doesn't understand why we don't."

"Really? Well, if that's so, he's sure got a lot to say."

"Of course," she said. "He's very bright."

Edward's mustache twitched. "You just have to look at his hair to know that."

She shot him a withering look. "I mean that he's very intelligent."

"Oh, well, of course. Goes without saying. Just last night we discussed Blackwell's theory of common law, and he made quite an impassioned argument for infants' rights."

Laurel put on a look of sheer horror. "Oh, no, not a budding lawyer!"

He made a grimace. "Better than a comedian."

"You're sure about that?"

The banter died on the air between them. His brow furrowed. "Actually," he said, "you have good reason to feel that way, and once I tell you just what I've done, you'll probably have more."

She arched a brow at him. What he didn't know, what she had held inside for some time now was that she couldn't help forgiving him whatever he might do. Quietly, her gaze on Barry, she said, "You brought my son back to me. Everything else pales in comparison to that."

"You won't think so when you understand that it was my fault he was taken to begin with," he said quietly.

Laurel cocked her head. "What do you mean?"

He lifted his gaze then, and she read apology and regret there. He licked his lips. "Bryce found out about him from me."

That seemed so unlikely that for a moment she merely blinked at him. "I don't understand."

"I came over to the apartment," he said rather harshly. "I wanted to talk to you, to apologize again. Your window was open. I heard Barry calling you Mama. I finally put two and two to-gether...."

"I should've told you," she said regretfully. "I meant to, but I kept putting it off, and then it didn't seem important anymore."

"Yeah," he rumbled, "and that was my fault, too."

"Let's forget about that," she said quickly. "I probably over-reacted anyway."

"No, you didn't," he said on a sigh, "and you may never speak to me again when I've told you the whole of it."

"I doubt that," she said lightly, pulling Barry onto her lap and smoothing down his hair, only to watch it rise again with a will of its own.

Edward put his hands to his hips and swallowed, obviously working up his courage. "I don't know what happened to me," he said hesitantly. "When I realized that Barry belonged to you, all I could think was..." He closed his eyes. "I don't know what I was thinking. The most important question seemed to be who the father was. I figured it was either Bryce or some other guy you hadn't told me about and—I don't know, I kind of lost it. I went right to Bryce and asked him. It was obvious that he didn't know anything about it. So I..." He gulped. "I went to Danny Hardacre."

She had been carefully taking it all in. Now she carefully, methodically thought it all over and drew some conclusions. "Danny told you about Avon."

"Yes, and that was when I realized what I'd done, and I actually went back to the apartment to explain and warn you, but you were asleep, and I figured it could wait until morning. I left a note in the door asking you to call me."

"I didn't see it," she said. "I guess it got blown away."

"Still, I should have followed up. Even if you didn't want to talk to me, I should have made you listen. I should have realized that Bryce would figure it out and call Kennison."

"Then it was Kennison who put him up to taking the baby?"

Ed nodded. "It's what I would have done—did do, in fact, when it was Parker and Darla. That way, he'd have physical custody. You'd have to sue him, instead of vice versa. It's the stronger position. Bryce went too far, though, forcing his way in and laying hands on you."

"Do you think he'll sue for custody now?"

He looked her square in the eye. "I don't doubt it. Kennison will see to it. It's their biggest gun, Laurel. They'll threaten to

use what they've got to prove your incompetence and Bryce's blood relationship to get you to drop your action for control of your inheritance.''

"And it'll work,'' Laurel said softly, hugging Barry to her. "It's been my biggest fear all along. Even with Avon's written preference, I don't see how I can win. I've given them too much ammunition and—''

Ed snapped his fingers. "Holy cow, I forgot about that letter!''

"Is it that important?'' she asked, her eyes wide.

"Sweetheart, it's our ace in the hole, especially since she mentions the benefits of that life insurance policy.''

"What difference does that make?''

"The difference it makes,'' he told her, "is that it constitutes a last will and testament, which makes it a valid court document in Texas. Handwritten wills are almost ironclad in this state, especially if they're notarized.''

"This one wasn't.''

"It's still valid,'' he stated flatly, "and we've got to go after it. I won't rest easy until I have it in hand.''

She looked down at the baby, who was beginning to fuss again and squirm around. "Suppose it'd be all right if I scrambled an egg for the baby?''

"Sure. In fact, I'll do it, if you want.''

"You could start it, if you don't mind, while I jump into some clothes.''

"No problem, give me a sec to wash up.''

She nodded and concentrated on the baby as Ed disappeared into the powder room. She poured some medicine down Barry while Edward took care of his most immediate needs. The poor little tyke was so hungry, he smacked his lips together in anticipation of more. Digging around in the diaper bag, she found a plastic margarine tub that she had packed with dry cereal for the baby-sitter to give Barry as a snack. She fed the teeny balls of corn to him one at a time, much to his frustration.

Edward returned a few moments later and picked up Barry and the cereal tub to carry them into the kitchen. Laurel hurried back to her room to dig through the things he'd brought her and find what she needed. It took longer than she wanted, but finally she

was dressed in jeans and a tank top, her hair combed, her teeth brushed, her feet encased in her sneakers. By the time she got to the kitchen, Barry had downed the scrambled egg and was trying out his first bowl of cereal with milk. Edward had him sitting in the middle of the table, a dish towel tied around his neck, and was spooning the mixture into his mouth, the milk running out the corners more often than not, much to Barry's delight. He somehow managed to chew and jabber and at the same time, keep his mouth open for more. Laurel laughed to see the two of them like that. Edward looked up.

"What? Am I doing it all wrong?"

"You're doing just fine," she told him, folding her arms and leaning back against the counter. He kept it up until Barry turned his head away, full to his ears, and reached for his mother. Laurel swung him onto her hip, dabbed at his face with the dish towel, took it off him, rinsed it in the sink and folded it, all with one hand. When she turned back to Edward, it was to find him finishing up Barry's cereal. Something about that, the intimacy and acceptance of it, tugged at her heartstrings. She swallowed a lump in her throat and said, "You must be hungry, too. Shall I fix you something?"

He shook his head and rose to put the empty bowl in the sink. "I'll keep. Let's get after that document."

Laurel nodded. Together they started for the front door. "Should we leave a note for the Sugarmans?"

"Naw, if we hurry we can be back before they get up. They sleep in mornings when Kendra has a late shift."

In the entryway, Laurel paused. "We need Barry's safety seat."

"It's already in the car," he said, opening the door.

They went out into brilliant sunshine. Barry hid his face against Laurel's breast until she handed him into the back seat of the car. Ed took him, put him in his seat, fastened the belt clip and patted him on the head before backing out and closing the door. Barry put his fingers in his mouth and began to swing one foot as if patiently waiting for the parade to begin. They got in and fastened their belts. Edward slid the key into the ignition switch, then

paused. He let his hand fall away from the key and leaned back, turning his head to look at Laurel.

"You're not upset with me," he said finally, and she knew it was as much question as statement. She shook her head.

"No."

"Why not?"

She felt the smile that tipped up her lips and lifted a finger to the place where it still pulled a little. She dropped her hand to her lap and lifted her chin, announcing, "Because you were jealous."

His eyes held hers for a long time, and then he reached out and clamped a hand around the nape of her neck, pulling her toward him. His mouth covered hers, sliding away from the corner where that little split was. He kept it light, flicking his tongue against the whole corner of her mouth, nipping at the underside of her upper lip with the edges of his teeth. Finally he sighed, slid his hand through her hair and sat back. She rubbed a hand over her chin and cheek and, smiling, said, "You need a shave."

He started the car and put it in reverse, then scraped his fingernails over his chin and throat, grinning at the resulting rasp. "What, this? This is just a little morning shadow. Give it a few days and see what you think then."

"I'll think you need a shave!" she said.

"Bad enough to shave me yourself?" he asked innocently, but the twinkle in his eye gave him away.

She laughed. "We'll see."

He winked, grinning, and started them on their way.

He carried his briefcase upstairs, pausing with her to tell the baby-sitter that Barry wouldn't be staying with her today. The pleasant woman made a big fuss about Laurel's bruises, which seemed to embarrass Laurel, and exclaimed her delight at knowing Barry was back where he belonged. At her prompting, Barry gave Libby Martinez messy, openmouthed kisses readily enough but held on tight to his mother's neck. Assured that he wasn't going to be dropped off, he relaxed and waved bye-bye as they climbed the remaining stairs to Laurel's apartment.

Laurel took a look around at the clutter that first Bryce had

strewn about and then he and Parker and said, "Heavens, it'll take hours to straighten this place."

Ed ducked his head apologetically. "Sorry, but we deal with this later. Right now just gather up whatever you think you'll need for the next few days."

"Why?" she asked in surprise.

"You can't stay here alone. It's not safe."

She bit her lip, thinking. "Fancy will put us up a few days."

"Will Fancy defend you against Bryce Miller if he comes around?"

She shot him an almost amused look. "Fancy will put a bullet in him."

"Oh, that's all we need," he said. "Bad enough I punched out his lights last night."

She smiled. "I assumed as much."

He shrugged. "Not the smartest move I've ever made—but I'd do it again."

Suddenly her brow furrowed. "Edward, you aren't in trouble, are you?"

He grimaced and slid an arm around her. "I figure we'll trade off assault charges," he said, "though I'd rather not. The rat ought to pay for what he did to you." He slid a thumb over the discoloration on her cheek. It wasn't as livid as he'd feared it would be, but it still made him want to make macaroni out of Bryce Miller.

She closed a fist in the back of his shirt, saying, "You can't go to jail, Ed. I won't let you. I need you too much."

He couldn't help that his smile was a little smug. "I know. That's the only reason I'll agree to the trade-off, but I'm going to make the son of a... I'll make him sweat over it first."

To his absolute delight, she laid her head against his chest. Barry mimicked her, doing the same but turning his face up to gaze at him with those big golden, trusting eyes. Ed's throat closed. Laurel said, "Don't put yourself at risk, please."

He wrapped his arms around them, thinking that he had too much to protect now to take chances. After some time, he cleared his throat and said, "Listen, I have an extra room. I want you two to stay at my place."

She pulled back in apparent shock. "We can't stay with you!"

"Why not?"

She stepped back, a hand going to her head as if he'd thrown her thoughts into a jumble. She looked around at her things, muttering, "We can't impose like that."

He made an impatient sound. "I won't rest for a single moment if I don't know you're somewhere safe. Where safer than with me?"

Her face was full of dismay. "Edward, I can't."

"Why not?" She turned away, but he followed, pressing her. "Give me one reason why not." She shook her head. "Laurel, I owe you this much."

"No!"

He turned her to face him. "Please, Laurel, it's the best answer for all of us. I want you near. I have to know the two of you are safe and together. Why not do it? Why not?"

She lifted tear-filled eyes to him. Her bottom lip quivered, and she whispered, "Edward, I'm already more than half in love with you. If I move in with you now, I'll—"

He didn't let her finish. Instead, he wrapped his arms around her and kissed her for all she was worth, ever mindful of that tear in the corner of her lip. He felt like shouting, like singing, like weeping. He broke apart their mouths finally, saying, "I'm not taking no for an answer."

She nodded, and he snatched Barry out of her arms and tossed him lightly into the air, catching him again with ease. Barry looked shocked, even a little frightened. Then he grinned and tried to throw himself up again. Laughing, Edward indulged him, stopping only because Laurel gasped and put a hand over her mouth to keep from ordering him to stop. He knew she didn't want to be overprotective or make him think she didn't trust him with this sort of thing.

"Get the letter," he said, parking Barry on his shoulder, where he promptly filled both hands with hair, holding on so tight that Ed could feel his scalp separating from his skull.

Laurel turned away to rummage in the overstuffed closet, coming out again with a blue baby book, which she quickly flipped through until she found the letter stuck behind some photos. Un-

folding it, she set the book aside then came to hand the letter to Edward. He read it over, well satisfied with the contents. It was even dated. Barry had incrementally loosened his hold on Edward's hair while this was going on, so it was no problem to hand him down to his mother while he placed the letter in his briefcase for safekeeping.

That done, he asked what she wanted to take with her. She grabbed the blue book then looked at the crib.

"Think we could take his bed? He'd sleep better nights."

Ed walked over and took a look. "Got a screwdriver? I think I can remove a few screws and break it down in parts small enough to get into the trunk of the car."

She dug through a drawer in the minuscule kitchen and came up with a small screwdriver. He went to work. She sat down in the rocker to play with Barry. After a bit she said, "I never really thanked you for the furniture."

"Don't need thanks," he said without looking up. "Besides, you're going home with me, and that's what counts."

Another period of silence passed, and then she said, "How will I get to and from work? Is there a bus stop near by? And what about Barry? It'll be so much harder to get him to and from the sitter."

He put down the screwdriver in exasperation. "None of that matters," he said. "You shouldn't be going to work anyway, and you certainly shouldn't be riding the bus."

"But I have to work," she said.

He picked up the screwdriver again. "I don't see why."

"They'll be shorthanded at the diner."

He rolled his eyes, then lifted away the side of the bed and placed it on the floor before turning to face her, his hands on his hips. "They'll manage."

She frowned. "But how am I going to pay my bills if I don't work? At least half my salary is tips!"

He shrugged. "We'll expense them."

"But that only works if we win. Otherwise, it'll come out of your pocket."

"We'll win," he said. If they didn't, he could afford to take

care of the two of them and had every intention of doing so, but now wasn't the time to explain that.

She sent him a doubtful look, but she said no more as he continued taking apart the bed and then carted it downstairs, load by load, to put into the car. Finally they were ready to go. Laurel looked around the single room as if for the last time, and if Edward had his way, it would be. He put his hands on her shoulders and squeezed comfortingly. He already knew what had to come eventually. It would solve all their problems, even tilt the scales in her favor from a legal standpoint, but even though it had been her idea originally, he didn't think she was quite ready to face it just yet. Oddly enough, it was an idea he welcomed, despite his initial reaction. He dropped a kiss onto the top of her head, wrapping an arm around her and Barry when she relaxed against him.

"We have to go, honey," he said gently. "I have important work to do."

She nodded and tilted her head back to look up at him. "I know. It's just all happening so fast."

"I guess that's how it's supposed to happen," he said, "but I'll admit, it takes some getting used to. It did me."

She half turned and searched his eyes. "Are you sure about this, Edward? Really sure?"

He tilted her head with his hand in order to kiss the corner of her mouth, then planted a kiss on Barry's forehead for good measure. "Very sure."

He opened the door, and she walked through without a backward glance. *Very sure,* he told himself once more, so sure that he never intended for her to set foot in this place ever again.

He drove her first to the diner, at her insistence. There much was made about the condition of her face and Edward's bravery. He felt like a fraud, but when he tried to explain, Laurel elbowed him neatly in the ribs and changed the subject.

"We're going to be away for a few days," Laurel told her friends and co-workers hesitantly. "Ed doesn't think it's safe for us to stay at the apartment, at least not until the restraining order comes through."

"That's right," he said, "at least."

Fancy immediately offered her place. "You know you can al-

ways stay with me, sugar, and don't worry about being safe. I keep a loaded gun in my bedside table.''

"I hope you have a permit for that," Edward said.

Fancy grimaced. "Lawyers."

Laurel changed the subject once again. "Ed has a spare room at his place, and, um, I guess we'll be staying there since we'll be working a lot on the case from now on."

"A lot," Edward echoed helpfully.

Fancy narrowed her eyes but kept silent. Shorty assured Laurel that they could get a substitute for a few days. It went without saying that after that, she'd have to rethink her options, which included taking an unpaid vacation, quitting or simply coming back to work. As far as Ed was concerned, she could quit now, but he couldn't very well say that just then. So he simply put her and Barry back in the car and drove them home.

Home.

That's exactly what he wanted it to be from then on—her home. Their home.

Chapter Thirteen

It was an interesting house, an old fire station converted with Parker's talented guidance, and Edward seemed anxious for her to like it. The sturdy redbrick facade had been altered to include a covered front garden and a skylight that filtered sunshine into an otherwise dark entry complete with slide pole, around which a spiral staircase turned. The first floor consisted of garage, entry, dining area and kitchen, a dream of efficiency in cream and blue and containing the original cookstove. The furniture in the dining area was all wrong—too much chrome and black slate—and the entry, which would have made an excellent gallery, was virtually empty, save for some utilitarian hooks screwed directly into plain white walls.

The upstairs was more spacious, with living area, two bed-rooms and the largest bath she'd ever seen. Indeed, the master suite was enormous, featured a lovely redbrick fireplace and was sparsely furnished. The huge walk-in closet was very nearly empty or looked it with only Edward's clothing hanging on a single rod. Edward's utilitarian decor left much to be desired, but the place had such wonderful possibilities that Laurel itched to

start looking at fabric swatches and paint samples. She couldn't help thinking what a wonderful studio and showroom this place would make, but she reminded herself that this was a temporary situation at best. This place was not hers and never would be. Nevertheless, certain realities had to be addressed.

The extra room was smallish, with a full-size bed and a mismatched dresser taking up most of the space. Laurel had Edward shove the bed into the corner and set up Barry's crib at its foot. It was cramped, but it would do. They had to share the bathroom with Ed, but space was no problem, and she figured they could keep out of each other's way.

Keeping out of the way was exactly what she intended to do as long as she was there, while pulling her own weight as much as possible at the same time. She figured she could at least put together some meals and do some light cleaning. Other than that, it would be very nice just to spend some time with Barry. Maybe she'd have Edward take her to the library for some reading material. It had been a long time since she'd had the pleasure of reading at her leisure. Other than that, she didn't know what she was going to do with herself for the next few days, or afterward for that matter, but she didn't have to think of that this first night.

At any rate, she was too tired to think that night. The emotional and physical toll together had sapped her strength. At her insistence, she put together a light dinner from the few ingredients in Edward's kitchen. Afterward, she and Barry retired to soak in a warm tub before bedding down in the same room.

She was even more exhausted than she thought, for she woke in the middle of the night to find Edward standing over Barry's crib in nothing more than pajama bottoms, Barry fussing against his bare chest. She tossed back the covers and reached for her robe, slinging it on over her cotton shorty.

"I'm sorry he woke you," she said, coming to stand beside them. "He's teething."

Edward juggled him up and down and patted his back to no avail. "Yeah, I know. Parker explained it to me. But he didn't wake me. I was working on a brief."

"Well, I'm sorry he disturbed you, anyway," she said, gingerly lifting him from Edward's arms. She was acutely aware of

the feel of his skin and the silky crispness of the hair that covered him in a triangle drawn from chest to navel. "I'll give him his medicine and get him back to sleep."

"I could do it," he said. "You're tired."

She shook her head. "No, I can't let you do that. Besides, I want to do it. I'm just so glad to have him with me."

Edward nodded. "Okay. Where is it? I'll get it."

"The medicine? On the dresser."

She sat down on the edge of the bed with Barry, who continued to fuss, and tried to calm him. Edward brought over the medicine and the measuring tube with its spoonlike extension. He poured the dose and handed her the tube. She got the dose down Barry but only with great effort and some spillage.

"Maybe he's hungry," Edward suggested helpfully.

"Maybe."

"I'll get a bottle out of the fridge while you change him."

"You don't have to do that," she protested, but he just shook his head and left the room, returning moments later with a bottle in hand.

"Do I have to heat it?" he asked uncertainly.

"No, the cold helps his gums," Laurel said, struggling to get Barry into a fresh sleeper while he squirmed around and reached for the bottle. She thought he was reaching for the bottle, but when he had the nipple clamped firmly between his front teeth, he surprised her by reaching up again—for Edward.

Edward scooped him up and cradled him against his chest. Barry lay along Edward's arm, one leg crossed nonchalantly over the other, the bottle held securely between both hands while he drank from it. He looked like a miniature couch potato kicking back in his favorite recliner.

"There, see," Edward said proudly. "He was hungry." He tickled Barry on the chin. Barry stopped sucking up milk long enough to grin around the nipple, then went right back to filling his belly. "A growing boy needs more for supper than some mashed peas and a few noodles, doesn't he? Yeah, tomorrow we're going grocery shopping, fill up our cart with..." He looked at Laurel. "What's he eat anyway?"

"Baby food mostly," she told him, straight-faced.

His own expression said, "Duh." He grinned at Barry and teased, "This ain't no *baby*. Uh-uh, this here is a *boy*, and boys need junk food, don't they? Lots and lots of junk food." He poked Barry in the belly with his finger and got a giggle for it.

Laurel rolled her eyes. She could see a case of hero worship developing—or the infant version of such—and she wasn't sure that she liked it. She was, in fact, just a little jealous. Barry had never preferred anyone to her. She started to reach for him, only to draw back when Edward frowned and said, "You know, Parker said that a bottle might not be good for him at this age if he's prone to ear infections. He said we might need to go to a cup with handles pretty quick."

We? Laurel thought. Who did he think he was? Never mind that David had said the very same thing to her. She got up in something of a huff, plucked Barry out of his arms and climbed back onto the bed, folding her legs beneath her. Barry was looking at her as if to ask what bug had bitten her, and she made an effort to put on a normal, adoring mommy face. Apparently satisfied that it had been a momentary aberration, he turned his attention to sucking vigorously on the bottle, getting as much of it down as he could before sleep pulled him under. Greedy little love. She almost forgot about Edward standing there. Almost.

She looked up to find him leaning one shoulder against the door frame, arms folded across his broad chest, one ankle crossed over the other. He had a sappy, kind of secretive smile on his face, and he had filled his gaze with her and only her. She felt it head to toe, and it was the most unsettling feeling she'd had yet. He looked so *male* standing there, so *proprietary*. It fairly took her breath away. She swallowed with a dry throat and softly said, "He'll be asleep again soon. You can go on back to what you were doing."

"I don't want to go back to what I was doing," he said.

She was momentarily at a loss. Surely he didn't mean to just stand there and stare. Sit and talk? Play a game? Go out for coffee? She had to ask. "What do you want to do?"

His expression said, "You know." He didn't move a muscle, and yet suddenly he felt so close, imminent. He was swamping her, overwhelming her with his male presence. His voice thick

and unusually deep. He said, "I want to crawl into that bed with you and stay the night—and I don't mean to sleep." Then he sighed and swung his big body away from the wall. A single, easy step brought him up to the bed. In one lithe, fluid, completely natural motion he bent and kissed her forehead, skimmed his fingers over Barry's dimpled cheek, and then he turned and walked out of the room.

She sat there with her mouth open, feeling so much at one time that she couldn't identify any of it. She held her baby in her arms and mentally counted the hard, erratic beats of her heart. She had suspected this was coming, and yet she hadn't expected it to feel like this, part thrill, part sadness. She wouldn't be stupid enough to think that it had anything to do with love. She had to accept that it didn't. Anything else was a sure ticket to misery, not that she could escape that particular fate now. It was already too late for that. It was already love on her part. Whatever happened now, she was going to get her heart broken. That's what always happened. That's what always would happen until she learned to guard her needy heart. She looked down at the sleeping baby in her arms and told herself that this was enough. For the first time, she didn't quite believe it. But it had to be enough. It just had to be. She couldn't bear to think that even this might be taken from her.

Edward wouldn't let it happen. That much she believed. She had to. She simply had to.

Despite a restless night, she got up early enough to make Edward's breakfast. It was the least she could do. After all, he was her white knight, her help, protector. He was also better looking than he had any right to be in a crisp, closely tailored shirt of dazzling white with vertical mauve stripes a half-inch wide, and with a mauve tie with narrow white diagonals. His mauve slacks fit superbly, soft despite the small precise pleats at the waist, and broke at the instep with a generous flow of fabric. He was wearing his hair a little shorter on top than current fashion trends dictated, but on him it somehow looked right. Cleanly shaved, his mustache neatly clipped and combed, he had a dangerous look about him, a look that said, "Beware. I take care of my own."

Barry kicked the overturned pot on which he was sitting and stuffed omelet into his mouth with his fist. She had tied him to the back of the chair with a dish towel, and he apparently thought it was all great fun. His eyes lit up when Edward came into the kitchen and sat down at the small table, smelling of something exotic that Laurel could only assume was in his after-shave. She had never smelled it before. Her hands shook a little as she offered up French toast and wedges of cheese omelet, with hot coffee and milk.

Edward smiled. "Looks good." His eyes were on her even as he picked up his knife and fork. "I think I could get used to this, but you don't have to cook my breakfast. I've been living without such luxuries a long time."

"No, I want to," she insisted, sitting down in her own place.

He shrugged and tucked in, eating with flattering gusto and more than a little haste. Finished, he got up and carried his plate to the sink, where he scraped and rinsed it before stashing it in the dishwasher. Then he fetched the coffeepot and carried it to the table, where he refilled Laurel's cup and finally his own. He put the coffeepot back on the burner, and on his way to the table again took a legal pad and a pencil from a drawer. Laurel smiled at that little idiosyncrasy.

"Do all attorneys keep legal pads as kitchen equipment?"

"They do if they can't remember what they need at the grocery store without writing it down first."

"Ah."

But a grocery list wasn't on his mind. He sat down, wrote something at the top of the page and then targeted her with his gaze, saying, "Tell me everything you can think of about Avon Miller."

Laurel cocked her head. "Why?"

"Because it's better to be safe than sorry," he said succinctly. "I've already got an investigator on her trail, but he can use all the help he can get—and so can we."

A small blot of panic burst in her chest. "W-why do we need to find Avon?"

"So she can tell the court that she wants you, and not her no-good brother, to raise Barry, just in case the letter is not enough."

"Oh." That didn't feel like much comfort somehow. Laurel tried to push away the fear that threatened to explode within her, but it was too strong. She gulped and leveled pleading eyes at Edward. "What if we find her and she's changed her mind?"

Edward shook his head. "With a brother like Bryce Miller as the alternative? No, I don't think so."

"I don't mean that. I mean, what if she changes her mind about not wanting to raise Barry herself?"

Edward put his pencil down. "I didn't think of that. I mean, I just assumed... Is she likely to change her mind?"

Laurel ran a fingertip around the rim of her cup. "I don't know. I don't think so, but I keep imagining myself in her place, and I know that nothing and no one could keep me from my son, no matter how difficult it might be to raise him on my own." She turned a bleak gaze on Barry who, sensing something afoot, had paused in the act of squishing syrupy French toast between his fingers and was dividing a stare between the two of them. "Do you think, if she sees him that she'll want him with her?"

Edward's big hand moved across the table and covered hers. "I don't know, honey. I only know that if she was like you, she wouldn't have left him in the first place, and since she had, we might have a good case to keep him even over her objections. But I won't lie to you. It would be a hell of a fight."

Laurel turned her hand in his and squeezed, grateful that he would go so far with it, but that didn't really help. "I couldn't do that," she said shakily. "Avon's the one person I couldn't fight for him."

"Because you can put yourself so easily in her place," Edward surmised correctly, and she nodded. "I'll call off the search," he said. "It was just a fail-safe bid, anyway. We can make do with the letter."

But Laurel heard a note of doubt in his voice. "Wouldn't it be better to have Avon here to testify, though?"

Reluctantly he looked her squarely in the eye. "I told you that I wouldn't lie to you. The answer is yes. But we'll take our chances with the letter anyway. We may have to. We may not even find her."

She leaned her bowed head against her free hand, elbow against

the table, and tried to think. "You can't know how I've lived in fear that Avon would show up again one day and demand to have her son back, and yet, she's my friend. I care about her. I want what's best for her, too."

Edward's grip on her hand was so tight that it was almost painful, but hers was equally tight. "She left him, Laurel. She abandoned him. She doesn't deserve—"

"Yes, she does," Laurel interrupted firmly. "Don't you see? No one's ever loved her. She's young, and she was scared that she didn't know how to be a mother, but that might have changed by now. She might have come to understand that no one really knows how to be a mother. It's a learn-as-you-go project. God knows I knew nothing about it when I began."

"But you did it," Edward argued.

"I didn't have any choice."

"Yes, you did. There are social agencies in place to—"

"I'd never just dump him—"

"I know that! That's my point exactly."

She looked down at their linked hands. "I was dumped," she said softly, "in one boarding school after the other. That's the way of it, you know. The wealthy dump their unwanted kids in boarding schools. The poor resort to social services."

"Or friends they can trust," Edward pointed out. "That's what makes me think that Avon is more responsible than some. She chose you. She knows you have a heart full of love for that little boy. I'm convinced that she couldn't have chosen a better mother for her son, and I'm going to convince a judge of that, too. All right?"

Laurel found herself able to smile, to hope. "All right."

"Good. So it's your call. Do we look for Avon Miller or not?"

Laurel bit her lip, thinking, and finally said, "Look for her. If she's having second thoughts, better to know it now than later."

He nodded, and gave her hand a final squeeze. "Wise choice. Now..." He released her hand and picked up the pencil again. "Tell me everything you know about Avon Miller."

It didn't take long. There wasn't much to tell. Not even nineteen when Barry was born, Avon hadn't had much time to acquire a history. What there was, though, was mostly sad. More than a

decade younger than Bryce, she hadn't developed any real ties with her older brother, who had left home early in order to escape their abusive father. Avon's mother died when she was eleven. She'd lasted two years alone with her father before running away for the first time. Her own experiences with social services after that had soured her on that course. They'd returned her to him. She'd run away from him the last time at sixteen.

At seventeen, social services had cut her loose and she'd eventually shown up on Bryce's doorstep, but it was Laurel who had insisted that she stay, and it was Laurel who had worked hard to create a stable life for her. Only after Avon had taken off again after an argument during which Bryce had slapped the girl had Laurel fully given up on her marriage and filed for divorce.

Avon had shown up once more, this time to find that Laurel and Bryce had split up. She had gone to Danny Hardacre and talked Laurel's address out of him. After she had told Laurel that she was pregnant, Laurel had moved them to her current apartment in an attempt to honor Avon's desire to keep Bryce from finding out. Bryce apparently hadn't cared enough to look for his wayward sister, much to Laurel's relief.

Avon had talked at times about Galveston, Texas, and had said that it was there on the beach one night when Barry had been conceived. She had stated baldly that she did not know his father's identity and did not desire to know. From this and other things she had let slip, Laurel had determined that Avon had been raped, even though Avon would not confirm her suspicion or consent to any sort of counseling on the subject. Only her physical description remained to be discussed, and Laurel pointed out that Barry was a small male version of her, from the top of his red head to the bottoms of his tiny feet. Then she remembered a photo of Avon that she had stuck in his baby book. She hurried away, found it and returned with it in only moments.

Edward studied the tall, slender girl in the photo, her red hair cropped short and worn close to her head, large amber eyes full of a saucy sadness, full mouth bracketed by dimples in freckled cheeks. Her neck was long, her shoulders, exposed by the tank top she wore with faded cutoffs, knobby and thin. She wasn't a

beauty, but she wasn't unattractive, either. More than anything else, she simply looked lost and somewhat defiant.

"May I keep this for a while?"

At Laurel's nod, he put the photo in his shirt pocket. Then he tore the sheet from the pad, folded it and put that in his pocket, too. He stood and reached for the suit coat that he had draped over the back of his chair, slinging it on as he came around to Laurel's side of the table.

"Do you need anything?" he asked. "I'd planned to do the shopping this evening, but if you'd rather, you can take me to the office and keep the car."

She was surprised by the generosity of that offer, though after everything else he'd done, she couldn't think why. She shook her head. "We'll be fine until this evening. I don't think there's anything here for dinner, though."

"We'll eat out," he said, standing just inches behind her left shoulder, "and do our shopping afterward."

She twisted her head around and tilted it back in order to look at him as they spoke. "We don't have to go out. It's difficult with a baby. I'll order in, if you like."

"No," he said, resting his hands lightly on her shoulders, "I want to take the two of you out, unless it's too much trouble for you."

"No, it's fine. Whatever you want."

He leaned down until his nose touched hers. "Careful," he said, "I happen to want a lot."

She pulled back a little and twisted around in her seat. "What is it you want, Edward?"

There was that secretive little smile again, and then he was cupping the back of her head with one hand and bringing his mouth down on hers for a long, sweet, gentle kiss. She wanted to get up and wrap her arms around him, but she knew that if she did, she would give him what he apparently wanted. She supposed that she would eventually anyway, despite what it would do to her heart to leave him afterward. She owed him, after all, and in all honesty, she wanted him. It was just too much enticement to be desired this way. Just once, she wanted to know what it meant to be truly, deeply wanted by someone, even if it

was only physical for him. And what else could it be? The fact that she was a Heffington obviously meant nothing to him or anyone now that her grandmother was no longer around to wield the family name like a cudgel. She had no money at the moment, and whether or not she ever would have was anybody's guess. Her fashion expertise was his for the asking. What else but her body was there to want?

She stayed in her chair, and he eventually broke the kiss, placed another in the center of her forehead, then did the same to Barry before walking to the door. "I'll try to be home by six," he said.

"We'll be ready," she assured him.

"Call the office if you need anything."

"We'll be fine."

"And don't open the door to anyone you don't know."

"I won't."

He winked and went out through the dining room, across the entry and through the door to the garage. A few moments later she heard the rumble of the car engine and then the clank and clatter of the garage door as it lifted.

It was a quarter to seven before she heard the garage door lifting again. She was sitting in the living room with Barry, trying to keep them both neat, not that her denim skirt and cotton, sleeveless sweater were likely to wrinkle. She had purposefully chosen her ensemble for its durability. If there was anything she'd learned about babies, it was that they tended to crawl all over you. Of more concern to her was her makeup. She had carefully applied it, after spending most of the day with an ice pack on her cheek and eye, to hide the bruising as much as possible. Her lip was already nearly healed, and the ice had taken care of most of the swelling and the worst of the discoloration. What remained was barely visible beneath the cosmetics, but if she couldn't keep Barry from rubbing them off her face, it wasn't going to matter. Added to that worry was another.

Earlier in the day, she had moved some of the furniture around, breaking up the boring, unimaginative arrangement of walls lined with whatever came next. The large, cream-colored, suede sofa now sat at a slight angle in the center of the room, a white, tan,

and orangish rug spread over the wood flooring before it. She placed the chrome-and-glass coffee table in the center of the rug, then arranged a tapestry armchair and small ottoman next to it. Edward's recliner, which she found a truly abhorrent piece of furniture, she placed at an angle opposite, pointing it toward the entertainment center across the room. A small writing desk and chair of exquisite rosewood had come out of the corner and taken center stage against the longest wall, surrounded by potted plants—silk, unfortunately—and overhung by a lovely sketch of the firehouse as it once was, framed in chrome—another unfortunate choice.

She'd moved the smaller tables, lamps, magazine caddy and various other pieces into small groupings that took them away from the walls and gave the room a comfortable, lived-in feeling. She'd also rehung several pictures, none of them extraordinary, but all more striking now that they'd been arranged properly.

Looking around the room, she knew that it was vastly improved, but she suddenly doubted whether Edward would think so or not. Nervously she jumped to her feet and gathered up Barry and baggage, hurrying toward the staircase, intending to meet Edward in the foyer and distract him until she could tell him calmly what she'd done to his house. Edward was already bounding up those same stairs, however, and practically bowled her over at the top, throwing his arms around her and baby to steady them.

His smile was warm and apologetic. "Sorry I'm late. I forgot about a consultation, and I didn't want to call you and have a private conversation in front of the guy, and the staff had already gone home, and..." He stopped in midexplanation and looked around him, mouth ajar.

Laurel's stomach dropped. "I'll move it all back," she said quickly. "I shouldn't have moved anything to begin with. I—I only—"

"This is great!" he exclaimed, interrupting her and taking a better look around. "Parker's always said I couldn't arrange a plate of cookies. Guess he's right. I'd never have thought of arranging it like this any more than I'd thought of dressing in double-breasted suits. But you've got the eye," he said. Turning back

to her, he looked at her as if seeing more than he had before. "Ken was right," he muttered mysteriously, and then he put his arms around her in a hug. "Listen," he said, after a moment, "I'd be pleased if you'd redo the whole house top to bottom, but then I'd be pleased if you never did anything but sit in that chair over there from now on. You'd still be nice to come home to. You're looking good, too, by the way. Bruises hardly show."

Laurel leaned back in his arms, Barry perched on her hip, and looked him in the face. "Thank you," she murmured.

He kissed her then, quickly but firmly, and said, "I'm starving. I know it's my own fault for being late, but can we go now?"

She nodded dumbly, and he lifted Barry from the crook of her arm, held him against his chest with one arm and slipped the other about her, moving them all toward the stairs. In short order, they were loaded in the car and backing out of the garage. He named a family-style restaurant up the street a few blocks and asked if that would do for dinner. She said it would, and he drove them there, parking and vaulting out. Before she could get her seat belt undone, her feet on the ground and her denim miniskirt straightened, he had Barry out and was locking the car. Together, they walked into the restaurant. Twenty minutes later, Edward began making a double order of chicken fried steak disappear while she fed Barry off her plate with mashed potatoes, pinches of soft dinner roll, carrots she mashed with a fork and minced grilled chicken.

Barry was fascinated with the restaurant, the people, the food, Edward. He hardly spared his mother a glance, even while obediently responding to her soft commands to eat by opening his mouth and leaning toward her while his inquisitive eyes followed the frenetic movements of a three-year-old child driving her parents nuts at the next table. Edward chuckled. "You'd think this was his first time out in public."

"It is," Laurel told him. "His first time in a public restaurant, anyway."

Edward's fork halted midway to his mouth. "You're kidding."

She concentrated on mashing a carrot with her fork. "We can't exactly afford evenings out."

Edward lowered his fork as if suddenly losing his appetite. "It's been pretty tough, hasn't it?"

She shrugged. "We've managed, but I can't pretend that the future hasn't worried me. He's outgrowing his shoes about every other month now. Fortunately they can be had pretty cheaply at this stage, but what about next year? And the year after that? I don't even want to think about five or ten down the road."

Edward held his hands poised over his plate. "That's why you're fighting for your inheritance."

She looked at Barry, her heart overflowing with love, and smiled at the way he tried to get that little girl's attention by smacking the table with the flats of his hands and making a tentative sound partway between a bark and a grunt. The girl didn't know he existed, but several adults were watching him with bemused expressions. Laurel felt a swell of pride. "Yes, I'm fighting for him," she said. "It's all for him."

After some time, she became aware that Edward was staring at her, and a faint blush of color stained her cheeks. She looked back to her plate.

"I understand now," he said. "I understand everything now."

She nodded briskly and focused on the food. She had just put a bite of chicken into her own mouth when a pair of women stopped by the table. One of them, a grandmotherly type, beamed down at Barry and said, "You have the sweetest little boy. He's so well behaved."

Laurel smiled and gulped and moved the chicken to one side of her mouth, but before she could manage to speak, Edward said, "Thank you. We're proud of him."

The woman cooed a moment and moved on, but Laurel could only stare at Edward. Had he meant that? Or had it merely been the expedient thing to do and say? She was afraid to think otherwise, and yet as the evening progressed, Edward showed every sign of intending to step into the role of doting father. He assumed responsibility for getting Barry in and out of his car seat as if that was the normal scheme of things, and insisted on filling their shopping cart at the grocery store with every conceivable food, beverage and snack suitable for a one-year-old.

Back at the firehouse, as Laurel had come to think of his home,

he spent a good half hour on the floor with Barry, playing. When Laurel announced that it was bath time, Edward carried Barry into the bathroom and hovered over them both while she ran a few inches of water into the obscenely large tub, disrobed Barry and began the arduous task of washing him. Soon, Edward had gotten into the fray himself, and soon after that, all three were soaked.

Edward even followed them into the bedroom and sat on the bed with Barry playing peekaboo with the towel while Laurel gathered up his nightclothes, diapers and all the requisite paraphernalia connected with putting a baby down for the night. Edward even gave him his medicine and put his diaper on him, but when putting his jammies on threatened to become a game of tickle, Laurel had to step in and take over, pointing out that it didn't help little boys sleep if they got all excited and stimulated just before the lights went out. With that new knowledge, Edward himself dimmed the lights and stood by to occasionally pat Barry's little back while Laurel cuddled him, humming softly, and tucked him into bed. As they tiptoed from the room minutes later, Edward slipped his arm around Laurel's shoulders. They moved down the short hall and turned into the living room, where Edward brushed his damp shirt and said, "We need one of those baby bathtubs."

"There's one under the kitchen sink at home," she answered distractedly.

"I'll get it tomorrow if you like."

She shook her head. "There's no point going to that trouble."

"You sure? I don't mind."

She shook her head more firmly. "We'll be going home soon."

Edward brought his hands to his hips, his face suddenly shuttered. "Do you really think that's wise? Bryce would be stupid not to make another grab for Barry if he thought he could, and I guarantee you, we wouldn't get him back so easily again."

She sighed. "I know you're right. I just don't want to impose on you any more than I have to. Maybe I should look for another apartment."

"You don't want to stay here?"

"It's not that."

"Then what is it?"

She shook her head, knowing she couldn't explain, and said again, "I just don't want to impose."

"You're not imposing," he told her softly. Stepping up beside her, he brushed his hands over her shoulders and down her bare arms. Her skin felt supersensitized, tingling. "I want you here with me," he said. "Both of you."

"I know you're trying to keep us safe," she said breathlessly, "but—"

"It's not that! Not only that."

"No? What is it then? Because—"

His hands slid up her arms, over her shoulders and up the smooth column of her throat to cup her face and tilt it. "You ought to know by now," he whispered, stepping closer still. "I haven't been able to keep my hands off you from the first. I didn't understand it myself in the beginning, and I made some stupid mistakes. I want to make up for that, though, and I want—"

"You don't have to do that."

"You," he said. "I want you."

Laurel caught her breath, mesmerized by the smiling warmth of those pale blue eyes and the feel of his hands against her skin, his big body standing next to hers, the male strength of him. She thought dimly that if she simply forgot for a moment that this wasn't love, then this would be a perfect moment. In some ways, it was as if her whole life had been about this moment, and she knew that when it passed she would never be the same. Then he brushed his thumb across her lower lip, and the moment became more. Not only was she safe, she was free. Not only was she desired, she desired, as well. Not only was she treasured... Such love for Edward White swelled her heart that it was almost painful. She gave a little sob as his mouth brushed against hers and felt the tickle and prickle of his mustache all through her body.

He tilted her face with his hands and settled his mouth against hers. Parting his lips and slanting them, he opened her mouth for the gentle exploration of his tongue, first touching the edges of her teeth. Slowly he licked the sensitive undersides of her lips and then the slick, silky walls of the cavern of her mouth.

Laurel slid her arms around him, locking herself tight against

the hard column of his body. Her eyes closed, and she gave herself up, finally, to the heady plunge of his tongue into the well of her mouth. What had been gentle exploration became savage thrusting. His hands dropped away, his arms closing around her. She knew then that she was going to give him any and everything he wanted of her. It was too late to worry about what came next. Whatever came, she'd have this. It would have to be enough.

Somehow, it would just have to be enough.

Chapter Fourteen

He felt ten feet tall and as strong as Atlas, especially when he swept her up into his arms and carried her swiftly to the bedroom. He left the doors open, mindful of Barry in the other room. He might need his mother. She would feel guilty and blame herself if he cried and she didn't hear. And it was Edward's self-appointed job to take care of them both. He had never embraced any responsibility more fully, had never cared so deeply, and he was grateful beyond words that she understood that, that she had forgiven him his stupidity and opened her heart to him. He was grateful. He was humbled. He was deliriously happy.

He didn't turn on the light in the bedroom. The light from the opened doorways to both the bath and living room provided the needed ambiance. On another evening, he would have built a fire and made love to her by the light of the flickering flames. This winter, he promised himself. He would make love to her in front of a fireplace this winter. He didn't doubt it.

Standing her beside the bed, he kissed her again with some urgency, lest she change her mind and walk out before he could make her understand what this meant to him. Then he didn't know what to do except undress and get into bed. Suddenly his hands

were shaking, but he backed away from her and began unbuttoning his shirt. In his haste, he forgot the two bottommost buttons, so that when he whipped the shirt back off his shoulders, they flew in opposite directions, plunking softly in the distance. He couldn't have cared less. He yanked his hands out of the still-buttoned cuffs and dropped the shirt on the floor. When he reached for her again, she stepped back.

His heart in his throat, he watched as she slipped off her sneakers, then pulled down the zipper on the side of her skirt and let it slip down her legs to the floor. She was wearing pale blue bikini panties beneath, and his mouth went dry at the sight of them. With achingly graceful movements, she crossed her arms over herself, lifted the edge of her small, white cotton, sleeveless sweater and peeled it up her torso and off over her head. The instant she was free of it, she dropped it and stood before him in panties and bra, a lacy little strip of a thing with a narrow band and tiny straps. She reached behind her and unfastened it. The straps slid off her shoulders as she brought her hands back to her sides. She shrugged and brought her arms in front of her. The straps slid over her fingertips and fell away.

For a moment, he could neither speak nor move. Then her hand lifted and timidly brushed across his chest, her fingertips fluttering lightly across his skin. To his surprise and embarrassment, his nipples tightened into small bumps thankfully hidden in swirls of chest hair. He reached for her, his hands skimming over the bare flesh of her shoulders and back. Pulling her to him, he looked down, watching as the soft mounds of her breasts flattened against his chest. He put his forehead to hers, breathing laboriously, his heart hammering as if he'd run for miles. "So beautiful," he whispered, dismayed at the inadequacy of the words. "You are so beautiful."

"Edward," she said. Just that. It was enough.

He kissed her slowly, thoroughly, savoring the feel of her body next to his, so warm and sleek. The perfume of her filled his head. Hers was a unique scent—light, musky, so very female. He had forgotten that women smelled differently than men, but he felt certain that no other woman smelled like this, his Laurel. His Laurel.

He lifted her into his arms again, liking the feel of her weight, the heat of her skin, the way her neck arched languidly when he

put his mouth to it and how she made startled, delighted little sounds when he nipped at her with his teeth. He leaned into the bed with one knee and carefully lowered her into the middle of it, tasting her mouth again briefly before pulling away to toss off his shoes and peel away his socks before wrenching his belt open and stripping out of his pants. He came back to her in only his briefs. She lifted her arms about his neck as he settled beside her and found her mouth again. He folded her close, wrapping his arms and even a leg about her, wanting to absorb her through his skin and mouth. Need ached in his groin and throbbed against his belly. He slid his hands down her body and hooked his fingers in the narrow elastic band of her panties, peeling them away as she lifted for him and curled her legs so he could slip them off. When they had joined the rest of their clothing on the floor, he caught one of her hands and brought it to his waist.

Unable to resist the taste of her, he helped himself to her mouth again as her fingers dug beneath the waistband of his briefs and tugged them down. After struggling a moment—he was bigger than her and harder to disrobe—she pulled her head back. Her mouth flattening in determination, one slender brow quirking up with intent, she pressed a hand to the center of his chest. Pushing him down onto his back, she rose into a semisitting position and, affording him a delightful view of her luscious breasts, employed both hands in easing off his underwear. They were a tighter fit than he'd realized. Of course, he didn't usually fill them quite so well. She'd barely gotten them to his thighs when he lost patience and finished the job himself. He'd wear boxers from now on.

Rising up, he swept an arm about her waist and pulled her down onto the bed, settling his body against hers once more. He could not get enough of the feel of her skin or the taste of her. He began with her mouth and worked his way to the tip of one breast, kissing and nipping and licking down the column of her throat and over the gentle swell of her collarbone to her chest. His hands were at work, as well, stroking and pressing and shaping until his fingers slid into the welcome heat between her legs.

Very deliberately, pulse pounding at every pressure point, he tugged her nipple into his mouth and at the same moment parted her silky curls with his thumb and slid his middle finger deeply inside her. She gasped and threw her head back, exquisitely responsive, wet and hot. He dragged his hand upward, trailing her

own moisture, until only the tip of his finger remained inside, then pushed downward again, curling his hand so that his finger penetrated deeply once more. Again and again he repeated the process until she was wet enough to allow his index finger to join his middle one. Only then did he let his thumb explore and find the nubbin of flesh hidden in those blond swirls. Gently, oh, so gently, he worked fingers and thumbs together, while kissing and sucking and bathing with his tongue every inch of her that he could reach. The pressure of her thigh rubbing against his arousal, lightly at first and then more roughly as her excitement built, nearly drove him mad, but it was a madness he embraced whole-heartedly.

When she began to buck rhythmically against his hand, he knew it was coming and rejoiced. When she began to gasp his name, he raised his head and looked into her lovely eyes. There was some question in the way she said his name, some uncertainty in her eyes. Only when it was fully upon her, when she shuddered and her body clenched around his fingers, only when her eyes went wide and a little wild and her nails dug into his shoulders, only when that question that was his name came fully into blossom did he understand that she had not felt this before, had never experienced what she had every right to know. He was stupefied. No one had ever loved this entirely lovable woman as she deserved. No one until now. He watched the tide of sensation sweep over her face, saw the tears well in her eyes and trickle from their corners, and realized that his own cheeks were wet.

He slid his arms around her and hugged her close, whispering words and phrases in short, probably unintelligible gasps. He didn't even know what he was saying, but it must have been right, for her hands bracketed his face and lifted it so that her mouth could stop his. He kissed her then as he had never kissed another woman in his life, and he didn't stop with her mouth. He didn't stop until he'd brought her to tears again and she lay splayed beneath him.

He positioned himself, one hand dropping down to lift her knee as he pushed up inside her body with one long, slow glide that was pure ecstasy. He didn't stop then until he was implanted as deeply as was possible and her legs were wrapped around his hips. And then he began again. This time when he brought her to that peak of existence he was there with her, humbled and

grateful that it was a peak no other man had climbed, and in the rush of winds he heard the words as clearly as if she had said them. *I love you, Edward. I love you.* In his mind and in his heart, he shouted *I love you* back to her, and then as he drifted down into warm, happy contentment, he warned himself not to wake the baby and smiled. Maybe they would have another nine months from now. They hadn't used any protection, so unless she was on the Pill, which he doubted, pregnancy was a very real possibility.

He stroked the top of her head, feeling her settle into the easy, floating rhythm of sleep, and told himself that it probably wasn't wise to rush into having a second child. Laurel might not want another child for some time—or at all. He would have to ask her when the right moment presented itself. Meanwhile, he had much to do, not only to secure Barry's adoption, for he had no intention of settling for anything less, but also to free himself from the unrelenting pressure of private practice. What he needed, he reflected for perhaps the dozenth time in the past twenty-four hours, was a partner, not to mention cocounsel. In fact, now that he really thought about it, cocounsel had to come first.

He couldn't tell himself any longer that he could be dispassionate and objective in this matter. He had to face the possibility that he very well might gloss over something too threatening to face or give more weight to a promising factor than he ought. His heart was involved as deeply as Laurel's now, and he knew from experience that it was best to step back in such a case. That's what he had done with the Sugarmans' fight for Darla, and he had been right to do it.

Of course! He nearly bolted upright in the bed as the answer presented itself, and it was the answer to not one problem but both. Only the pressure of Laurel's head against the hollow of his shoulder prevented it, and even then he lifted a hand to smack himself in the forehead. Why hadn't he thought of this sooner? It was perfect! Utterly perfect! He put a fist to his mouth, muffling the chuckles of relieved joy that gurgled up from the deep well of his chest. For the first time in weeks, his full-to-bursting heart was light as a feather. For the first time since Laurel Heffington Miller had walked into his office, he knew exactly what he should do, and he was only too happy to do it.

* * *

She woke alone in the big, rumpled bed and knew instantly that she had made perhaps the biggest mistake of her life. The wonder of the night before swept over her in a great, poignant wave. The only term she could think of to express what she had experienced in Edward's arms was *physical joy,* but the melding of ultimate physical sensation with that of pure emotional joy was beyond anything mere words could adequately convey. And it could only be hers for the moment, then never again.

Suddenly she knew why such intimacies as she and Edward had shared should be confined to marriage. They weren't meant to be temporary. In her case, they were not, for she knew with awful certainty that she would never love another man as she loved Edward White, and yet one day soon she would have to go back to her real life. It hardly mattered anymore whether she went back to that shabby little apartment or the mansion in Highland Park, for whenever she went, she would undoubtedly go alone. No, not alone. She would still have Barry. Wouldn't she? She refused to think that she might not, for that she knew she could not bear. She could not lose Edward and Barry, too. She simply couldn't, and yet... Oh, God. Oh, God. Oh, God.

She threw back the covers fiercely and scrambled from the bed, determined not to cry. She had brought this on herself. She would not die of it. She would not. If only for Barry, she would not. Barry. She needed to hold him suddenly, to feel and smell and snuggle him. Almost running, she tore across the master bedroom, through the bath, across the hall and into the small bedroom to the crib. Barry lay on his tummy, blissfully sucking his finger in his sleep. He was wearing a fresh cotton sleeper and, from appearances, a dry diaper. Edward.

A feeling of intense love welled up in her. She staggered beneath the weight of it and backed against the end of the bed, collapsing there. A bittersweet moment from the night before found her, and she relived it with aching resignation. She felt the shockingly giddy euphoria, the overwhelming sensations, the wringing depth of emotion. She heard herself sobbing out the wrenching truth, "I love you, Edward. I love you." She experienced the hard, empty silence that followed, so much sharper and uglier now, so much more cruel and disappointing.

At least, she told herself, he hadn't lied to her. But then he wouldn't, not Edward, not her white knight. Except he wasn't

hers. No, if Edward loved anyone, it was his best friend's wife. No doubt, Laurel was nothing more than a substitute for the woman he couldn't have, because, man that he was, Edward would never let himself come between Parker and Kendra. Edward had more integrity than that. He had more integrity than Laurel herself, or she wouldn't be in this position now. She had told herself last night that she was doing it for him, because it was what he wanted. She had seen it as a selfless act on her part; an act of gratitude, but she knew now that that wasn't so. She had made love with Edward because she had desperately wanted to, and she knew that in the back of her mind she had been hoping that it would be enough to make him fall in love with her.

Well, it hadn't worked. Obviously he hadn't known how to face her in the cold light of morning after she'd blurted out her feelings last night. She didn't blame him for slipping away before she woke. They both needed some absence in order to put perspective back into the situation. She would be ready when he came home, ready to pretend that he hadn't said a word about love, that he hadn't answered her with telling silence, that her heart wasn't broken and he wasn't uneasy. She would use these hours well, so that when he came home, she would be what she needed to be. Until then... She lay back, put her fist to her mouth, curled into a ball and surrendered to the agony of tears.

Kate Ridley Ballard leaned forward over her slender, crossed legs and placed her empty ice tea glass precisely in the center of a round cork-and-felt coaster. Straightening again, she swept her long blond ponytail off her shoulder and fixed Edward with her cool gray-blue eyes. Kendra's stepmother was older than him by some ten years—ten years of experience enhanced with a formidable intelligence, keen insight and fierce competitiveness. He could see the wheels turning behind that assessing gaze, processing all that he'd told her and much that he hadn't. As an attorney, no one rated more of his respect than this tall, handsome woman.

"Well," she said, "you seem to have a knack for involving yourself in unusual custody cases. Tell me, are you in love with the foster mother again?"

He'd expected this, and still she'd somehow caught him unaware. It took a moment to get himself in hand. The answer,

however, was never in question. He sipped ice tea, one brow cocked in silent congratulation, and said, "Yes."

Kate stared a moment longer, then a smile curled the corners of her mouth. "At least you're consistent, Ed. I'll give you that."

He chuckled and shook his head. "Actually, last time didn't count." He leaned forward then, elbows on knees and addressed her with all earnestness. "I can't tell you how important it is that we win this one. Laurel's taken too many emotional blows already. She can't take another. She's cared for this kid since even before he was born. I can't let her lose him. I need your help. Again."

Kate smiled supportively. "I'd be glad to help." She folded her arms. "To tell you the truth, I'm ready to get back into a courtroom. Dan and I needed this last year together, and we've had great fun, but I need the stimulation of practicing law again."

"Does that mean you're ready to go back to work full-time?"

She grimaced, hedging a bit. "Yes and no. I guess it depends on your definition of 'full-time.'"

Edward chuckled and shook his head. Not too long ago, he wouldn't have understood what she was getting at. Now he did. "I'm not too enthused by the idea of burning the midnight oil anymore, either. I love practicing law, and I doubt I'll ever fully retire, but there is life outside the office and the courtroom."

She appeared appropriately shocked. "Why, Edward, I do believe you mean that." She sat up very straight then and cocked her head to one side. "You really are in love this time. Edward, are those wedding bells I hear?"

He knew he was grinning like an idiot, but he couldn't seem to help himself. He wasn't even sure that he wanted to. Dignity be damned. "I told you I was much too close to this one to handle it on my own."

"Do you mean you've actually asked this woman to marry you?"

He was surprised at what pleasure he took in saying this. "Actually, no. She asked me."

He had never expected to see Kate Ballard speechless, but doing so, he had to laugh. "Now you know why I'm thinking of taking someone new into the practice. Full-time doesn't mean quite what it used to now that I have a real personal life, a *family* life. And that's another reason I came to you, Kate."

Kate shook her head. "I—I'm not sure I understand."

"It's surprisingly simple," he said. "I need someone experienced and objective to guide this custody case for me, someone fiercely dedicated to fight for Laurel's right to control her own inheritance—and a partner I respect and trust."

Kate stared at him a moment longer, and then she stuck out her hand, smiling. "Seems we've got our work cut out for us, partner."

Ed was surprised and pleased by the strength of her grip. He'd have the papers drawn before he called it a day, even if it took all night. He envisioned the new shingle. White And Ballard, Attorneys At Law. Then he put his head back and laughed because if he knew Kate, that new sign was going to read Ballard And White.

It all seemed to happen at once. He called late in the afternoon to tell her that the restraining order had come through, some of the other papers had been filed and he was working with a new attorney on the rest. Then they were going to personally serve Bryce and track down a couple of potential witnesses. He called again near ten in the evening to say that she shouldn't wait up for him, that he was likely to be at it all night. The background noise told her that he wasn't at the office. The laughter and the music and the crack of billiard balls was all too audible. Didn't he know that, or didn't he care? She tried not to think about it, but when morning came and he did not, she could no longer pretend that it didn't matter.

It was nearly lunchtime when he finally came dragging through the door. He was too tired to eat, he said, and too tired to talk, but she should take heart from the fact that it was all working out better than he'd even hoped. Soon, he mumbled, scratching at nearly two days' growth of beard, she could go back to living a normal life again. Then, placating a reaching Barry with a clumsy pat on the head, he shuffled off to bed.

A normal life. To Laurel that meant a life alone. Peeking in at him near dinnertime, she saw that he had not done more than step out of his shoes and throw off his coat before tumbling facedown onto the bed. He had clearly worked himself to the point of exhaustion over these past few days, and she knew that she ought to be grateful. She was grateful, and yet she could not help wish-

ing that their time together could have been longer. But her "normal life" beckoned, and she reasoned that the sooner she got back to it, the better for everyone.

Edward woke around two in the afternoon, showered, shaved, changed and gulped down a turkey sandwich, talking hurriedly the whole time about a Kate Ballard and possible leads and affidavits from Danny Hardacre, which meant they would not be pressing charges. Now if only the maid would cooperate, he muttered. But it was all terribly confusing to Laurel. Beginning at the beginning, she tried to question him.

"Who," she asked, following him down the spiral staircase to the entry, Barry on her hip, "is Kate Ballard?"

He paused in the dual act of digging the car keys out of his pocket and reaching for the doorknob to give her an odd, almost censorious look, and dropped the bombshell. "She's the new attorney who's taken over your case."

Laurel rocked back on her heels. New attorney. "But I thought you were handling everything."

He made an impatient sound and said, "I'll still be in it up to my elbows, but Kate's making the tough decisions now. Look, she's had more experience at this sort of thing than I have, and she's a damned fine attorney. I wouldn't have turned it over to her otherwise. It'll be fine. It's best this way. Trust me."

She bit her lip and nodded. Yes, she trusted him. If she was disappointed or hurt, it was her own fault. How many times had she been in this same spot? Looked like she'd learn one day not to hope for too much. Funny thing was, she hadn't thought she had.

He went on about something else, but she found it too difficult to pay attention and merely batted back tears. Finally he caught her face in his hands and lifted it for a brief, cool kiss, saying, "I have to get back to the office. Kate's downtown shopping for an immediate court date. We want to catch Kennison off guard, but there's still much to do if we're going to be prepared ourselves, and as far as I'm concerned, the sooner this is over with, the better. Don't you agree?"

Gently she extricated herself from his grasp and nodded. "Yes, I see that now. You're right, it's time to get back to a normal routine."

He murmured something about everything happening so fast and there being no time for long explanations, but she put on a brave face and told him that he should just get to it then and not worry about her. He went out the door saying that he'd known she would understand. He was thankful, it seemed, that she wasn't going to try to hang on to him when all was said and done.

Been there, done that, she told herself resolutely, and she had learned from the experience. God knew she had.

She called Fancy at the diner and explained that it was safe now for her to return to her own apartment and her job, the restraining order having been served. Fancy agreed to come for her at the end of her shift, and Laurel began packing the things she and Barry had brought with them.

Edward took the stairs two at a time, whistling. He was tired but satisfied, even excited, and to think that he had Kate and none other than Danny Hardacre to thank for it. Danny had done considerably more than stipulate his own complicity with Abelard Kennison in the matter of Laurel's divorce settlement. He had let Kate alternately charm and bully him into telling everything he knew about Abelard Kennison's dealings, and he knew quite a lot. Hardacre had first-hand knowledge, for instance, about two other cases where Kennison had persuaded elderly clients into setting up trusts controlled by himself or a handpicked minion. He had then proceeded to milk each estate dry, leaving the supposed inheritors broke and confused. He had names, dates, strategies, and he was willing to tell them all in a bid to keep his license to practice. In addition, Pamela Scott, Bryce's former maid and girlfriend, had also given them a detailed and very damning statement. It was, figuratively speaking, the mother lode, and Edward could not have been more pleased. It was all over now but the shouting, and he couldn't wait to tell Laurel. She would be as delighted as he and Kate, and that being the case, they were due a small celebration. He had agreed to meet the Ballards at a local supper club and, pending Laurel's permission, had arranged for the Sugarmans to keep Barry for the evening. He meant it to be more of a personal celebration than even the Ballards or Sugarmans might suspect, and he was eager to begin the festivities.

He was just about to take a chance on disturbing the baby by calling Laurel's name when he spied the note taped to the top of

the stair rail. A shiver of unease passed through him. Why had she gone out? Hadn't he told her that a restraining order was no guarantee of safety? He couldn't actually remember if he had or not, but he knew that this note did not bode well for his peace of mind. Carefully he peeled it off the railing and held it up to the light, expecting to find a hastily scribbled message saying that she would return from the corner market in ten minutes or less. Instead, it was a carefully penned note.

Dearest Edward,
You were right about getting on with our normal lives. I certainly cannot go on living here on your goodwill indefinitely, and my job at the diner cannot be held open for me much longer. As I am well enough and the legal pieces seem to be falling together, no good reason exists for me to continue as I am. You can, of course, find me at the apartment or reach me via the diner or Fancy. Thank you from the bottom of my heart. You have truly been my White Knight. I'll never forget you.

Laurel

He could not quite comprehend that she had gone back to her old life until he read the note through again, and even then he merely looked around him at first in a kind of emotional stupor. She had left him. After everything, she had left him. He sat down heavily on the top step to think what to do next, but what was there to do? He looked down at the note crumpled in his hand, and all the cogs and wheels of his mind seemed to grind to a slow, paralyzing stop. When next he looked up, the house was dark, and a deep, angry desperation settled over him. Surprisingly, he could think of only one place to go, only one thing to do. Blindly, he stuffed the note into his coat pocket and stumbled down the stairs and out the door.

Parker stepped down into the large, dimly lit room and looked around. Sitting at the bar, Edward tossed back a jigger of straight bourbon and followed it with a swig of cold lager, watching as Parker scanned the pool tables and electronic game machines before spotting him at the bar. The expression on Parker's face told Edward that he had been looking for him for some time, but Ed

was too far-gone to much care. He pushed the shot glass in the bartender's direction and ordered another shot. With a glance in Parker's direction, the pretty little blonde named Cathy complied. Ed tossed it back while Parker removed a flip phone from his pocket and dialed a number, speaking briefly before folding up the phone and stashing it.

"Broke mine," Ed said sluggishly as Parker walked up to the bar. "Damned thing kept ringing."

"Yeah? How come you didn't just answer it?"

"Why would I want to do that?" Edward said, and swallowed a big mouthful of beer to cool the burn in his gut.

Parker smiled at Cathy and leaned over the bar to give her a peck on the cheek. "How you been, Cath?"

"Same old same old," she said brightly. "How's the family?"

"Couldn't be better. Well, Ken has been worried about this big galoot."

Cathy sighed. "Yeah, me, too." She cocked a hip and cracked her chewing gum. "I haven't seen him like this since... Nope, I haven't ever seen him like this. Somebody pulled his chain, huh?"

"Must have," Parker replied noncommittally, stepping over the stool next to Ed and taking a seat. He shook his head when Cathy laid a napkin down in front of him. Shrugging, she turned away and began polishing the glasses brought in from the dishwasher in the back. Edward ignored them both and nursed his beer. After a moment, Parker took some peanuts from the basket at Ed's elbow, popped them into his mouth and said, "Well, is this déjà vu all over again or what?"

Ed tapped his shot glass on the counter to get Cathy's attention and ordered another. She looked at Parker. "You driving him?"

"Yeah."

Ed said nothing as she filled the glass. He was already fairly drunk, but not nearly as drunk as he intended to be. Parker ate a few more peanuts and said, "Want to talk about it?"

Ed sucked up half the bourbon and took a deep breath. Fishing in his pocket, he took out the crumpled note and tossed it onto the bar. "Nothing to talk about."

Parker smoothed out the note and bent his head over it, reading it by the meager light. Finished, he pushed it away with his fin-

gertips and smoothed an eyebrow. "I thought you two were getting married. That's what Kate said anyway."

"Yeah, well, I thought so, too," Edward said, slamming back the last of the bourbon. It went down hard, and he shuddered when it hit his stomach and started to roil.

Parker scratched his head. "So, um, when did you ask her?"

"Ask her who?"

"Laurel."

"Ah. What was the question again?"

Parker rolled his eyes and carefully said, "When did you ask Laurel to marry you?"

Ed frowned and waved a hand, feeling decidedly woozy. "I didn't ask her. She asked me. Remember? That was the whole damned deal. She asked me!"

Parker nodded, clearly having trouble putting it all together. "Okay. So, um, when did you agree to it?"

Ed tried to think that one over but quickly gave it up. "I don't know."

"You don't know when you agreed to marry her?"

Ed shook his head impatiently. "Look, it wasn't like that, all right? I didn't say, 'Oh, by the way, I've thought it over, and I will marry you, after all.' I didn't say that."

"What did you say, then?"

"I didn't say anything! No. I mean, I didn't have to *say* anything." He swallowed beer and sighed. "Actions speak louder than words, you know—and that's all I have to say about *that*."

Parker rubbed the back of his neck like he was getting a headache or something. "So what did you *do* that let her know you wanted to marry her?"

Edward couldn't believe he was hearing this. He looked Parker squarely in the eye—or as squarely as he could manage with his neck starting to feel like it was rubber—and said, "You don't really expect me to tell you that I made love to her, do you?"

Parker's mouth compressed like he was trying to hide a yawn or something, and he quickly turned his head away, saying in a choked voice, "No, no. Wouldn't dream of demanding details."

Ed nodded decisively. "'Course not. Anyway, it doesn't make any difference. She left anyway."

Parker inclined his head. "Well, maybe she didn't understand exactly what you were telling her when you...you know."

Edward snorted and wondered briefly which of the two beers in front of him was his, or even which hand was his, for that matter. He shook his head, and the two beers became four, so he closed his eyes. "Whadda you mean, she didn' unnerstan'?"

Parker sighed and confessed, "I've discovered an odd thing about women, old friend. They have to be told point-blank what's on a fellow's mind. Even now I find myself explaining to my own wife, in minute detail, just what it is I mean. And who, I ask you, could know me better than Ken?"

Edward peeked out from beneath heavy eyelids, pleased to see only one of Parker on the stool next to him. "She made it sound like it was me," he said, and when Parker looked at him like he'd grown a second head, he added, "In the note, that stuff about 'normal lives.' I didn't say that. Well, I did say it, but not like that, not like she should go back to what was her normal life before *our* normal life that started when she came home with me, and for sure then when she let me make love to her. See?"

Parker started a nod and ended with a shake. "Nope. Uh-uh."

Edward rolled his eyes and nearly fell backward off his stool, catching himself at the last moment. Something new occurred to him. "Hey, you 'member that night we was in here jus' before Darla's custody hearing?"

Parker laughed. "Yeah. I remember you told me I had to tell Kendra that I wanted her to stay. You implied, in fact, that I had to do more than tell her, I had to make her believe it, even if it meant seducing her repeatedly. At least that's the way I took it."

"So what're you sayin'?"

"I'm saying, maybe she just hasn't gotten it yet. Maybe Laurel needs now what Kendra needed back then. Maybe you just have to spell it out."

"You mean I should ask 'er t' marry me?"

Parker shrugged. "Why not, if that's what it takes?"

Edward frowned at the empty bottom of his glass. He'd heard somewhere that you could drown in an inch of water, but only, he supposed, if you didn't want to. That's how this stuff usually worked, and since that was the case, he might as well drink it. It was kind of like getting married—she only wanted you to until you wanted to, too. He shook his head and said something he'd never thought he'd ever say. "I liked it better that she asked me. It was kinda nice, her askin' me, you know? Made me proud.

Scared the hell outta me, but it was nice, too, even when I thought she was nuts because she asked me, unnerstan'?''

Parker was hiding a yawn again. ''I understand,'' he said, reaching up to pat Ed's shoulder. Unfortunately, that was all it took to tip Ed forward off his stool. Fortunately, he was out before his head even hit the bar.

Chapter Fifteen

"Rise and shine, partner. You've had all the rest and recuperation I can give you."

Edward groaned and rolled over, hitting the floor with a foundation-shaking thud. Laughter echoed and reverberated inside his head, which he tried to hold together with his hands. If he ever made sure it would stay in place, he'd get up and throttle whoever was doing this to him. Where the hell was he anyway? Gingerly he cracked open one eyelid, moaning when pain lanced his head in a bright ray of light. He was dying. No other explanation of sufficient import existed—until he remembered the bourbon and beer he'd slugged back at Patrick's Place last night. Was it only last night? Had to have been. He distinctly remembered sitting next to Parker at Cathy's bar station and being asked if he'd *told* Laurel that he wanted to marry her, like you could tell that woman anything. He snorted at the idea, and pain shot up his nose and exploded inside his skull. Damn.

"Okay, pea brain, let's try this again."

He vaguely recognized the voice, not that he cared to. Then numerous hands reached down and tugged him up off the floor onto...a couch. When his head stopped swimming, he cupped his

hands around his eyes protect: : 'y and carefully opened them. Kendra and Parker stood in his direct line of fire. He groaned, understanding at last. "Couldn't you have taken me back to my place?"

"And do what with you?" Parker asked. "Lay you out on the dining room table? Have you ever tried to lug two hundred and fifty pounds up a spiral staircase? It was all I could do to get you this far."

He remembered none of what it had taken to get him here to Parker's multipurpose room. The very last thing he remembered, in fact, was wondering if he was going to drown in the bottom of his glass—and telling someone how proud and happy he'd been that Laurel had asked him to marry her. Remembering it all now, he leaned forward, elbows on knees and supported his hanging head with his hands, groaning. "Somebody get me water and aspirin, please."

They were thrust into his hands almost immediately. Steeling himself, he put his head back, shoved the aspirin into his mouth and thirstily drank down almost the whole glass of water, which began to roll around in his gut and threaten to come up.

"Here." Kendra dumped saltines into his hands.

Blearily, Edward stared down at them. "What are these for?"

"Nausea," she said. "Well, they help with pregnancy-related morning sickness, I thought they might help with hangovers, too."

Willing to try anything, he was chewing the first one when it hit him. He jerked his gaze up, the pain in his head somewhat less than blinding. "Hey, are you having morning sickness?"

Kendra grinned, and Parker slid an arm protectively around her shoulders. "Is it great or what? I'm going to be a dad again, this time the regular way, and Darla is just as thrilled as we are."

Edward smiled, on his way to a chuckle, consequences be damned, when a wave of envy so strong that it brought tears to his eyes hit him. He lurched forward, groaning to cover his embarrassment, and saw a pair of women's feet in pale gray, two-inch heels cross his view.

"Oh, I'm so happy for you!"

Oddly, he knew those feet, or rather, the shoes, and he knew that voice.

"Your father will be ecstatic when he hears!"

Edward groaned again, inwardly this time. This was all he needed, Kate to view his ignominy. He sighed and rubbed his stinging eyes with the backs of his hands. The babble of three happy voices died away, and the squared-off toes of those extremely uncomfortable-looking shoes inserted themselves once more into his eyesight.

"Think you can manage now?" she said. "Actually, you'd better be able to do more than that. We have a court date, my friend."

Edward moaned. He wanted to tell her to take that court date and shove it. But he wasn't going to. This was Laurel's life they were talking about—Laurel's and Barry's. His throat closed up momentarily at the thought of that boy. He guessed he'd started thinking of the little redheaded scamp as his. True or not, he felt the loss dearly. He couldn't help thinking what a similar loss would be like for Laurel. No, he couldn't—wouldn't—let that happen to her. He cleared his throat and managed to ask, "When?"

"Oh, in about three hours."

His head shot up, pain bouncing off the top of his head. "Three hours!"

Kate grinned that cold, courtroom smile of hers. "That's not the best of it. Judge Halstead is sitting."

Hal Halstead. Holy cow. Halstead adored Kate, called her his "little darling" in the most obnoxious, sexist, condescending manner possible. She hated it, but she used it to her advantage. Oh, brother, did she use it!

"And there's more," she went on. "Hal's agreed to arbitrate the inheritance matter."

"Arbitrate!" Ed exclaimed, frowning. "We don't want arbitration!"

"Yes, we do," Kate told him smugly, "because Hal's promised me that if we present incriminating evidence, he'll convene a grand jury."

Edward caught his breath. A grand jury. That meant, not just a civil suit but criminal charges. Completely ignoring the state of his head, he surged to his feet, threw both arms around Kate Ballard and kissed her soundly in the center of her forehead. "Yes!" he fairly crowed. Kennison was going down big-time.

And Laurel was going to get everything she had coming to her—
Barry, the inheritance, the house, the cars. Everything.

"Now," Kate was saying, "all we have to do is get Laurel
and the baby there on time. You know the drill—a nice conservative suit, not too much makeup, the baby needs to be clean and
neat and, if possible, happy. And you warn her, Ed. No matter
what anybody says or does, she's to keep her cool. And I'd really
appreciate it if you could get us there early enough for me to talk
to her. I don't like representing a client I haven't even met!"

Ed nodded, remembering that Kate and her husband were to
have met Laurel last night. Well, last night was behind them.
Today was the key to the future, and nothing was going to keep
him from ensuring Laurel's future. Nothing—not even pride. He
was already moving in the direction of the shower. Ripping off
the tie someone had loosened, he tossed it over his shoulder.
"Someone press this," he said and began peeling off his shirt,
"and this. And find my coat!"

"There's a razor in the cabinet above the sink!" Parker called.

"And an extra toothbrush!" Kendra added, while Kate gathered up the articles of clothing he'd left behind.

"Someone better get in there and catch his pants," Kate said
wryly.

Parker started off behind him, muttering, "I draw the line at
his underwear," but he was grinning when he said it.

Ed walked into the diner like he owned the place, a cool blonde
several years older on his heels. He walked right up to Laurel,
took out of her hand the coffeepot from which she was about to
pour a refill and set it on the table in front of her startled customer.
"You're coming with me." He clamped a hand on her wrist and
began to turn away.

"Hold on!" She yanked back, trying to divine this strange
mood of his and casting a curious look at the blonde. "I can't
just walk out."

"You'd better," the blonde said flatly. "We're due in court in
just over two hours."

"We?"

Edward set his jaw and jerked a thumb in the blond's direction.
"This is my new partner, Kate Ridley Ballard. I told you about
her the other day."

"No, you didn't."

"I did!"

"You only mentioned that you were turning my case over to another attorney. You didn't say anything about having a partner."

A muscle jumped in the hollow of his jaw. "Evidently I failed to mention quite a few things, so obviously we have a lot to talk about. Of course," he added sarcastically, "we could have talked about it *last night* at dinner with Kate and her husband, but you were gone when I got home."

"And then *you* got stinking drunk," Kate pointed out helpfully, a fingertip imbedded in the top of his shoulder.

Laurel's startled gaze flew right back to Edward's reddening face. "You got drunk?"

Edward closed his eyes. "Could we discuss this later, perhaps? Right now we have to get you ready for court."

Court. Laurel's hands were shaking as she untied her apron strings. They were going to court and Edward had gotten drunk, *stinking drunk,* according to...Kate? "I won't be a minute."

She hurried around the end of the counter and through the swinging metal doors into the kitchen, where Fancy had disappeared minutes earlier. "Fancy, I have to go. I'm sorry, but Edward and the new attorney are here, and they say we have to go to court!"

"Today?" Fancy said, pausing in the act of ladling gravy over an open-faced steak sandwich.

Laurel nodded and glanced at her wristwatch. "I have two hours to change and get to the courthouse."

Fancy's heavily made-up eyes narrowed dangerously. "You don't suppose he did this on purpose, do you?"

"Edward? Why on earth?"

Fancy considered and apparently rejected the notion. "Yeah, I guess you're right. It's just that any guy who'd take advantage of a helpless woman to—"

Laurel rolled her eyes. "Oh, please! If anyone took advantage it was me. But I don't have time to argue with you. I have to go."

Clucking worriedly, Fancy followed her into the other room. "You let me know how it turns out, hear? I won't rest easy for

a minute until I know.'' She stopped and glared up at Edward. ''And you just keep your hands to yourself, mister.''

''Fancy!'' Laurel scolded. Shrugging apologetically at Edward, she gave her head a small shake, trying to tell him without words that she hadn't complained about his treatment of her—quite the opposite, in fact.

He leaned close and angrily hissed, ''I didn't exactly force myself on you!''

''I never said you did,'' Laurel replied quietly through her teeth.

''Okay, kiddies,'' Kate Ballard interrupted, ''this will have to wait. We've more immediate problems to discuss.'' Elbowing Edward out of the way, she stuck out a hand to Laurel. ''It's nice to meet you, Laurel. May I call you Laurel? Good. Now then, I want you to listen very carefully.'' So saying, she took Laurel by the arm and turned her resolutely toward the door.

Kate talked all through the car trip to Laurel's apartment, explaining in detail what she expected Laurel to say and what she was not to say or do under any circumstances. Edward drove, silent as stone and seemingly as impervious. Laurel listened and nodded and made copious mental notes—until Kate got to the part about having to take Barry with them.

''It's just a formality,'' she assured Laurel, seeing her alarm, ''but it's also the law, and we've skirted enough of the regulations as it is.''

''I don't understand.''

Kate tamped down her impatience with visible effort. ''I've convinced Judge Halstead that a home study would be counter-productive as this point. Instead, he's agreed to judge your fitness as a parent on a report we've elicited from David Greenlea and his own personal observation, as well as—'' She shot a look in Edward's direction, and finished, ''As well as Edward's reputation.''

''Edward?''

''Yeah, go figure,'' Edward all but snarled.

Laurel had the dreadful feeling that she'd missed something, something important, but she didn't have time to think on it as Kate kept drumming away at what she was to expect and how she was to react. Her head was whirling by the time they reached the apartment complex. Hurrying ahead, she had explained mat-

ters to the sitter and had Barry on her hip by the time the others arrived. She watched Edward's face change from sullen to winsome as Barry put up his little arms and silently begged to be held by him. Edward swung him up into his arms, smacked a kiss between his eyes and smoothed down the hair that seemed to stand on end no matter what Laurel did to it. Barry dug a finger into the knot of Edward's tie and jabbered as if the sounds themselves were meant only for the two of them. Laurel felt her heart squeeze painfully in her chest and turned away before she was reduced to tears.

She led the way up the stairs and unlocked the apartment. It was steamy hot inside, but she couldn't bring herself to turn on the air-conditioning just yet. The thought of paying those outlandish electric bills made her shudder. Edward, with Barry in tow, and Kate were right on her heels. Edward immediately took over.

"Let's find something for the baby first. Kate can dress him while we look through your wardrobe. She can use the practice, seeing as how she's going to be a grandmother—again."

Laurel couldn't help an exclamation of surprise. She had never seen a less grandmotherly-looking female. "Th-that's wonderful. You just don't seem old enough to be anyone's grandparent."

"Well, thank you," Kate purred. "Actually, I'm a stepgrandmother. I think you know our little Darla."

"Darla Sugarman?"

"Kate is Kendra's stepmother," Edward explained.

The implications became clear immediately. "Is Kendra going to have another baby?"

"They just told us," Kate confirmed. "I doubt her father even knows yet."

Edward didn't say anything, just stared at Laurel almost accusingly. She cocked her head to one side, wondering what that was all about. He looked away, moving to Barry's dresser. Quickly he went through the top drawer, pulling out a navy blue short suit with a lapelless jacket and a white, round-collared shirt. "Can he wear this?"

"It might be a little big yet. The sitter bought it as a gift for his birthday."

Edward held it up to Barry as best he could. "We'll try it."

She went over and dug out socks, shoes and a pair of small

red suspenders. Edward found a white sailor cap with an elastic strap to go under the chin. He plopped it on Barry's head and pronounced it "better than that rooster's comb you've got on top." Barry's eyes sparkled with delight. He always thought he was something special in a hat. Delivering all into the unlikely hands of Kate Ballard, Edward then turned his attention to Laurel's wardrobe. He tore through the hangers, rejecting first one garment then another until his patience ran out.

"Don't you have anything conservative?"

She glared at him, feeling more than a bit on edge herself. "Do I strike you as the conservative type, Edward?"

"Only if you consider Mae West conservative," he grumbled, tearing through her clothes again.

"I resent that! What's wrong with you anyway? You used to like the way I dress!"

"That was before I came home, brimming with good news, to find you'd moved out without so much as a word!"

"I never moved *in!*" she reminded him. "And you as good as told me—"

"I never told you anything, damn it, because I didn't have a chance!"

"We don't have time for this!" Kate shouted, startling the baby into sudden cries.

"Now look what you've done!" Edward accused, stomping across the room to sweep up Barry and quiet him, for all the world, just like a...father.

The fight went right out of Laurel, tears suddenly brimming in her eyes. She whirled around and began digging through her clothes. She jerked out the olive green number she'd worn to his office that first day and held it up for approval. He grimaced.

"Too short." In an aside to Kate he said waspishly, "Her whole damned wardrobe's too short."

Just for spite, Laurel pulled out a long black jersey knit with a plunging neckline and overlong sleeves belled at the ends. "Oh, that's perfect," Edward snipped. "Have you got fangs to go with it? Or maybe you could hang a funeral wreath around your neck."

"Maybe I could hang a noose around yours?"

"As if you haven't all ready!"

"Oh, for Pete's sake!" Kate said, practically snatching Barry out of Edward's arms. "Wear pants!"

That gave Laurel an immediate idea. It just might do, too. Quickly she pulled out a sleek fawn-colored silk suit with a soft shawl collar and loose, wide-legged pants. She put a cream white, cowl-necked, sleeveless blouse with it and unearthed a pair of matching shoes with sturdy platform heels and ankle straps. Adding a wide, leather belt, a long gold chain and a pair of gold oval disk earrings banded with pearls, she held the whole ensemble up for approval. "What do you think?"

Edward cocked a brow at Kate, who rolled her eyes heavenward. "Thank God. Now do you think we can get you dressed without the two of you drawing blood, or shall I send Edward down to the car?"

Edward took back Barry and plopped down in the rocker. "I'm not going anywhere." The look he gave Laurel said, "And neither are you until we settle a few things."

A thrill of anticipation skipped up her spine. Had she misread him, after all? Had he really meant for her stay, perhaps permanently? She knew suddenly that if Kate hadn't been there, she'd have walked across the room and sat herself down on his other knee, staying put until she had a full explanation. As it was, though, she merely turned and went into the bathroom to change.

When she returned, it was to find Kate packing a diaper bag and Edward cooing to Barry. Kate looked her over and said she'd do. Edward merely glanced her way and said nothing. Laurel changed purses and gave her hair a thorough combing so that it lay softly against her head while Kate dropped the diaper bag in Edward's lap, picked up Barry and announced they'd wait outside before leaving.

For a long moment, neither Laurel nor Edward spoke or moved. Then suddenly he got up and cleared his throat, his hands going to his waist. Taking that as her cue, she walked briskly across the apartment and toward the door. Just as she moved past him, his hand shot out, clamped over her forearm and yanked her back. Groaning, he framed her face with his hands and covered her mouth with his. Tremulously exultant, she threw herself against him, her arms locking around his torso.

"Oh, Edward!" she gasped when next he let her breathe.

"I'm an idiot," he said at the same time. "I thought you understood that—"

"I love you!"

"I love you!"

She laughed, and he kissed her again, his hands roaming possessively over her body. Kate beat on the door, reminding them that they didn't have the time to indulge in explanations or recriminations just now. Sighing, Edward turned her toward the door and escorted her out.

Laurel began to shake with nerves on the drive to the courthouse. She kept telling herself that everything was going her way finally, but the very notion itself was so new that she couldn't quite trust it yet. So she reminded herself that Edward was there, her white knight, and he loved her. He wouldn't let anything bad happen to her or Barry if he could help it, and there was Kate, too—a veritable tiger. Grandma Tigress. The sheer incongruity of the picture made her smile. Her mood lightened a bit, but that only lasted until they got off the elevator at the courthouse and found Danny Hardacre waiting for them. Laurel physically recoiled.

"Relax," Edward said, his arm sliding about her shoulders. "He's here as our witness."

"*Our* witness?"

"He won't testify today," Kate explained briskly, "but his presence in the courtroom can only add weight to his deposition."

Danny stepped up then to add his own clarification. "The whole thing was a setup, Laurel. I'm really sorry. I didn't want to hurt you, but Kennison convinced me that I didn't have another option. Edward made me understand that I did." He clapped Edward on the shoulder, reaching up considerably in order to do so. "You're getting a good guy," he went on. "The best."

As he shambled off, Laurel looked up at Edward in confusion. "What's that all about?"

He shrugged uneasily. "Aw, heck, rescue a drunk and you wind up with a new best friend."

"Glad to hear it!" Parker exclaimed, appearing at Edward's elbow. "Maybe I'll get the respect I'm due now."

Edward shook his head and said to Laurel, "Don't ask."

Before she could, David Greenlea appeared. He kissed her cheek and shook Edward's hand. Laurel looked around for any more new arrivals and spied Kendra holding Barry and talking nonsense to him, her eyes skittering back and forth between Laurel and Edward. Every once in a while, she'd point at one or the

other of them and whisper something in Barry's ear. He was absorbing every word.

"The bailiff's opened the doors, folks," Kate announced, herding everyone in that direction. "Time to go in."

Laurel moved up next to Kendra and held out her arms for Barry. "Mama," he said decisively, and Kendra whispered something in his ear before handing him over. Edward plunked the sailor cap onto his head and arranged the chin strap. Laurel said to Kendra, "I understand that congratulations are in order."

Kendra beamed. "Uh-huh. And I understand that the same thing is in order for you guys." Before Laurel could make solid sense of that, Kendra leaned forward and kissed her cheek, whispering, "I'm so happy for you. He deserves the best, and I think he's got it."

"Thanks, kid," Edward rumbled, one hand on Laurel's shoulder and the other patting the top of Kendra's head. Laurel rolled her eyes up at him, but he was looking at Barry and grinning.

Kate led them down the aisle to a small rectangular table at the front of the courtroom. They were barely seated before the bailiff appeared in front of the bench and said, "All rise." They got up again as he rattled off a pompous-sounding announcement signifying that court was in session with the Honorable Harold Halstead presiding.

"This guy loves Kate," Edward whispered as the judge swept in and climbed up to his seat, black robes flying.

He waved them down into their chairs and signaled the bailiff to read off the docket number of the case before nodding in the direction of what Laurel took to be the defense table. For the first time, she realized that Abelard Kennison and her ex-husband were in attendance. Kennison was the picture of lawyerly dignity. Dressed all in cool gray and white, with a black tie and highly polished shoes, he appeared as coolly confident as ever, his sleek white hair swept back to expose the patrician features of a face still handsome despite his years. Bryce, by comparison, looked decidedly uncomfortable in an expensive, well-tailored pin-striped suit of navy blue serge, a pale blue shirt and a red-striped tie. His shoes looked new. She hoped they pinched.

As if sensing her ill wishes, he turned his gaze directly at her. Laurel gasped. His nose was swollen and blue, a butterfly strip across a hump in the bridge that had decidedly not been there

before. In addition, the flesh around one eye had turned a sickly
yellow veined with angry-looking scratches. Edward clasped her
hand in his and pointedly looked at Bryce, who craned his neck,
straightened his tie and turned back to the front, while Kennison,
who was standing, said something to the judge.

Laurel widened her eyes at Edward, who winked and allowed
a smug smile to briefly lift the corners of his mouth. She'd known
that there had been a scuffle but she'd assumed that it hadn't
amounted to much. Seeing Bryce, though, she knew that wasn't
so, and the knowledge that assault charges had been written off
on both sides suddenly held new significance. She leaned a little
closer to Edward, relieved that he hadn't wound up in jail because
of her. Barry looked up from her lap, pushing his hat down over
his eyes and happily babbled, "Mamamamama." Edward looked
down, smiled, and adjusted the baby's hat. Barry babbled something unintelligible. "Dddduummphd."

Laurel bounced him on her knee and whispered that he should
be quiet, ignoring what seemed like a bunch of preliminaries to
her. Suddenly, a sharp crack made her jump. She looked up to
find the judge glaring down at her. He had sparse white hair and
bushy black eyebrows that looked as though they belonged to
someone else, and he was frowning.

"I don't like repeating myself, young woman, so pay attention."

"Yes, sir."

"Your Honor," Edward whispered out of the corner of his
mouth.

"Er, yes, Your Honor."

The judge nodded and leaned forward over the bench. "I take
it this is the minor child whose custody is in question?"

Laurel nodded, and the judge barked, "Speak up. The clerk
can't hear nods."

"Yes, Your Honor."

Apparently satisfied, the judge nodded and signaled the bailiff,
who put them all on their feet again and swore in the witnesses.
Laurel was surprised when Edward raised his hand and repeated
the vow along with everyone else but the two attorneys of record,
the judge, the clerk and the bailiff himself. Oh, and Barry.

Then everyone but Kate sat down and Kate made a long statement about how Laurel had cared for Barry since even before he

came into the world by providing for his birth mother during her pregnancy. She said they'd prove that Avon hadn't trusted her own brother to do so and why, and that Avon had named Laurel as the child's sole custodian in a document that she called a hand-written will.

Afterward, Abelard Kennison got up and said that Avon Miller was an even more pathetically unstable individual than Laurel herself and custody should be given to the child's natural uncle.

Then Kate got up again and asked to have a deposition entered as evidence of Bryce Miller's "venal nature" and his "sole reason for seeking custody of his nephew." Kennison objected, saying that he had not had a chance to look over the evidence. Kate then offered to dispose of the deposition and have the witness, one Daniel L. Hardacre, testify in person. Kennison paled and vociferously objected. To Laurel's surprise, and apparently to Kennison's, as well, the judge told Kennison to sit down and shut up. Banging his gavel, he said, "Objection denied. I've read said deposition and it's clear to me that Bryce Miller engaged in dishonest, unlawful, malicious activity for personal gain. Furthermore, I've examined the handwritten will wherein the child's mother specified guardianship to petitioner Laurel Miller, and I consider it valid."

Kennison shot to his feet once more. "But Your Honor, I have proof of Mrs. Miller's emotional instability."

The judge narrowed his eyes. "Is that so?"

Kennison climbed up onto his oratorical pedestal and held forth in grand style, citing the instances in Laurel's youth when she had been hospitalized, and the opinion of her own grandmother. After he'd said enough to hang her—or so Laurel thought—Kate neatly looped the noose around his own neck, pointing out that the grandmother's opinion was clearly rebutted in Mr. Hardacre's deposition and announcing that she had statements from several doctors who had treated Laurel and the unanimous conclusion was that Laurel was remarkably well-anchored considering her grandmother's obvious mental and emotional abuse. Even Laurel gaped at that one. Edward, however, settled back in his chair and sighed with immense satisfaction, a smile on his face.

Kennison sputtered objections and pontificated about nothing much until the judge pointed his gavel and told him to wrap it up or forget it. Red in the face and hanging on to his temper

apparently by sheer dint of will, Kennison snarled that as a single woman barely able to support herself by waitressing, Laurel had no means by which to support a child. The judge waggled his eyebrows at Laurel who opened her mouth to defend herself, only to feel Edward's large hand clamp down warningly on her forearm as Kate again got to her feet.

"With all due respect, Your Honor," she said mildly, "it is our considered opinion that my client will shortly have control of the inheritance of which her ex-husband and his counsel have tried so hard to bilk her."

"Objection!" roared Kennison, shooting to his feet. "Your Honor, these allegations are substantiated only by the deposition of a known alcoholic, who has himself admitted incompetence!"

"We have other evidence, Your Honor," Kate rebuffed smoothly, "which we'd be glad to present."

The judge smiled and decided this would be an excellent idea. Kennison declared the proceedings an outrage, not that anyone paid the least attention to him. When Kate submitted the sworn deposition of one Pamela Scott, currently employed as a housemaid, Bryce audibly groaned and slid down in his chair. Receiving a whispered tongue lashing from Kennison, he hung his head and sulked, defeat screaming from every line of his posture and expression. Laurel could only look on in confused wonder. It was obvious to everyone that Judge Halstead had already read the deposition now entered into evidence, for he merely glanced over it before leaning forward and fixing Abelard Kennison with a baleful, gleeful glare.

"Getting a bit sloppy in our old age, are we, Counselor?"

Kennison was already spouting off about women scorned and single-digit IQs that would never bear up under cross-examination. The judge banged his gavel and said, "Tell it to the D.A.'s office, Counselor, for that's exactly where these documents are headed next. As to the matter at hand—"

"That woman couldn't raise tomatoes properly on her own!" Kennison screamed, pointing at Laurel.

Edward surged to his feet, face suffused with rage, hands balling into fists. Laurel grabbed his arm and hung on for dear life, crying, "Edward, no!" He was yelling at Kennison, though, and seemed not to hear her. For several moments, it was utter chaos with Edward and Kennison shouting at one another and Judge

Halstead banging his gavel continually while Kate and Laurel ineffectually urged restraint. Finally Halstead stood up and threw his gavel at the floor in front of the bench, at which point the bailiff jumped up, yanked out a whistle and tried to burst the eardrums of everyone present.

Silence gradually ensued. Judge Halstead folded his arms and sat down. "Good." He pointed at his gavel, and the bailiff retrieved it, handing it over. The judge snatched it out of his hand, ordering, "Shoot the next person who speaks out of turn!"

Nodding, the bailiff clumsily drew his pistol. Kate paled. "Uh, Your Honor, sir..."

Halstead made a face. "Oh, relax. It isn't loaded." Then he drew a gun from beneath his robes and plunked it onto the bench. Grinning, he added, "But this one is." He glared at the entire room and sat back in his chair, his gaze coming to rest on Kennison. His smile was absolutely chilling. Oddly, however, it was Laurel he addressed.

"As to the matter of single motherhood," he said, "I understand, Ms. Miller, that best wishes are actually in order, hmm?"

Laurel blinked uncertainly. "I—I beg your p-pardon?"

Halstead switched his glare to Kate and then Edward. "Well, attorney White, is it wedding bells or not?"

Edward's eyebrows shot up. He looked accusingly at Kate, who shrugged as if to say it couldn't be helped, then he turned to Laurel. For a long moment, his pale blue eyes plumbed hers, then his arm slid around her shoulders and he looked up to the bench. "It definitely is, Your Honor. That is, if Ms. Miller's proposal is still valid."

The judge abruptly targeted Laurel again. "Well?"

Laurel couldn't seem to get her mouth closed in order to reply. They were talking about marriage, weren't they? She had asked him to marry her—ages ago. And in all that time she hadn't changed her mind. She still felt that Edward White was the best possible candidate for a husband that a girl could have. Marriage to him still seemed like the answer to all her problems and, even more so, the embodiment of all her dreams. What she couldn't seem to grasp was that he might actually want to marry her. That, it turned out, was the only thing that seemed to matter. She turned a questioning gaze on the man of her dreams and whispered, "Edward, do you want to marry me?"

For answer, he stared a moment into her hopeful eyes, then lifted a hand to tilt her chin and tuck her head back into the crook of his arm, at which point he kissed her until her toes curled and laughter erupted from the gallery. He kissed her still, until a tiny, probing finger dug its way between their mouths and finally separated them. Edward looked down into Barry's upturned face. His sailor hat had tumbled off into his lap and now slid unheeded to the floor. "Killjoy," Edward muttered, his arm tight about Laurel's shoulder.

Barry reached up with that intruding little finger and touched it to the tip of Edward's nose, saying as clearly as sunshine, "Dada."

Edward put his head back and laughed before snatching up Barry and lifting him high overhead. "That's right, son!" Behind them, a triumphantly delighted Kendra applauded. Laurel laughed, understanding now what all that whispering was about.

The judge cleared his throat, and all eyes turned his way. Looking down at the court clerk he said, "Did you get all that?" Fingers flying, eyes wide, she nodded. Kennison sneered. Miller laid his head on the table and rolled it morosely side to side. Edward sat Barry in his lap and smiled at Laurel.

The judge banged his gavel and said, "I rule in favor of the plaintiff. To wit, I grant custody of said minor, Barry Lawrence Miller, to Laurel Heffington Miller—pending her marriage to Edward Patrick White, attorney."

Kate gasped. "Your Honor!"

Confused, Laurel looked to Edward. "What?"

"The judge just granted you conditional custody."

"Conditional?"

"Mm-hmm, the condition being that you marry me."

"Oh." She grinned her broadest.

"Now," the judge said, producing an official-looking paper with a flourish. "Having been assured by counsel—who's entirely too confident of her abilities as well as her personal charms—that this union was in the offing, I've taken the liberty of having the county clerk's office send over a license." He rustled the paper at Edward as if it were a red cape and Edward the bull.

Edward slid a look at Laurel. "It's not a big fancy wedding," he said lightly, "but it's unique. How about it?"

Laurel felt happiness like a physical entity, embracing her,

holding her. Oddly, it felt like an old and trusted friend. She smiled at Edward and leaned close until she could rub noses with him. "I love you," she said, "but I reserve the right to make all the marriage proposals in this family."

He laughed and said, "Propose away."

"Then I propose we let this nice judge marry us—right now."

The place erupted in pandemonium, with laughter and applause carrying the wave. Kennison provided the only sour note, however. Slamming his materials together and snarling about officious conduct and backstabbing weasels, he stormed out of the courtroom, Bryce following like a whipped puppy. The judge hooted at them, literally, and ordered loudly for the bailiff to call someone in the D.A.'s office to come down for the incriminating documents immediately. He winked at Kate and said, "He won't get far. They'll have his assets frozen by the close of business."

Juggling Barry between them, they filled out the license and stood shoulder to shoulder in front of the judge, who looked them over and asked, "I don't suppose you have any rings on you?"

At that, Parker spoke up. "They can use ours, Your Honor." After a moment, during which he worked his ring off his finger and collected Kendra's, he came forward. Dropping them into Edward's palm, he said, "Just a loan, mind you, but maybe they'll bring you two the same happiness they've brought us."

Edward clapped him on the shoulder in appreciation, then said to Laurel, "We'll pick out our own this afternoon. I promise."

She nodded and accepted Parker's ring, eying it doubtfully. It looked much too small for her Eddie, but what the heck. She wouldn't have cared if they'd used rubber bands. Kate took Barry into her arms and stood to one side, talking softly to him about what was going on, not that he understood any of it, but he kept pointing at Laurel and Edward and babbling, "Mama," and "Dada," sometimes not in the proper order. it was sweet music as far as Laurel was concerned.

"Now then," the judge said, "let's choose your witnesses and get on with it."

Edward nodded at Parker, who stepped immediately to his side, beaming and back-slapping. Laurel glanced around. Kate? She seemed to have a large hand in all this. Kendra? Clearly, she wished them only the best. Then again the court clerk was sitting there with big tears in her eyes. Before she could make up her

mind, a bright familiar voice from the back of the room said, "Let me."

Laurel gasped and spun around. Avon stood in the back near the door, having slipped in unnoticed some time before. She hadn't changed a bit, except that her curly bright red hair was inches longer and quite flattering, frothing around her shoulders. Otherwise, she might not have even changed her clothes since Laurel had last seen her. Her jeans were worn and artfully tattered, her flowered blouse small and clinging.

"I'd love to stand witness for Barry's mother," she said. "God knows she's the best friend either of us ever had."

Laurel reached out with both arms and Avon hurried into them. "I knew even when I was carrying him that he really belonged to you," she whispered. Then louder she cracked, "And now you've got him a lawyer for a dad, huh? Boy, I don't know about that, but if you think he's the one..."

Everyone laughed.

Laurel said, "He's the one. He's the only one. He's my white knight, and he always will be."

The judge said later that it was the first time in his court that the groom had kissed the bride without compunction or any sense for the propriety of the thing—which meant that he couldn't keep his hands or his mouth off her, either before, during or after. Especially after. Ever after.

* * * * *

Share in the joy of yuletide romance with brand-new stories by two of the genre's most beloved writers

DIANA PALMER
and
JOAN JOHNSTON
in

Diana Palmer and Joan Johnston share their favorite Christmas anecdotes and personal stories in this *special hardbound edition.*

Diana Palmer delivers an irresistible spin-off of her **LONG, TALL TEXANS** series and Joan Johnston crafts an unforgettable new chapter to **HAWK'S WAY** in this wonderful keepsake edition celebrating the holiday season. So perfect for gift giving, you'll want one for yourself...and one to give to a special friend!

Available in November at your favorite retail outlet!

Only from
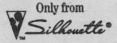

Silhouette

SPECIAL EDITION™®

That
SPECIAL
Woman!

**These delightful titles are coming soon to
THAT SPECIAL WOMAN!—only from
Silhouette Special Edition!**

**September 1997 THE SECRET WIFE
by Susan Mallery (SE#1123)**

Five years ago Elissa's dreams came true when she married
her true love—but their honeymoon was short-lived. Could
she and Cole Stephenson get a second shot at happiness?

**November 1997 WHITE WOLF
by Lindsay McKenna (SE#1135)**

Hard-core cynic Dain Phillips turned to mystical medicine
woman Erin Wolf for a "miracle" cure. But he never suspected
that Erin's spiritual healing would alter him—body and soul!

**January 1998 TENDERLY
by Cheryl Reavis (SE#1147)**

Socialite Eden Trevoy was powerfully drawn to Navajo
policeman Ben Toomey when he helped her uncover her half-
Navajo roots. Could her journey of self-discovery lead to full-
fledged love?

**IT TAKES A VERY SPECIAL MAN TO WIN THAT
SPECIAL WOMAN....** Don't miss THAT SPECIAL WOMAN!
every other month from some of your favorite authors!

SHARON SALA

Continues the twelve-book series—36 HOURS— in October 1997 with Book Four

FOR HER EYES ONLY

The storm was over. The mayor was dead. Jessica Hanson had an aching head...and sinister visions of murder. And only one man was willing to take her seriously— Detective Stone Richardson. He knew that unlocking Jessica's secrets would put him in danger, but the rugged cop had never expected to fall for her, too. Danger he could handle. But love...?

For Stone and Jessica and *all* the residents of Grand Springs, Colorado, the storm-induced blackout was just the beginning of 36 Hours that changed *everything!* You won't want to miss a single book.

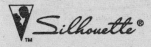

36HRS4

COMING NEXT MONTH

#1135 WHITE WOLF—Lindsay McKenna
That Special Woman!
Hardened corporate raider Dain Phillips turned to mystical medicine woman Erin Wolf for a "miracle" cure. But he never expected to care so deeply for Erin—or that her spiritual healing would forever alter him body and soul!

#1136 THE RANCHER AND THE SCHOOLMARM—
Penny Richards
Switched at Birth
Schoolteacher Georgia Williams was stunned when her fiancé passed her in the airport, got attacked and suffered amnesia. How would she handle the revelation that this riveting man who stole her heart was *not* her groom-to-be—but instead his long-lost identical twin?

#1137 A COWBOY'S TEARS—Anne McAllister
Code of the West
Mace and Jenny Nichols had the *perfect* marriage—until Mace discovered some sad news. Jenny was determined to convince her brooding cowboy of her unfaltering love—and that there was more than one way to capture their dreams....

#1138 THE PATERNITY TEST—Pamela Toth
Powerful Nick Kincaid could handle anything—except his mischievous twins. His new nanny, Cassie Wainright, could handle everything—except her attraction to Nick. Now Cassie was pregnant, and Nick was being put to the *ultimate* test.

#1139 HUSBAND: BOUGHT AND PAID FOR—Laurie Paige
Fearing for her life, heiress Jessica Lockhart hired P.I. Brody Smith—and then proposed marriage. Her aloof bodyguard agreed to a platonic union, but that didn't mean the lovely lady had the right to wiggle her way into his heart.

#1140 MOUNTAIN MAN—Doris Rangel
Gloria Pellman was a single mom, raising her young son, Jamey—alone, thank you very much! She didn't need a husband! But when Hank Mason rescued them from his rugged mountain, Jamey discovered a friend...and Gloria discovered her heart was in danger!

Daniel MacGregor is at it again…

New York Times bestselling author

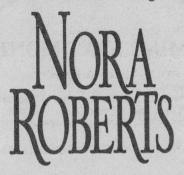

NORA ROBERTS

introduces us to a new generation of MacGregors
as the lovable patriarch of the illustrious MacGregor
clan plays matchmaker again, this time to his three
gorgeous granddaughters in

From Silhouette Books

Don't miss this brand-new continuation of Nora Roberts's
enormously popular *MacGregor* miniseries.

Available November 1997 at your favorite retail outlet.